Other Titles by *Langaa* RPCIG

Francis B. Nyamnjoh
Stories from Abakwa
Mind Searching
The Disillusioned African
The Convert
Souls Forgotten
Married But Available

Dibussi Tande
No Turning Back. Poems of Freedom 1990-1993
Scribbles from the Den: Essays on Politics and Collective Memory in Cameroon

Kangsen Feka Wakai
Fragmented Melodies

Ntemfac Ofege
Namondo. Child of the Water Spirits
Hot Water for the Famous Seven

Emmanuel Fru Doh
Not Yet Damascus
The Fire Within
Africa's Political Wastelands: The Bastardization of Cameroon
Oriki'badan
Wading the Tide
Stereotyping Africa: Surprising Answers to Surprising Questions

Thomas Jing
Tale of an African Woman

Peter Wuteh Vakunta
Grassfields Stories from Cameroon
Green Rape: Poetry for the Environment
Majunga Tok: Poems in Pidgin English
Cry, My Beloved Africa
No Love Lost
Straddling The Mungo: A Book of Poems in English & French

Ba'bila Mutia
Coils of Mortal Flesh

Kehbuma Langmia
Titabet and the Takumbeng
An Evil Meal of Evil

Victor Elame Musinga
The Barn
The Tragedy of Mr. No Balance

Ngessimo Mathe Mutaka
Building Capacity: Using TEFL and African Languages as Development-oriented Literacy Tools

Milton Krieger
Cameroon's Social Democratic Front: Its History and Prospects as an Opposition Political Party, 1990-2011

Sammy Oke Akombi
The Raped Amulet
The Woman Who Ate Python
Beware the Drives: Book of Verse
The Wages of Corruption

Susan Nkwentie Nde
Precipice
Second Engagement

Francis B. Nyamnjoh & Richard Fonteh Akum
The Cameroon GCE Crisis: A Test of Anglophone Solidarity

Joyce Ashuntantang & Dibussi Tande
Their Champagne Party Will End! Poems in Honor of Bate Besong

Emmanuel Achu
Disturbing the Peace

Rosemary Ekosso
The House of Falling Women

Peterkins Manyong
God the Politician

George Ngwane
The Power in the Writer: Collected Essays on Culture, Democracy & Development in Africa

John Percival
The 1961 Cameroon Plebiscite: Choice or Betrayal

Albert Azeyeh
Réussite scolaire, faillite sociale : généalogie mentale de la crise de l'Afrique noire francophone

Aloysius Ajab Amin & Jean-Luc Dubois
Croissance et développement au Cameroun : d'une croissance équilibrée à un développement équitable

Carlson Anyangwe
Imperialistic Politics in Cameroun: Resistance & the Inception of the Restoration of the Statehood of Southern Cameroons
Betrayal of Too Trusting a People: The UN, the UK and the Trust Territory of the Southen Cameroons

Bill F. Ndi
K'Cracy, Trees in the Storm and Other Poems
Map: Musings On Ars Poetica
Thomas Lurting: The Fighting Sailor Turn'd Peaceable /Le marin combattant devenu paisible

Kathryn Toure, Therese Mungah Shalo Tchombe & Thierry Karsenti
ICT and Changing Mindsets in Education

Charles Alobwed'Epie
The Day God Blinked
The Bad Samaritan

G. D. Nyamndi
Babi Yar Symphony
Whether losing, Whether winning
Tussles: Collected Plays
Dogs in the Sun

Samuel Ebelle Kingue
Si Dieu était tout un chacun de nous ?

Ignasio Malizani Jimu
Urban Appropriation and Transformation: bicycle, taxi and handcart operators in Mzuzu, Malawi

Justice Nyo' Wakai
Under the Broken Scale of Justice: The Law and My Times

John Eyong Mengot
A Pact of Ages

Ignasio Malizani Jimu
Urban Appropriation and Transformation: Bicycle Taxi and Handcart Operators

Joyce B. Ashuntantang
Landscaping and Coloniality: The Dissemination of Cameroon Anglophone Literature

Jude Fokwang
Mediating Legitimacy: Chieftaincy and Democratisation in Two African Chiefdoms

Michael A. Yanou
Dispossession and Access to Land in South Africa: an African Perspevctive

Tikum Mbah Azonga
Cup Man and Other Stories
The Wooden Bicycle and Other Stories

John Nkemngong Nkengasong
Letters to Marions (And the Coming Generations)

Amady Aly Dieng
Les étudiants africains et la littérature négro-africaine d'expression française

Tah Asongwed
Born to Rule: Autobiography of a life President
Child of Earth

Frida Menkan Mbunda
Shadows From The Abyss

Bongasu Tanla Kishani
A Basket of Kola Nuts

Fo Angwafo III S.A.N of Mankon
Royalty and Politics: The Story of My Life

Basil Diki
The Lord of Anomy

Churchill Ewumbue-Monono
Youth and Nation-Building in Cameroon: A Study of National Youth Day Messages and Leadership Discourse (1949-2009)

Emmanuel N. Chia, Joseph C. Suh & Alexandre Ndeffo Tene
Perspectives on Translation and Interpretation in Cameroon

Linus T. Asong
The Crown of Thorns
No Way to Die
A Legend of the Dead: Sequel of *The Crown of Thorns*
The Akroma File
Salvation Colony: Sequel to *No Way to Die*

Vivian Sihshu Yenika
Imitation Whiteman
Press Lake Varsity Girls: The Freshman Year

Beatrice Fri Bime
Someplace, Somewhere
Mystique: A Collection of Lake Myths

Shadrach A. Ambanasom
Son of the Native Soil
The Cameroonian Novel of English Expression: An Introduction

Tangie Nsoh Fonchingong and Gemandze John Bobuin
Cameroon: The Stakes and Challenges of Governance and Development

Tatah Mentan
Democratizing or Reconfiguring Predatory Autocracy? Myths and Realities in Africa Today

Roselyne M. Jua & Bate Besong
To the Budding Creative Writer: A Handbook

Albert Mukong
Prisonner without a Crime: Disciplining Dissent in Ahidjo's Cameroon

Mbuh Tennu Mbuh
In the Shadow of my Country

Bernard Nsokika Fonlon
Genuine Intellectuals: Academic and Social Responsibilities of Universities in Africa

Lilian Lem Atanga
Gender, Discourse and Power in the Cameroonian Parliament

Cornelius Mbifung Lambi & Emmanuel Neba Ndenecho
Ecology and Natural Resource Development in the Western Highlands of Cameroon: Issues in Natural Resource Managment

Gideon F. For-mukwai
Facing Adversity with Audacity

Child of Earth

Tah Asongwed

Langaa Research & Publishing CIG
Mankon, Bamenda

Publisher:
Langaa RPCIG
Langaa Research & Publishing Common Initiative Group
P.O. Box 902 Mankon
Bamenda
North West Region
Cameroon
Langaagrp@gmail.com
www.langaa-rpcig.net

Distributed outside N. America by African Books Collective
orders@africanbookscollective.com
www.africanbookscollective.com

Distributed in N. America by Michigan State University Press
msupress@msu.edu
www.msupress.msu.edu

ISBN: 9956-616-01-X

First Published 2008

DISCLAIMER

The names, characters, places and incidents in this book are either the product of the author's imagination or are used fictitiously. Accordingly, any resemblance to actual persons, living or dead, events, or locales is entirely one of incredible coincidence.

Content

By the same author

Born to Rule (Autobiography of a Life President)

Guide to Electoral Fraud (Winner Take all)

Chapter One

That Saturday morning was going to be particularly busy for the Asaah family as a whole. The Asaah children startled out of bed just when the morning mist had wrapped the village in its cold embrace as pelting, raging rain rapped the zinc roofs in their father's compound with all its blighted fury. The children would have to brave the elements to carry out their normal weekend chores. As far as they were concerned, that, in any case, was something they had grown accustomed to doing at that time of the year. For them, rain was after all nothing more than tears that heaven shed to water the crops and provide sustenance to the entire village. Moreover, they always counted themselves blessed in that, while drought pursued some other parts of the country and the world at large with pitiless vindictive vigour, it had so far spared them.

As usual, after twitching their eyes, after yawning and stretching to wake up numb parts of the body, the Asaah children ran outside and looked upwards towards Fomusongma, the towering and imposing boulder shrine that stood majestically, almost imperially, on the forbidding hills that dominated the village. That shrine was the pride of the Ndzahma clan for only they could go there to pour libations and appease the gods of the village. The hills themselves looked like phalanxes of gallant soldiers cordoning off marauding invaders. Too bad the morning mist that was drifting erratically had enveloped them. On a much-clearer morning, one could behold them from the distance as they ring the village like some natural fortifications standing cheek to cheek with the horizon.

Those venerable hills were once the abode of various forms of wildlife and especially of those sly and arrogant baboons that had nothing but contemptuous disrespect for the villagers. Until the very recent past, one could contemplate the baboons tanning themselves on the rocks and grooming their babies with self-possessing imperturbability. But then hunters from neighbouring villages had embarked on a grotesque and gruesome slaughter, decimating the baboon population in their mad quest to satisfy the insatiable desire of the village folk for baboon meat. Too bad younger generations of Chuforba children would not be privileged to see their cousins of the animal kingdom.

As if to protest the disappearance of their once-teeming baboon population, the Boza Hill and Fomusongma boulder shrine are said to rumble and grumble from time to time which, according to the villagers, is proof that they hold within their cavernous entrails mineral gems of all kinds. No wonder every villager upon waking up always looked upwards towards Boza and Fomusongma.

The Asaah children definitely had a busy day ahead of them. Not that their other Saturdays were really not busy. After all, it had become a weekly ritual for them to accompany their mothers to the farm early every Saturday morning to either slash and burn or to bring home the harvest. That particular Saturday morning though was unlike the others because of the family reunion that was going to take place the following day. The Asaah children dashed to the shallow tadpole-rich stream that snaked its way proudly through the palm wine bush that their father used to tap behind his compound. As the water spluttered noisily amidst the croaking of frogs, the children washed their clothes in preparation for the family reunion.

The Asaah children were very excited about the meeting because a family reunion was an occasion that usually took place only once every three years unless there was a compelling reason to convene one earlier. Family reunions afforded the entire family an occasion during which relatives from far-flung villages and from all over the country congregated in the main family compound to discuss family matters, settle palavers, and engender a sense of family in everyone. The Asaah children looked forward to that family reunion with utmost expectancy because of the importance of the items on the agenda. In a year of tumultuous political changes taking place in the country, invidious rumours of all kind were going round, which sowed the seed of fear in everybody.

Of great concern to the Asaah family was the misunderstanding that had broken out between Ma Naah, the eldest of Pa Asaah's daughters, and Ni Achiri, the eldest boy. It would appear that Ni Achiri had fought with Naah's husband, Leviticus Ngu, in the presence of younger Asaah children because Leviticus Ngu was accused of always maltreating Naah. That palaver had become so hot that it almost divided the Asaah family. While the overwhelming majority of the Asaah family members wanted Naah to leave her dreaded husband and return to the family fold, she stuck by him and asked the family not to meddle in her marital life. And her mother supported her.

There were other problems. Ngum, one of Pa Asaah's favourite daughters, refused obstinately to marry the person the family had groomed her for from the time she was born. Yet everybody knew that Mr. Abraham Fon, alias Money Miss Road, the family anointed husband to be, was one of the richest men in Chuforba. The Asaah family had been counting on the money Money Miss Road would pay as bride price to renovate the compound. Furthermore, one of Pa Asaah's most successful children, Dr. Zacheus Akum, a well-known history lecturer at the Meroonca National University, had joined the newly formed opposition party—the Social Front for Democracy (SFD), popularly known as Suffer for Democracy—much against his father's wish. While his father, Pa Asaah, didn't particularly like the ruling United People's Movement (UPM), he was afraid that as what had happened to many sons and daughters of Chuforba and other Merooncans who had showed open support for the SFD, his son would be victimised, blacklisted, and kicked out of his teaching position as evidenced by the opposition bashing that was going on in the progovernment press.

Then there was also the problem of Ruth Ngwe, who had been dismissed from Our Lady of Love's Secondary School because Mr. Innocent Fru, the biology teacher, had put her in the family way at age fourteen. Ruth wasn't Mr. Fru's first victim, but nothing could be done about it because no law court in the country had ever convicted a man for sleeping with an underage girl. Men, especially those in positions of authority, could cavort with girls of any age and get away with it. After all, innocent schoolgirls are sitting ducks for errant rich men, whose standing pricks have no conscience.

Pa Asaah had, out of anger, refused to send Ruth Ngwe to another secondary school because he said he would be wasting his money. He had even driven her out of the compound to go and live with Mr. Fru, but Mr. Fru had, once he knew that Ruth was pregnant, disowned her and taken in Lum, whom everybody knew was engaged to Job Mokom. The family was therefore divided between those who—while not approving of what Ruth Ngwe had done—sympathised with her, and those who simply didn't want to see her at all.

Lastly, the family had to discuss the hottest political news in the country. It would seem that the ruling political party, the United People's Movement (UPM), had sent out well-armed exuberant soldiers in excess anger to hunt and track down opposition leaders as if they were prized game. Apparently the chairman of the UPM took very unkindly to the opposition's call for nationwide strikes to protest against rampant corruption and against the arrest of opposition supporters during a peaceful demonstration. As everyone in the country knew, the chairman of the UPM, Chief Dr. Prof. Jean de Dieu Amot's main claim to intellectualism resided in bogus honorary degrees and titles he had received from nondescript universities that dished them out in return for money. Chief Doctor Professor Amot also happened to be an insult-hardened man with an implant of wickedness drilled into him. He was said to be a turgid personality, clamped up and locked up in fear of himself.

As the Asaah children washed their clothes, they were careful not to venture near the pond downstream. It was sacred, and no one was allowed to disturb the peace of the wild ducks that swam in the placid water freely. The week before, a curious and inquisitive little boy had accidentally drowned in the pond, and his parents had alleged that their neighbour, one Ni Kweti, was responsible in that he had bewitched the boy and sold him to the water mermaid, Mami Water, in return for fame and wealth.

After rinsing their clothes, the Asaah children squeezed and wrung them until all the water in them had dripped. They then returned home and hung them on some coffee plants in the yard to dry. Thereafter, the children wended their way into the neighbouring forest, fending off thorns, in search of firewood, while their mothers whisked off to their farms to gather the harvest and bring home the cocoyam, beans, potatoes, vegetables, and other foodstuffs that would be prepared for the entire family and guests the following day. Since the harvest that year had been exceptionally bountiful, the villagers planned to make sacrifices to their ancestral god of fertility. They would also take some of the harvest to the chief as their token of appreciation to him for the prayers he always made, on their behalf, to his late father who no doubt was in communication with the god of fertility. It was said that the late chief inhabited a dark, eerie-looking pond not far away from the chief 's palace.

According to tradition, the villagers believed that the late chief had not really died but was simply missing. Consequently, his successor was considered a caretaker chief, and it was therefore appropriate that the villagers should offer the missing chief some of their choicest foodstuffs, especially in years of plenty.

As the Asaah children combed the forest in search of firewood, they came to an old dangling bridge of twines that swayed hypnotically from side to side as the fuming Gyi Shum Waterfall raged beneath. They crossed briskly with the dexterity of circus tightrope walkers. The forest at that time of the year was full of transcendent splendour and, as usual, of intriguing aesthetic beauty. It was unspoiled because no backpack-toting tourists had ever been there to desecrate it and destroy its pristine beauty. Here and there, one could see squirrels with kola nuts between their teeth flapping and then scurrying in rhythmic and graceful movements as if teasing the Asaah children to run after them up the kola nut trees the way they were doing.

The romantic flight of the birds coupled with their chirping; the melodious sound of the wind as it hummed past while the trees, even the regal mahogany that reigned supreme, kowtowed reverently to it; the artful composition of mellifluous notes and tunes being played by nature in this sublimely remote forest tucked away behind the hills; the water skipping gracefully over the large stones and strutting down the steep slopes gaily and merrily all transformed the forest into a lavishly exuberant screen before which the Asaah children, enraptured, seemed to be watching the sleek performance of a celebrated concert. This was nature in all its finery, and the Asaah children contemplated its awesomely overwhelming presence. Only Almighty God—the god of all creation, not the imaginary deity of some silly crackpots—could have, in his infinite wisdom, designed intricate webs of nature of such breathtaking magnificence.

Given every living being's creative instinct for survival and preservation, little wonder that the Mamben forest should be serving as a sanctuary or refugee centre, so to speak, for all those bird and animal species fleeing from the human race's choleric tendency to overpower nature. Mamben was a world of its own, much tamer than the world of human beings with its variegated inhabitants living in peaceful communion with each other, their race and the colour of their skin counting for nought. Maybe it was the peace that reigned in the Mamben forest that made its soil so fertile and gave it so much biodiversity. No doubt all the villagers always went there as a matter of course to farm and to harvest the well-known health-restoring herbs and elixir plants that Mamben gave freely to the village.

There were also the shrines dotted here and there where the old men of the village—so full of age, so full of wisdom—usually retired to in the dead of night to pray and make their offerings. On a hearth at the trunk of a gigantic mahogany tree could be seen, sleeping by the side of the remains of a goat very likely sacrificed the day before, an inert saw that must have been used by those intrepid sawyers from neighbouring villages to maim and destroy the mahogany tree. The children passed by, taking note that someone had been there to say his prayers and had, thanks to his vigilance, chased away the surreptitious sawyers whose avowed aim was to hew down all the mahogany trees for timber. It wasn't for nothing that the Chuforba Village Traditional Council had decreed that no one should cut down any tree without the permission of the chief because at the rate at which sawyers fronting for some lumber companies were going, Chuforba would not have any more forest to speak of in a few years.

Also, the fact that someone had been there very early in the morning to make sacrifices to his ancestral god meant that the forest had been purified and that the Asaah children had nothing to fear all the more as all the evil spirits that would normally roam and prowl aimlessly at that time of the day must have been chased away. When the children came to the small Lechoro stream, they recited some incantations and waited for the edge of the water's anger to wear off before crossing.

Some of the children then drifted like the early morning mist to Shum in Leka, the rock shelter cave discovered by archaeologists, to visit the well-preserved abode of their ancestors buried there between 7000 BP and 3000 BP, making the burial site and the eighteen human skeletons of children discovered there the most ancient fossils in West Central Africa. For the Asaah children, visiting the sacred remains of their ancestors was one way of building their future on the remains of the past.

Chapter Two

Pa Asaah, patriarch of the Asaah family, was busy making a bamboo fence round the compound where the family members and guests would sit the following day for the family reunion. The younger children had stayed back home to take care of the coffee beans that had been left to dry in the sun on a cemented porch.

The Asaah children continued to force their way through the thickets, following fresh-meandering footpaths left by those who, the night before, had gone to pick kola nuts. They would occasionally trample on some thorns that pierced their bare feet and would let the blood flow like water from a spring. They groped on until they came to a spot where a feeble old man dressed in skimpy loincloth hanging dejectedly on his body was invoking the name of his ancestral god.

When the man saw the gaping sore on the feet of some of the children, he dashed behind a tree and returned with a smoke-stained gourd containing some slimy substances he had concocted from the bark of some trees. He washed the cuts and bruises with it and then squeezed some liquid from herbs and plants he was boiling unto the sores. The children thanked him and scampered for some succulent berries that they ate.

Before sunset, when witches and evil spirits eat dinner, dress, and prepare to make their rounds, when the sun's incandescent smile turns sullen as the sun shrinks, retreats, and tries to hide its face coyly in the horizon, the Asaah children emerged from the forest tired and exhausted, each of them toting a bundle of firewood well balanced on the head. For the Asaah children, it had been a gruelling day in the forest. And with the bundles of firewood on their head weighing them down, they sang some traditional folk songs and the latest Ni Kyen bottle dance hits as they trotted along in order to banish from their thoughts the uncomfortable feeling that the trip had been long and dreary.

When they finally reached home, they all heaved a sigh of relief and treated themselves to a heavy meal of akwa—that is, pounded cocoyam with okra soup—giant bowls of beans, and fufu corn. Each of Pa Asaah's wives had brought in a basketful of food. The Asaah children ate ravenously, smacked their lips, and then left their revered father to go and greet their mothers.

Pa Asaah was a high-yielding man at age seventy-eight. Not to be undone by age, he had begotten twenty-four children of whom sixteen were females or, as he liked to describe his female children, fee males. With a splinter of firewood in his hand, Pa Asaah rose slowly from his mahogany stool on which no one else had a right to sit; he then crept into a small, dark corner of his mud-walled house and brought back from his well-stacked palm wine cellar five calabashes of palm wine he had tapped that very evening in his farm in Tanjim. Tanjim was his favourite farm because it was like a staging post from which he could spy the well-known cow thieves that fled and retreated to neighbouring villages. Tanjim also brought back to him memories handed down by past generations. It was there that criminals in times past, such as villagers found guilty of practising witchcraft, were hanged and dumped.

The palm wine was still so fresh and young that it was foaming at the mouth of the calabash. A few bees were swimming in it with jubilant ecstasy after tasting the sweet aromatic stuff. Achu, one of Pa Asaah's sons—a student at Cohesa College in Konman—who had arrived in the village the day before for the family reunion, loved to clutch snugly at his father's legs by the fireside. When he saw the palm wine, he smirked and then ran outside to summon all his brothers and sisters who were in their mothers' houses. Within a minute, everyone dropped whatever they were doing and ran to their father's house. Even small Anjei, at barely fourteen months, came staggering in, not to be left out of the celebration. The smell of fresh palm wine, especially that wrought by their father's hand, always beckoned to them.

Pa Asaah was a wiry old man described as few because of his diminutive figure that fitted his small frame. His legs were fairly thin and scotched because he spent most of his time by the fireside. He looked time beaten and weathered by scores of years of hard life and drudgery in the village, but he still retained his outgoing and engaging personality. In fact, he had been kept alive by a combination of traditional and modern medicine. For several years, he had been so ill that the family had on many occasions given him up for dead, but somehow he always miraculously sprang back to life and mesmerised everybody with his prodigious knowledge of family and Chuforba history.

Pa Asaah liked to describe himself self-deprecatingly by saying he was living on spare parts. This wasn't entirely false. He had had most of his teeth replaced, and some were cobbled together by wires. Then he had also undergone a kidney transplant and had his hip bone grafted. Yet when anybody saw him, it was clear to them that Pa Asaah must have been very handsome in his youth because the remnants of his good looks were etched on his face. He had a small round face, well-defined facial features, and prominent cheekbones. His ginger beard was well manicured, and the small patches of grey hair that dotted his head looked well groomed. On occasion, he would dye his hair black, although it was not the case that evening. His once-fat and rounded jaws had now dropped, but for someone his age, he surprisingly had virtually no wrinkles because most of his life he had been an exercise buff. He used to like walking, jogging, and doing yoga. His large glowing and prominent black eyes were somewhat tired, but it was evident that they must have served him well as a radar to detect and track down all the beautiful women he was alleged to have caught in the net of seduction he cast wherever he went. He still had his elongated neck, which he wheeled from side to side, as well as that trademark glint that proved to be a fatal bait for many a woman.

Pa Asaah remained an imposing presence in Chuforba not only because of his age, since most people his age had already passed away, but also in part because of his past glory. He had served as the chairman of the Chuforba Traditional Council, but the position that shot him to prominence was that of interpreter to the British governor when Britain held sway over Southern Merooncа. Pa Asaah had been privileged to tour all parts of the country in the company of the governor and to rub shoulders with all the influential white men at the time. It was therefore not for nothing that the villagers delighted in calling him their "black man white man."

The children always liked to crowd around him, as they always did every evening, to listen to folktales, riddles, and stories of all kinds and also to pick up the wisdom-laden words that dropped from his lips each time he opened his mouth to speak. They particularly cherished his jokes because he considered jokes to be the yeast that leavens speeches and stories. Pa Asaah, on this occasion, raised his eyes towards his children, clasped his hands together, and bestowed manifold blessings on them. Then he piled some of the firewood they had brought home that evening into the fire to evict the stubborn Chuforba cold and to dry the corn that had been brought into the barn by the women.

As the blaze from the fire illuminated the house, he took a pinch of snuff from a rusty old cigarette cup that was hidden under his bamboo bed, and sniffed. Then turning his scarlet red eyes in the direction of his children—who, assembled, looked like a small village congregation—he ponderously raised his finger to his lips and hissed in the manner of a snake. Eloquent silence fell on the children. Smarting under the weight of his old age, he cleared his throat and allowed his tender glances to wander about in the room, settling on each of his children for a flashing moment; the soft glow of the fire also seemed to venerate the moment by refusing to crackle, as if it had decided to join the children in a sort of conspiratorial silence.

"My children, oh my dear children," Pa Asaah began in a deep drowning voice as he struck the spotty white patches of hair on his chin. "This fire is warming my heart and this house because of the firewood that all of you fetched today. The fact that all of you went as far away as to the Mamben bush today to bring back all this firewood is a sign that you love me. After all, what are children made for if not to help their parents in old age. I think I can be deservedly proud among my few remaining friends who always complain that their children are very stubborn. Well, I know there are times when I have chided all of you for disobedience and stubbornness, but this is because I love you. I thank God for giving all twenty-four of you to me; but as I have always complained, well, I . . . I . . . wish I had more of you."

Just then, Sah, one of Pa Asaah's daughters, interjected. "Nei, you are always complaining that you only have twenty-four of us. What of your friends and others who don't have any children at all? I think you should rather be thankful to God that he gave you this number."

"Thank you, my daughter," Pa Asaah responded, half closing his eyes and nodding. "Thank you, my beloved children. Your sister here has spoken not like a girl but like a woman. Yes, she has spoken words of wisdom, and I say this is a sign of maturity on her part. Indeed, we should be grateful and thankful to our Lord for everything he has given us. The way Sah has spoken shows you what education can do, and that is why I have always counselled you to take your book thing very seriously. You see me. I could have been a better person than what I am if I had had a very good education. It is true that I used to be the interpreter to the British commissioners, but what has that given me? I learned English like that, you know . . . just from working with white people. Since the white commissioners left, what do I have? What has become of me? What did the new government do to show that they were grateful for all the work I did? Nothing. And I mean it. Nothing at all, nothing kwata kwata. Yet if I had had the proper education and training, I probably would have been governor myself today."

"You really mean it, Papa?" enquired Achu, intrigued. "You mean you too could have been governor?"

"Of course. Why not?"

"But, Papa, I really don't see what education has to do with it. Don't you think that what one needs to be a governor is mostly experience?" Achu pursued matter-of-factly.

"There's no doubt that experience is necessary, but one needs a minimum level of education," answered Nei Asaah absently.

"But, Papa, you have more than the minimum. After all, you attended the Chuforba Presbyterian School in those days and later on became a pupil teacher for many years following the departure of the British commissioners. I don't see why you are berating yourself."

Just then Arimboh interrupted, "Apart from that, Papa, we have had some governors in this country that neither had your educational background nor experience. Even some ministers and the president himself. In what way are they better than you?"

"Well, they are better in that they are in power and I am not. And they're making a fortune from it. My children, whether you like it or not, education is the ticket to a first-class life even though education too can bar the way to one's success in that in this country, one sometimes has to be stupendously dull to be admitted into the charmed circles of politics and positions."

"In that case, I don't have to be highly educated to be a politician since that's what I plan to be," Achu offered with self-assurance. "Son, listen," Nei Asaah spoke guardedly."When you have a good educational background, you can do many things and adapt to many situations."

"But the politicians can frustrate you," Achu returned. "Papa, look at all the big intellectuals in this country and see how they are prostituting themselves to the politicians just because they want jobs, positions, and power."

"You are right, but this country will change someday," Nei Asaah predicted triumphantly. "Things can't go this way indefinitely."

"I hope God will listen to you, Papa, because the way things are going on in this country, we're in a great mess," Achu returned with grim diffidence.

"It is precisely for that reason that young people like you should be highly educated so that when the time comes, you will be able to take over the country and run it well."

"Papa, but you have lots of intellectuals in the government and in the private sector. Yet nothing seems to be working."

"That's in part because the politicians are making life difficult for them. Remember that education is expensive, but stupidity is more expensive. Plus there's a total breakdown of discipline. Moreover, everyone is scrambling to get rich quick, and no one cares about the future of the country. No one cares about future generations. There's a high-speed chase for wealth at every level from the top to the bottom. Don't forget that the rich climb to wealth on the corpses of the poor. Now just imagine what would have happened if I had been made governor."

Pa Asaah spoke bitterly with a sinister look on his face. His eyes breathed bitter regrets. "All this suffering would not be there."

Pa Asaah ran his left thumb and index finger over the bridge of his nose, which he squeezed, and then he sniffed. After a short pause, he looked up wanly at his children. Just when he was about to continue, Achu cut in. "But it doesn't matter, Papa," he said trying to lift up his father's flagging spirits. "The whole village knows who you are and what you have done for this country."

"Thank you, son, for the nice words, but you and I know that one doesn't eat nice words. Money is what makes the world go round, and if I had money, you wouldn't have been suffering the way you are doing. I really don't think all of you know what I go through every time the school year is about to begin. I never know in advance where I'm going to get the money to pay your fees." Pa Asaah took in a deep breath, exhaled heavily, and then sighed.

"But somehow you've always managed, Papa, so I don't think you should feel that bad," Achu responded in a whisper as he almost choked. He bit his lower lip, and tears started to form in his soulful eyes.

"Maybe so," Pa Asaah said unconvinced. "But how can I not feel bad when you, Achu, had to be sent away from school last year because I couldn't afford the fees? And you were one of the best students in your class. Here I am—a retired civil servant who gave all his life to the service of his country. Today I can't even take care of my own children. And you expect me to be happy?" he spoke nervously.

"But, Papa, that is behind us now since I will be writing my GCE A level exams at the end of this school year. By God's grace, if I pass, I'll enter university, and then you don't have to worry about me." Achu tried to cheer up his father.

"That's precisely the problem," Pa Asaah said pensively. "You may not be aware, but I still owe part of last year's fees and part of this year's fees; and at this very moment that I'm talking to you, I don't know where I'm going to get the money." Pa Asaah said and pinned an icy stare on Achu and continued, "You know that since the government liberalised coffee prices, life hasn't been the same for us, the poor farmers."

Achu's heartbeat galloped because what his father said was an ominous message to him that he might not write the GCE. His heart sank as his father's words struck him harshly in the face like a serious blow, bludgeoning him to silence. His sad eyes stared in the middle distance blankly.

"Anyway, I thank God for giving all of you to me and for giving me the knowledge and wisdom to bring all of you up to know the truth and what is right," Pa Asaah managed to say. "Remember, my dear children, that one hand cannot tie a bundle. As long as all of you are united, nothing will divide you. You have always heard the catechist say that a house divided between itself cannot stand," Nei Asaah said as he turned his face away and cupped his hand to his jaw to cough. Ndi, one of his sons, cut in to speak.

"But, Papa, Papa, you know that—"

"But papa you know that nothing, Ndi," Pa Asaah quipped seething with anger. "You shut up those busy fangs of yours and let all of you listen. Have trust and confidence in yourselves, and let there be no misgivings amongst you. As you all know, I will not be around eternally to shepherd all of you in life; hence, in this my old age, all I can do is hope that you will all live by the precepts I have taught you and that all of you will forever abide by our traditions."

Ndi, flummoxed as he was, said nothing further. He dared not to. There was an uneasy silence as the other members of the family made faces at him because he had been humiliatingly silenced. Ndi's eyes gorged with tears, and he hung his head in shame and chewed on his nails. His pressure-cooker personality seemed to have been doused with water.

Outside the house, the moon shimmered and cast its rays like a net on the countryside, which stretched for miles on end. On such a radiant night, one could see the moon perched on the kola nut trees that stood akimbo in the far distance, and the green pastures rambling on and on to the edge of the horizon. Down below in the valley, where the war-hardened Babli people who had confiscated the fertile land of the Chuforbas set out to build settlements, faint lights emerged from the sprawling mansion of Honourable Nguked, a dishonourable minister of Public Works and Procurement who had transformed his small village into a modern town overnight and, as rumour had it, skimmed millions from government coffers to build a mansion for himself.

As everyone knew from the anonymous leaflets that were always circulating in the country, Honourable Nguked was said to be involved in every major shady deal that involved government contracts and procurement. He was accused of building for himself a huge bank account abroad from monies squirreled away from his ministry's budget and also of putting up an extravagantly ostentatious mansion that was perched on a small hill in his wife's village. That mansion was the talk of the town, and some of the flap-jawed tabloids took great delight in publishing its picture. In his attempt to squelch what he said were invidious rumours about his wealth, Honourable Nguked issued a number of sometimes contradictory press statements in which he claimed that his wealth had been accumulated before he became minister. But then everybody knew that he was lying between his teeth because it was common knowledge that he had only been a petty trader before his appointment and thus couldn't have garnered so much money from his petty trading business. In any case, he had been appointed to the juicy position of minister of public works and procurement because he had been a loudmouthed vocal leader of a fringe opposition party that had entered into an alliance with the ruling party to form a so-called government of national unity. People had been scandalised by the rapid pace with which Honourable Nguked enriched himself, but then nobody could do anything about it. Milking the government and bilking the treasury was no big deal. After all, all his colleagues were doing the same thing, taking the cue from the president of the country and paying a deaf ear to the opposition's call for ministers and the president to declare their assets.

Honourable Nguked continued to flaunt his wealth with ill grace in the full glare of the public's eyes and was reported to have said to some of his friends that politics will no longer be politics if the nation's high-ranking officials were asked to declare their assets. It was even said that when Honourable Nguked had initially heard about his appointment on the evening news of the North West Radio and Television Network (NWRTV), he had fainted because he hadn't been expecting to be appointed to such a succulent position. Usually when fringe opposition parties joined the ruling party to form a government, they were given inconsequential ministries to run. Everyone was therefore surprised that Honourable Nguked's party—the People's Convention Party (PCP), which had virtually no following—had been honoured with such a lucrative position. But then again, Honourable Nguked must have been given the position because he had swum against the tide of opposition to the government in a province where the ruling party and government were considered enemy territory. So the position was blood money for him betraying his people.

From cracks in the wall of Pa Asaah's house that served both as a chimney as well as a busy thoroughfare for cockroaches, some of the moon's rays trickled into the house. The evening was lulling and quiet and calm, with fireflies dancing enchantingly in the air and neon lighting the sky. The Asaah children decided that while they awaited the arrival of the distant relatives for the following day's family reunion, they would take leave of their father to go out and play hide and seek.

The Asaah boys dived under Arabica coffee shrubs and also lurked in the foliage of some cassava plants. The girls for their part, in their skimpy loincloths, covered their faces with a piece of cloth and staggered through the plants looking for their brothers. As the game seemed to grow increasingly violent but exciting, the air was soon charged with their uproarious laughter and high-voltage screams. The noise of distant children playing te-tekam filled the air too, shattering the placid atmosphere.

Unable to withstand the strain of the hubbub any longer, Pa Asaah crawled out of his house and, supporting himself with his cane walking stick, yelled at his children. They came out of their hiding places instantly, obediently, and respectfully.

"When will you all learn to grow?" Pa Asaah pealed like the rainy season thunder. "What opinion do you want the guests we are expecting to have of us? That I run a brood of unruly, ill-bred whelps?" When his eyes picked out Achu, he bawled, "And you, Achu, as small as a broomstick, how many times have I told you not to play with these big fools? Soon you will, as usual, run to me in tears, nursing a bruise."

The other children grumbled, but none of them said a word. They knew their father always had a soft spot for Achu. Pa Asaah turned his back slowly and hitched waveringly on his walking stick and entered the house.

The children began to shuffle the stools and benches in position in readiness for the family reunion that all of them looked forward to with great anxiety. After they had done that, they all poured into their father's house and took their usual places. As they mended the fire, their father treated them to one of his favourite yarns, "Sense Pass King", the story of his father's enlistment into the Southern Meroonca's police force.

Pa Asaah told his children that a British officer known simply as Lieutenant James had visited Chuforba during World War II in search of sturdy, hefty male villagers to recruit into the police force. When the then-reigning chief had been informed, he asked one of his special assistants—that is, one of his chindas—to beat the palace drum and summon all the young able-bodied men to the palace. When the young men arrived at the palace, the chief told them that the white man commissioner at the time had sent Lieutenant James to speak to them about their possible recruitment into the colonial force.

"For an officer in the colonial army," Pa Asaah said, "Lieutenant James was a dull man in an advanced state of intellectual benightedness who was not conversant with the Chuforba language. He, therefore, requested the chief to serve as his interpreter."

According to Pa Asaah, Lieutenant James was the kind of guy who, like ignorant members of his kindred race, expected black people to be mesmerised by his presence. He always spoke with authority, behaving as if he was a bomb ready to explode at the slightest provocation. Pa Asaah explained that since black people could not readily discern a white man's age, the villagers had assumed that because Lieutenant James wore a shabby beard and raised an unkempt moustache that looked more like whiskers, he must be quite an elderly man. Accordingly, the villagers bestowed on him all the respect that was due a man of a certain age. Lieutenant James, however, mistakenly assumed that the overt respect the villagers were showing him was a sign that they were afraid of him. He, therefore, carried himself around with insolent pride, and it wasn't until much later in life after Pa Asaah's father had joined the police force that he got to know that Lieutenant James was simply an oversized boy with an impetuous character.

When Lieutenant James started to address the villagers, he paused after every sentence to enable the chief to translate what he was saying into Ngamebene, the Chuforba language.

"You people of Chuforba," Lieutenant James began as he exposed his medals. "Yes, you people of Chuforba, you are a marvellous people, but you are very lazy."

The chief licked his lips, rubbed his eyes, and turned to his subjects and translated, "The white man has said that the light of our village is shining so brightly that it can be seen all over the world, even in the white man's country where we are considered to be very industrious people."

Lieutenant James continued, "Look at your roads—very bumpy and very narrow. Two days ago, I was taking one of the chief 's wives to the maternity at the general hospital, but she delivered in the Land Rover because it was shaking her too much. If we had had a smoother road surface, I'm sure that wouldn't have happened."

The chief chuckled and then translated, "The white man has said that I should tell you that I, your chief, am the best ruler God has ever given to this village. That I am a wise man, a very good man, and all of you must continue to respect me."

On hearing this, the villagers broke out into lavish and spirited dancing amidst squealing and squabbling to the pulsating and throbbing beat of drums and xylophones, praising and extolling their chief as God's divine messenger.

Lieutenant James's bulbous ears stood up as his eyes whispered with anger. He could not fathom why the villagers would be so happy as to dissolve into such a fit of elation because of their bad roads. He shook his head incredulously from side to side, and he continued, "You people of Chuforba will be expected to turn out tomorrow en masse with your spades and hoes, cutlasses and palm wine at the chief 's palace. We must repair this road and open up your village to development. We need to market your kola nuts for you."

The chief went on with the translation, "The white man has said that tomorrow all the young men in this village who have the interest of their birth place at heart should each take one pig or fowl to the chief. The white man says he will bring a machine that will remove all the big trees and dig our road for us. That way we will be able to reach the coast very easily."

The villagers burst into spontaneous applause and screamed with joy. The shrill voices of some women could be heard yelling ulililililililili while the men in unison responded to the chief with mbe, chamufor, and various titles of respect and reverence.

Pa Atanga, president of the Chuforba Traditional and Cultural Society, took the floor and spoke on behalf of the villagers; he assured the chief, His Royal Highness, the Leopard Tamer and Rain Maker, Fon Tsugmoh, that his will would be done.

"But before I go," Lieutenant James added, "I must say one more important thing. Next week, I shall come and select from your midst sturdy and hefty men that will join the Southern Merooncа's police force. It is the wish of the government for every village in this country to be represented on the force. We are for democracy. Full democracy. That's why we shall continue to rule you until we think you are mature enough to rule yourselves. And that is why we want you to fight for us. We want you to fight for democracy. We want a force that is capable of winning any war, and from my experience in this country, I believe I can say convincingly that some of this country's best elements are from this village."

So saying, he turned to the chief to translate.

The chief translated, "The white man has said that only those of our people who have given the chief pigs and fowls will be selected to join the police force. No one else. Mark my words. No one else. Those of you who are always refusing to help your chief will miss this opportunity. This is therefore your last chance to show the world that you love your chief. And the chief too will, of course, show you that he loves his subjects. You see, I brought this white man here today to give our young people jobs."

The villagers dispersed. Many of them beat their breasts and promised to bring their fattened pigs and chickens to their beloved chief. Some of them said if that was all the white man wanted them to give their chief, it was nothing compared to the valued traditional treasures that the white man himself had plundered and spirited away to his country.

The next day, some of the male villagers brought their fattened animals to the chief, and the women brought food and kola nuts. Full of the wisdom invested in him by age, the chief lumbered and sat in his rickety old chair on which some leopard skin had been spread. There was complete silence as he peered down at the assembled villagers searchingly as if probing some unfathomable depths of thought.

"Thank you, my citizens. Thank you, my subjects. All of you deserve to be enlisted into the police force, but since it is the white man's force, there is pretty little I can do. The only advice I can give you is that when the white man comes, he will say, 'Left right, left right.' Those who do not know their left from their right will, of course, not be taken. Left is the woman hand and right is the man hand. So when the white man says 'left turn,' turn to the woman hand; and when he says 'right turn,' turn to the man hand."

A week later, Lieutenant James returned to the village for the recruitment drive. The villagers who had been selected by the chief stood in a single file, and when the willowy white man with his pointed nose and overflowing jaws ordered left turn, the villagers executed the order with military precision. Lieutenant James was lost for words. Not believing his eyes, he ordered right turn, and again the villagers turned right with skill as if they had just returned from military training. Lieutenant James was delighted and switched on one of his rare smiles that lit up his face and showed his flashing teeth, which are arranged like corn on a cob. He was amazed at the villagers' skills and praised the young men for being the only ones in the entire country who had all, to a man, executed the order without a fault.

All the villagers the chief had selected were thus recruited into the Southern Meroonca's police force, and Pa Asaah's father, Nei Asangwa, was one such lucky recruit.

Chapter Three

As the story dragged on, someone knocked on the door. Kwa kwa kwa. The story was so interesting that none of the children heard the knocking. There was another knock followed by another in rapid succession. Pa Asaah stopped talking and craned his long neck in the direction of the door.

"I think there's someone at the door," said Pa Asaah. The children pricked their ears and listened. No one moved, and not even an eyelid batted.

There was another knock, and then the person spoke, "You mean there's no one in this house?"

Still no one spoke nor moved, frozen as they were with fear. Death is, after all, just a heartbeat away from life. The only noise that could be heard was the commotion from the mice in the ceiling. They must have had their fill after feasting on the groundnuts and maize that had been kept up there to be smoked. And having eaten to their hearts content, they were now playing hide and seek, tackling each other, and making fun of the Asaah household. One week after, Pa Asaah had set a trap in the ceiling to reduce their numbers; only one dumb mouse had had the ill luck to be caught in it because of its greediness. It had, after feasting on the corn, gone after the meat that had been used as a bait.

As the knocking resumed, Achu—always the daredevil—jumped up to open the door; and Pa Asaah pulled him back by the sleeve. Achu staggered backwards, lost his balance, and bumped his buttocks on the floor at the spot where Pa Asaah had just poured some dirty water to send the dust to sleep and also to drown the ubiquitous jiggers. The Asaah children burst out in raucous laughter.

The knocking persisted but was somewhat drowned by the high-pitched laughter and squawking of the children. Suddenly there was a lull in the knocking as if the knocker wanted to be certain it wasn't the wrong door he or she had been knocking on all this time.

Pa Asaah took his finger to his lips and hissed in the manner of a snake. The children glued their lips, and there was total silence. No one stirred.

"Who are you, and what do you want?" Pa Asaah ventured.

"You mean that you no longer recognise my voice again?" the knocker responded tartly. Evidently it was a feminine voice but with a manly, commanding tone.

At that time of the night, no one trusted anyone. Ma Sah's daughter had died the year before and, characteristically, the village had been rife with rumours that the girl, though dead, was roaming from house to house at night, disturbing the peace of the entire village. And since the villagers had succeeded in elevating gossiping and rumour mongering to a pure art form, no one wanted to believe that death, for all its daring, could be natural. You died because someone wanted you to die. Period.

Whoever was knocking continued to knock but with reinforced strength. Ni Gwebei, brother of Pa Asaah, grabbed a spear and cutlass and dashed for the door. Taking cover behind it, he unbolted it slowly while his hands trembled in fright. As he opened it, two ladies, both lavishly dressed, strolled in, preceded by the sensuous aroma of a spicy perfume they were wearing.

All eyes turned in the direction of the ladies. The one leading the way was, of course, familiar to everybody. She was tall by Chuforba standards, lavishly pretty, and considered by most Chuforbas as an irresistible woman with a voracious appetite for sensuality. Lush black hair hung irresponsibly down her back. She waved the pair of customised dark glasses she had just peeled from her face when she entered as a mischievous grin kept her company. One of the Asaah children rose to give her a seat as she made her way through the crowd of children.

The brown shawl she had negligently thrown over her shoulder fell. Foti dived to pick it up; and she barked, "Leave it before I bash your head in, you clown. Can your mother buy it?" Foti retreated immediately, and she bent down to pick it. Her low-cut top, sumptuously laced and bristling with bright buttons, revealed a matching brown bra. Two pompous breasts jutted out to be noticed, and she scrambled to shove them back to where they belonged. Just at the same time, the hairpin holding her hairpiece in place so the unruly Chuforba wind wouldn't run away with it, dropped. No one dared make an attempt to pick it up for fear of incurring her wrath.

"Pick it up quick, you idiot," she thundered. "You expect me to bend down twice?" Foti bent down and picked it up with fumbling fingers, and he was shaking with fright as he handed it to her. The eyes of the entire household peered at her. She grabbed the hairpin gruffly and threw the shawl over her shoulder in an attempt to cover her exposed chest.

Mrs. Akwen Ndefru, Pa Asaah's youngest sister, always dressed suggestively and never cared a hoot what people thought of her, not even her family.

Mrs. Akwen Ndefru's friend was a no-less-flamboyant woman. She was lofty and had extraordinary grandeur, although she was slightly heavily set. She walked with short measured steps, her neatly cut green suit made from African wax lappa material matched her green hat that had a tassel dangling from the top. The hat, for its part, hid her fine silky hair that had been damaged by her continuous use of heated appliances and chemicals. Her face showed signs of skin discoloration from skin lightening creams, but it was adorned with a broad, elegant, and vivacious smile. The green dress hugged her body in a sensuous manner, and a large heart-shaped gold pendant dangled from her neck.

The Asaah children steered their eyes away from Mrs. Ndefru whom they knew very well as their aunt and gazed at Mrs. Grace Mokom, a twice-divorced and youthful-looking woman of fifty-one years who was well-known for her romantic escapades. She usually crossed the manned border of marriage where conscience stands on guard into the unmanned territory of infidelity with ease.

When she realised that all stares were pinned on her, she looked somewhat ill at ease and out of place in the crowded one-room mud house. She fixed the blue barrette that had clipped her hair in place, and her wandering voluptuous eyes ping-ponged around the room as she and Mrs. Ndefru sat down on Pa Asaah's creaking wooden bed that agonised and ached with pain whenever someone moved their buttocks. Pa Asaah's bed was full of endurance and had known untold pain and hardship from overuse. The seeds from which the twenty-four Asaah children were born had been sown in their mothers' wombs as they lay in that bed.

After the two women sat down, Pa Asaah squinted as he looked at them. "Who is this like, Akwen?" Pa Asaah enquired. "Why did you have to scare us like that? This is your house, and you want to knock it down before entering? Don't you know that at this time of the night, people don't open their doors anyhow?" Then he turned to the other lady and greeted, "Welcome, madam."

"Thank you, Pa. Good evening," Mrs. Mokom responded and stretched her hand. Pa Asaah held it for a while and shook it lightly. The hand was baby soft as if she was not used to pounding achuh, one of the local staple foods.

Mrs. Ndefru drew a sullen countenance and turned her face away. She removed a perfumed handkerchief from her snakeskin purse and began to wipe her glasses. Pa Asaah blinked and looked at her with circumspection, awaiting a reply. Mrs. Ndefru did not respond. In the meantime, Mrs. Mokom began fidgeting with the heart-shaped pendant that hung from her neck.

"Akwen," Pa Asaah blurted out, "I just asked you a question, and you are looking at me as if I am some kind of statue. I hope you are not having problems again with your husband."

Mrs. Ndefru pouted her lips and still said nothing. Pa Asaah rubbed his hands together and mended the fire. There, Mrs. Ndefru sat almost apologetically although she looked sweet and tender as always. She stole a smile when her eyes met with those of Anyim, one of the older daughters of Pa Asaah. Mrs. Ndefru had always liked Anyim, and so when their eyes met, her face radiated good cheer.

When Mrs. Ndefru had been much younger, the local Damenba newspaper, the Grass Fields Times, had compared her to a blooming hibiscus flower in the heart of the rainy season, especially after she had won the much-coveted Miss Chuforba Bottle Dance Beauty Pageant. That bottle dance beauty pageant had been the talk of the village and of the country as a whole. While some people had opposed the idea of a pageant because they felt it belittled women, others had gone out in arms in support of it because they said it was an opportunity for the village and the nation to admire God's creation. Women, after all, were flowers that God had created to adorn the earth. And men, like bees, flocked to them to suck the life-sustaining nectar that they held in their bosoms.

Mrs. Ndefru had run for the Miss Chuforba Bottle Dance Beauty Pageant when she was a ravishing seventeen-year-old girl with the kind of warm personality that melted men's hearts the first time they laid eyes on her. And she had won very easily. Her glamorous looks and tall and overarching figure had dwarfed all the other girls. It did not matter at the time that she could not answer most of the questions that were asked. She was pretty, and she danced good. Full stop.

Mrs. Ndefru leaned sideways to whisper something to Mrs. Mokom, and her earrings trembled and dangled like a fern that yields to the strength of the passing wind. Pa Asaah's eyes peered from behind the sockets, and he threw a curt glance at his little sister. Still she said nothing but took out a wooden comb from the bag that was resting on her lap and began to arrange her hair. Then suddenly, as if seized by some spasm, she said starchily in a stammer, "Nei, Nei, I came to see you for another problem."

"I guessed it," Pa Asaah replied sarcastically. "I hope it is not the same perennial problem between you and Ndefru. By the way, where is that husband of yours? Isn't he supposed to be here with everybody else? The way both of you are dressed, I am sure you must be returning from some great official party."

"Please, Nei, you mustn't say that," Mrs. Ndefru cut in sardonically. "Yes, we are coming from the VIP bash that takes place at this time of the year. But surely you don't expect Ndefru and I to be going all over the place together at night as if I am a dog on a leash. Ndefru leaves the house every morning and doesn't return until late at night, and you expect me to stay at home waiting for him? Ask Grace here to tell you since when Ndefru left the house today. I haven't laid my eyes on him since then. But then you know as well as I do that he wants to marry that whore of a girl who claims to be the daughter of Mr. Achiri, the well-known traditional doctor from Baba. Nei, the problem between Ndefru and I is becoming more and more serious, and I'm not sure I want to play second fiddle."

"Akwen, I understand, but this wound has been festering now for quite some time," Pa Asaah snapped sharply. "I have always told you that there is no couple without problems, and I do not see why you should be bothered by the fact that Ndefru wants to marry another woman. Why can't he? Isn't he a man? Don't you know that the number of women a man marries is a measure of his manhood and wealth? I don't understand the reason for all the fuss. Ndefru is free to marry whomever he pleases. You will recall that when you were about to marry him, the family refused because he comes from a family with a background of witchcraft. You said at the time that we had no business meddling in your private affairs with Ndefru and that you were highly educated enough to know what you wanted. You refused to listen to the voice of reason because you were in love, and now . . . well, this is what happens to children who don't listen to their family."

Mrs. Ndefru clenched her teeth and sucked in her overlapping upper lip. Blood thumped hard in her heart, and she mobbed the beads of sweat that had just formed on her brow. She then turned towards her friend whose head was bowed. She wanted to reach out to her from the bottomless well of depression in which Pa Asaah's words had dumped her. She needed her friend to utter some soothing words that would fortify her, but Mrs. Mokom was so taken off guard by Pa Asaah's remark that all she could do was stare at her friend blankly. Suddenly, Mrs. Ndefru exploded.

"Anyway, Nei, whether you think my problem is serious or not," she gurgled fitfully, "I have one thing to say and that is that I cannot continue with Ndefru anymore. At least not the living me. Uh-uh, not me. A toad likes water but not when the water is boiling."

Pa Asaah smiled wanly, looked up at the ceiling, and fawned on his beard. "Akwen, I think this is a fairly serious matter that we can't possibly discuss tonight, especially with all these children around. Delicate subjects like this should not be discussed in the presence of children. I, therefore, suggest that we discuss this tomorrow during the family meeting, in the absence of these children. This means that you will have to go and inform that errant and stray husband of yours to be here tomorrow because the family will like to meet him so that we can solve this problem once and for all. I hear he might be going to Victoria tomorrow. Tell him to postpone the trip."

"That's your problem, not mine," Mrs. Ndefru shot back squeamishly. "I don't care. After all, why can't we discuss it now? Haven't you always said that in this family we have nothing to hide?

In any case, to cut a long story short, I think I have decided to leave Ndefru once and for all. I can't catch up with his running around with girls his children's age. Just imagine. What kind of a man did I marry? After making just two children, Ndefru turns round and says he doesn't want more children. He says he is happy with two children, but that is a big white lie because while he is refusing to make another child with me, he is running round naked in every woman's bed."

"Yes, Akwen, but surely you can't say that two children are too small, especially in this day and age of economic hardship. Okay, everybody knows that Ndefru is a very rich and powerful man but all the same," Pa Asaah quipped. "You should be thankful to God for what he has done to you."

"I don't like you to preach to me," Mrs Ndefru burst out."What you are saying is very true, but haven't you been complaining that you only have twenty-four children? In my case, don't forget that Cho is over seventeen years old now while Fri is eleven. Yet Ndefru refuses to make another child."

"How do you know that he doesn't want to make more children?"

"You mean how do I know that Ndefru does not want to make another child with me? Well, for your information, in case you did not know, I am still married to Ndefru. I know him well enough. Besides, we have fought over this issue many times."

"If you know him so well," Pa Asaah interjected angrily as spittle dripped from his mouth, "then you should know that you can't eat and break the dish from which you've just eaten."

"What! See who's speaking," Mrs Ndefru thundered. "Speaking of dishes, how many have you broken? How many wives have you sent away, let alone those who left you because of your unacceptable behaviour? Did you not send away Ma Ngum because you said she couldn't give you a male issue? And what of Ma Neh who died from an overdose of gossip. Everyone claims you sold her to the infamous Zeg secret society because you wanted wealth and fame. But what has it given you if not abject poverty? And just recently, wasn't everyone in the village talking about you because Ma Atog, the mother of Achiri, reported you to the chief because you had accused her falsely of sleeping with Ni Fon? And just a few weeks ago, for that matter, didn't Pa Tingoh, the witch doctor, say that if you continue to defy traditions your late father will send lightning to burn all the hair under your armpits and private parts as a warning unless you make some traditional sacrifices? So see who is talking of breaking dishes. What also of Ma Susa, Ma Kyen, Ma Akwen, Ma Pauline, Ma—"

"All right, all right, Akwen," Ni Ngwed, her elder brother screamed as he squinted and squirmed. "Akwen, that does it. That ends it. You can't and shouldn't talk to our father like that, just as if you are talking to one of these children. You should not even be comparing yourself to him. You are a woman, Akwen, and don't let Ndefru's money go into your head because if you ever leave him, you will have to return to this compound. You shouldn't bite the finger that fed you. Apart from that, you are much younger than me. Who gave you the authority to speak to Nei in this manner? I don't know what is wrong with this country. Disrespectful and ill-brought-up children have arrogated to themselves the right to chastise their parents and elders just because they have money or they occupy positions of influence. And they claim it is education. Education my foot."

Mrs. Ndefru looked overcome by a strange and unfamiliar feeling of helplessness. She gave a sickly smile, bit her lower lip, and her cloudy and lacklustre eyes stared in the distance blankly. The unusual silence in the house seemed to deal her an added blow. Seething with anger, she looked like someone suffering from some outrageous misfortune. The veins on her hands and face were all drawn out and her normally youthful countenance faded. Tears gushed from her eyes, and she wiped them meekly with the back of her palm. When her friend, Mrs. Mokom, turned towards her compassionately, she drew her closer to her chest and, between sobs, whispered something into her ear. Both of them sighed.

Just then there was the drone of a Land Rover hurrying downhill from the schoolyard to the compound. The neighbourhood dogs, as usual, were barking and chasing it. The Land Rover approached the Asaah compound, pulled up to the compound, and parked. Some of the dogs rushed to it and sniffed its tires, presumably trying to discern the markings left by other dogs or trying to leave messages of their own to their canine friends.

Inside the Asaah compound, the entire Asaah household was quiet. There was a tap on the door followed by an accented voice. Ni Ngwed darted to the door and opened it gingerly. In strode the divisional officer (dio), Mr. Mofor, followed by his bosom—booze-som—friend Reverend Ndumbe, a young charismatic pastor ordained just a few months earlier.

Pastor Ndumbe had been the talk of the country because of the highly popular mammoth prayer and spiritual healing and cleansing rallies he organised. The officials of his church—the African Church of the Living God—had on several occasions asked him to desist from organising the rallies, but Pastor Ndumbe had maintained that he would rather listen to the voice of God than to that of man.

As the dio and the reverend pastor strolled in to take their seats, all the Asaah children stood up as a sign of respect. Mrs. Ndefru waved a smile at the pastor as he passed, and the gallant young man doffed his hat, nodded, and moved on to his seat.

"Mr. Asaah, we're terribly sorry we came this late." The dio mumbled as he leaned his walking stick against the wall. "You see, Pastor Ndumbe was busy at home entertaining the Christian women who had gone for confession. You know those poor women are usually dog-tired after working so hard on the mission farm, doing penance for their sins. I don't know who invented that form of confession, but I must say it is an ingenious way invented by the church for Christians to confess their sins. What could I do? I couldn't have abandoned them to the pastor alone so I stayed behind too. After all, I am the dio for everybody, whether they are Christians or non-Christians. Pastor Ndumbe has told me that the Christian women will take communion tomorrow, knowing that not only did they confess their sins, but that they also did penance. I think this country needs young, energetic, far-sighted, and revolutionary pastors like our friend here to revive our churches."

Pa Asaah looked bafflingly nervous as he stroked his beard. Mrs. Ndefru flung a glance at the pastor and looked at him longingly and with avidity. She let her voluptuously luring eyes rest perfunctorily on the pastor's tantalising lips. Pastor Ndumbe played with the gold clip that held his silk print tie in place. A warm and sensuous feeling approached him as he beheld Mrs. Ndefru's bulging and dominant breasts jutting unobtrusively from her dress.

"Don't . . . don't worry," Pa Asaah stammered hesitantly as his nostrils twinkled. "The important thing is the fact that you are here. After all, you are like family members, and you can walk in here at any time. The family reunion that will take place tomorrow is an occasion we've all been looking forward to. I'm excited about it myself because I'll be seeing most of my children and grandchildren. You know we didn't meet last year because of the death of Ngu Bot, the son of Tabe. I mean Tabe, the famous bottle dance guitarist whose daughter is married to Kweti, the man to whom I gave my palm wine bush at Koyimi to be tapped for me. I'm sure you will recall that because of the ban on meetings that the government imposed on the entire country following the riots that took place last year, we had to cancel the last reunion at the last minute."

Pastor Ndumbe snatched the cigarette he had been puffing on from his lips and stubbed it out under his shoes. And then as if someone had just reminded him that he shouldn't have been donning his hat in the presence of Pa Asaah, he wrested it from his head and bared a receding hairline that exposed a completely barren forehead. He pulled a white handkerchief from his vest pocket, ran it across his forehead mechanically and then began to wipe his eyeglasses. Achu shrank back petrified. The pastor's face, bereft of its glasses, resembled that of an owl with its eyes deep down in the sockets. Meanwhile the dio was exchanging warm, flirtatious, and endearing glances with Mrs. Mokom. She gave him a generous and amorous grin, and her glittering eyes sparkled in the dim light. Each time she moved her left hand, her diamond wedding ring emitted iridescent rays.

Achu poked the fire and pawed on his father's leg to which he was clutching.

Pa Asaah had an old raffia bag that had been hanging on the wall behind his bed for years. He got up slowly as his bones creaked at the joints, and plucked it down. Dipping his hand into it, he brought out two cow-horn cups and wiped the soot off. Then he blew into them feebly to expel any stubborn remnants of soot and handed them to the visitors.

Dio Mofor looked at the cups intently while Pastor Ndumbe removed a handkerchief from his pocket and wiped his own cup lackadaisically as if it were some tedious chore he'd rather dispense with. Turning towards Pa Asaah and hoisting the soot-darkened cup, the pastor said reflectively, "Mr. Asaah, I think our people are the greatest improvisers anywhere on earth. Just look at the work of their hands, and behold how well crafted these cups are."

"Sure," Pa Asaah replied casually, matter-of-factly."Aren't educated people like you the ones who say this is primitive? Aren't you the ones who cast aspersions on our traditions because you claim that we are behind the times and live in the past? You recall, Pastor. I don't quite remember when it was, but it must have been some time last year when you visited me and this same issue came up. I recall saying that the problem is not that we do not want to modernise but that modernising should not necessarily mean a rejection of our past. Our present is built on our past, and our future will be built on our present. Let none of you ever forget that, because one has the feeling that the present generation is being taught to abandon anything that has something to do with our past."

Both Dio Mofor and Pastor Ndumbe nodded their approval as the thought of what Pa Asaah had just said rang true in their heads. As the visitors mulled over Pa Asaah's words, he uncorked one of the jugs of palm wine, poured some of the wine into his own cup, and rose slowly, painfully. He took a few steps to the door as all eyes focussed on him. In a gruff voice, he called everyone's attention to rivet on what he was about to do.

Raising the cup listlessly and peering down at everyone, he first rushed his hand impatiently into the loincloth he had tied loosely around his waist, which barely covered his private parts from the peeping children flanking him. He scratched himself generously and self-deprecatingly with his long pawlike nails. Then slowly and meticulously, he lowered the cup to his lips, took a mouthful, summoned all his energy, and, as if activating an inner pump, sprinkled the wine on the children. Then clasping the cup in his two hands, Pa Asaah looked up momentarily, poured some of the wine to the ground as a libation, and said solemnly, "This is for our ancestors, those without whom we wouldn't have been here in the first place. As we drink tonight, we must remember them because this earth in which they are buried is the same earth that gives us our means of sustenance. In everything we do, we must ever be mindful that without our ancestors, we are nothing."

Ni Ngwed gave Pa Asaah some kola nuts. Pa Asaah split them into pieces and passed them round, first to his guests and then to everyone in the house. Then he chewed a few pieces and blew them on his children, thus bestowing on them his manifold blessings. They needed his blessings especially now in his old age.

Achu sat there crawling in the dust and clutching like a tick to his father's leg while Pastor Ndumbe and Mrs. Ndefru seemed to have been swept in a tide of intimate conversation. Seemingly oblivious of the presence of the Asaah children, they exchanged glances and yearning eyes that were pregnant with sensuality. At one point, Pastor Ndumbe stooped over and tendered his right ear to Mrs. Ndefru, who eyed him lovingly with gleaming eyes and beamed exuberantly. After Mrs. Ndefru whispered something into Pastor Ndumbe's ear, he tore back to his seat swiftly and burst out tempestuously in a defiant and tart voice.

"Mr. Asaah, what is this I am hearing again? That errant brother-in-law of yours, Ndefru, is now scheming to send away Akwen so that he can take in that prostitute of a girl? And you're sitting here almost unconcerned even though this is going to affect your sister? I can't believe my ears."

Turning to the dio, Pastor Ndumbe continued, "Dio, I can't believe this. Akwen is the one who has made Ndefru what he is, and because Ndefru thinks that he is sufficiently rich and politically powerful now, he thinks he can just drop her like that and nothing will happen to him. Dio, I think we must do something about this. We must otherwise . . . well, I don't know, but I think we have a duty to do something about it. We can't let Ndefru treat Akwen as if she is nothing."

"Yes, Pastor," Pa Asaah responded with a blazing hot temper. "What's the big deal? After all, this is not the first time that Akwen and Ndefru are at it again. Nor is this the proper time to discuss this palaver. I have already told Akwen that we can't discuss such a critically important family matter in the presence of these children. I have accordingly requested her to bring Ndefru here tomorrow so that we can discuss the matter during the family reunion. I don't understand why she had to bring up the matter again. Besides, let's face it, why are both of you so concerned about what is happening to Akwen? Does it concern you?" Pa Asaah looked at his two visitors with a contemptuous stare for it was clear that they had lit the flame of his anger.

Mrs. Ndefru immediately snapped and answered brusquely. "Nei, you are wasting your time because Ndefru and I have already come to the inescapable conclusion that we can no longer make it together. We've been going forwards and backwards on this issue all the time, blowing hot and cold with no satisfactory result. In case you want to know why the dio and pastor are involved, well, I'll tell you. They are both my friends, and Ndefru knows it. They have an obligation to come to my rescue. Moreover, I think Ndefru may be a dead battery."

Anger claimed Pa Asaah's senses and gloom swept across his face as he shivered tremulously. His heart pounded hard, and his heartbeat quickened while blood swished through his taut veins. Gloomily, he tried to push the thought of what he had just heard further back into the inner recesses of his mind but, disconsolately, the thought kept on surging forward ever more forcefully, refusing stubbornly to be restrained. Theirs had been a family untainted by scandal; now his little sister was just about to splatter dishonour on the family name.

Pa Asaah tried restlessly to impart a faint smile to his guests, but his writhing countenance chased it away. His piercing eyes scanned his sister, x-raying her to detect what it was in her that always made her so tempestuous, so imperious in speaking, and so impervious in receiving advice.

Looking a little withdrawn, as if burrowing into an isolation that only he knew the limits, Pa Asaah sat in abject forlornness, somewhat distant from himself, unmoving. The Asaah children began to whisper in hushed, soft tones. In the meantime, a smile flew past and settled on the pastor's lips. His eyes caught those of Mrs. Ndefru, and the smile retreated abruptly when Pa Asaah turned absently in the pastor's direction. The pastor dragged away his eyes from him and whimpered something only he himself could hear.

As Pa Asaah's eyes crinkled, he struggled slowly to gather himself, straining under the weight of the thought that fully possessed him as if some fettered shackles had bound him. He chuckled dimly and shook his head. Then he looked unenthusiastically in the direction of Mrs. Mokom and responded cuttingly in a choked voice as his lips trembled, "Okay, Akwen, I have heard you say all sorts of things about Ndefru but none so irreparably damaging as what you have just said today in the presence of these children and our visitors."

Before Pa Asaah could continue, Mrs. Ndefru shot back defiantly, an evil and mischievous grin walking lithely on her lips, "For your information, the dio and Pastor Ndumbe are not visitors. They are my friends. So correct what you are saying. As for these idiots sitting down here that you are calling children, I wouldn't call them children if I were you. Some of their age-mates already have children." The dio and Pastor Ndumbe laughed derisively and outrageously.

Pa Asaah stared at his little sister blankly with a puzzled look. And even though he made efforts to appear calm on the surface, undercurrent waves of anger convulsed the tectonic plates of his mind. He managed to mutter a withering response to Mrs. Ndefru. "Even if my children have grand—and great-grandchildren, they are still my children. Children are children no matter how big they have grown. Shoulders can never grow taller than the head." There was no immediate response from Mrs. Ndefru.

The silence was soon broken by a burp from the dio. It was so loud it sounded like the peal of thunder. Everyone turned in his direction. He shook off embarrassment and offered apologies in a tremulous voice, "I am sorry. I had some beans and potatoes for dinner. Each time I eat them, they betray me." A nervous smile hovered around his face.

"That's okay, Dio," Pa Asaah responded reluctantly. "It can happen to any of us."

"Not to any of us," Mrs. Ndefru said sarcastically, rubbing her chest on which two silicone-implanted breasts were mounted."Well-brought-up people don't go round burping all over the place just because they ate beans and potatoes."

"Akwen, that's a very uncharitable remark," Ni Ngwed said firmly. "The dio is our guest, and you should, please, mind your language."

"I'm sorry," Mrs. Ndefru replied. "As I told you, the dio is not a guest. He is my friend." She blew her nose into a white-starched handkerchief.

"But the dio is not in your house," Ni Ngwed responded. Mrs. Ndefru glanced at her brother with a scornful look and didn't respond. She raised her right hand and treaded her jaws. After an uneasy pause, Pa Asaah spoke up in a harried voice.

"Going back to what you said about Ndefru, I don't think it is fair for you to call him a dead battery. I concede that he may be a weak battery."

"But that is exactly what he is. A dead battery. Anyway, who told you that I only want two children?" she answered back cheerlessly. "While he is refusing to make more children with me, isn't he going round like a dog in heat? Didn't he make a baby with that filthy coastal girl in Our Lady of Love's College? And didn't one little girl of just about sixteen years who sells oranges come and insult me that I have no reason to be proud because she and I have the same husband? And, of course, I'm sure all of you have heard about the rumour that he is going out with Mrs. Fru, his so-called secretary. Am I not the butt of ridicule when everyone tells me that Mrs. Fru's child is not Mr. Fru's but my husband's? Enough is enough. I think I have had my own share of shame in this country."

"In that case you can't say Ndefru is a dead battery. A dead battery can't function unless it is charged," Pa Asaah suggested with diffident self-assurance, pinning his sister in the same position with a stare.

"I say he is a dead battery, and I'm not going to change what I'm saying,"

Mrs. Ndefru answered with an indomitable voice. "But then who can be sure that that prostitute girl from Our Lady of Love's College is speaking the truth?" she enquired rather ruefully with a shrug.

Before Pa Asaah could say anything, Pastor Ndumbe immediately jumped into the fray and responded in an offhanded manner, "Mrs. Ndefru, I don't think it is fair to—"

Mrs. Ndefru didn't wait for the pastor to finish. "And you, Pastor Ndumbe, you are always giving advice, but you forget that I know all about you. You are always giving people advice you yourself can't follow. Where is Grace, your first wife? I hope you haven't forgotten the scandal you caused a few years ago when you and the choir leader were caught in church red-handed, and Florence walked out on you. You're not yet a televangelist, but you're already doing exactly what televangelists are supposed to do so well. Please keep your mouth out of this because I don't think I need you to tell me what to do."

Pastor Ndumbe hung his head in shame, and the entire house was clobbered by disabling silence for a minute or so.

The dio tried to intervene to cool tempers down. "Don't let anything bother you, Mrs. Ndefru," he said. "I think my friend, the pastor, was just trying to help. I don't think he meant any harm. But one thing is clear, and that's that if that so-called husband of yours does not want to respect you as his wife, he at least knows that I am the dio of this province and that I have to be respected. I can't tolerate husbands who kick and toss their wives around like shells. Our women are inviolable. I will be summoning Ndefru to my office to lay the cards on the table.

We all know that most of Ndefru's wealth comes from government contracts that I myself have intervened for him to have. Ndefru has not been paying his taxes for the past five years, and I have been covering him up. Secondly, Ndefru has been involved in the illegal importation of firearms into this country and should normally have been locked up for life, if not executed. I personally intervened, and he was allowed to go scot-free. In other words, I saved him from the gallows.

Thirdly, Ndefru is known to be friendly with some opposition leaders. But for me he would have been accused of involvement in the last abortive coup d'état that failed miserably. Again, I am the one who told the investigating team of experts not to name Ndefru among the alleged ringleaders that were summarily executed. You know how things work in this country. Ndefru has stepped on too many toes, and out of jealousy, his enemies would have successfully involved him in that coup thing. You know better than I do what a coup attempt is and how this government treats coup people. But then enough is enough. How far is my generosity supposed to go? I have been doing all these things to help Ndefru because I consider this family like mine. And everybody knows this. What do I get from it? Have I ever drank a glass of wine given me by Ndefru? Yet people I don't know from Adam bring gifts of all kinds to me. Well, I don't want to end up losing my own head because of Ndefru. People have been wondering why I am always standing by the man. Some of them even think I am on Ndefru's payroll."

A smile approached Mrs. Ndefru's lips, and just as it was about to land, it whizzed past. She tried to beckon to it, but it was gone. Her face glistened as she looked at Pa Asaah and didn't say anything.

Pa Asaah coughed and said resignedly, somewhat dismissively, "It is true my father used to say that if you see a rat making fun of a cat, it is because there is a hole nearby."

The house rocked with instantaneous laughter, and Mrs. Mokom smiled elegantly as if to reassure everyone that she was following the conversation with rapt attention. Anger sat on the edge of Mrs. Ndefru's forehead ready to tumble down at any time.

Pastor Ndumbe, for his part, flicked his eyelids and trained his eyes on Mrs. Ndefru affectionately. Mrs. Ndefru caught the smile with her infrared eyes that could see far into any form of darkness that trapped a handsome man. A smile ran to her mouth and settled on it for a while. The pastor gave a nervous smile and stretched out his cup for a refill. As the pastor took a sip, Pa Asaah clicked his cup.

"Pastor Ndumbe, drink to the health of my family. These days, children no longer believe in what we the parents say, much less what the church preaches. This is the education they get nowadays."

Pastor Ndumbe shifted in his chair uncomfortably. He ran his hand across his face and took a deep breath. He was about to say something, but Pa Asaah cut him short.

"Don't mind it, Pastor, don't mind it. If this generation does not want to do as you and the church have commanded, it is their problem. One thing I tell my children is that whatever they do, they must venerate our traditions."

Chapter Four

One after the other, Pa Asaah called his children to approach him for a drink. They approached, knelt down before him, and wiped their hands on their buttocks. Then each one joined their hands together and cupped them. Pa Asaah poured some palm wine into them, and they drank in silence, reverently as Christians do when they are drinking the communion wine. After that, they licked their hands and the back of their palms like a dog to its cubs.

When the children had all drank, it was the turn of the women, the mothers of the children. All six of them were called in. They walked in—marching in a single file—and sat down. Some of them were bare chested, and their breasts hung loosely. They bowed to the visitors meekly and knelt down humbly before their husband. Ma Agyen, the youngest wife, placed a headpanful of warm water in front of Pa Asaah. He dipped his feet into the water and sat back leisurely as she bent down to wash and massage his feet.

Pa Asaah started to introduce the women to the visitors.

"I begin with Sah, who is my first wife. Call her the queen if you like. She is the head wife in this compound and is, in fact, the one who recommended most of her mates to me to marry. The next one is Arimboh. She was brought in when she was twelve years old. She had been engaged to me from the day she was born. You see the one over there, the one kneeling next to the pastor, she is the doctor's mother. By doctor I mean my eldest son, Dr. Akum Asaah. I hope you know that he is a doctor in white man's country. Too bad he wouldn't be here with us for this year's family reunion. I had been hoping that he would be here, but he sent me a message to be read to the entire family during the reunion. He says he cannot be with us physically though he is with us in spirit because he and his colleagues are busy on one sick man. They are trying to put a black man's heart into a white man who needs it badly to stay alive. I think he called the operation heart transpam, or something like that.

I don't really remember what he called it, but Achu and those of you going to school, what do you call it again? Heart trans . . . transpan—"

"Papa, I think it is called heart transplant," Achu responded.

"That's correct, my son. Yes, it is called heart transpalm."

"But, Papa," Moma, one of Pa Asaah's youngest children, asked searchingly.

"How come they are putting a black man's heart into a white man? Are the hearts the same?"

"Yes, of course," the dio cut in and answered swiftly. "They are the same. Don't mind all the bluffing of white people. If you cut them, they will also bleed, and the blood will be red like ours. They are the same like us."

Moma threw up his hands in the air. He couldn't believe what he was hearing. But he dared not say anything, let alone challenge the dio. But how come, he asked himself, could the dio, who was supposed to know better, say that the white man and the black man are the same? Moma couldn't understand.

Shaking his head as if to loosen the grip of the thoughts that bound and gnawed away at him, Moma exclaimed, "Papa, if it is true that the white man and the black man are the same, I too would like to have a white man's heart. That way, everybody will respect and fear me since we fear the white man."

"Shut up, shut up, and don't let me hear you ever say such a stupid thing again," Pa Asaah bawled out, his eyes darting across the room. "Even if you take a white man's heart, you will still be a black man. Being black or white is not a matter of colour alone. Being black is also a state of mind because we have some black-skinned people who are, to all intents and purposes, white in mind and character. My children, listen. You will be judged not by the colour of your heart or skin but by the purity of your acts. Remember that black never fades and that you must be proud of your blackness just as the white man is proud of his whiteness. The only thing is that you must work hard. Look at your oldest brother, Dr. Akum Asaah. He is a doctor in white man's country. And we are told that he is in charge there of the hospital where they are going to put a black man's heart into a white man. It shows you that where there is a will, there is a way. The white man will respect you when he sees that you are as good as he is, or better than he is. In fact, we are not, as far as I know, afraid of the white man. If anything, they are the ones who are afraid of us because they think that if we are strong and united, we might do to them what they have been doing to us. Anyhow, let us go back to where we were, and I hope this time, none of you will sidetrack me. If I am not mistaken, I think I was introducing your mothers to the dio and the reverend. Yes, Dio, the next one is Lum, the daughter of Papa Ngwa Timotias. You remember Papa Timotias, I'm sure. He is the one whose grandparents come from Njinmambang. Sitting next to her is Ufei, the wife of my late junior brother whom you should know very well. You remember the man whom that police officer shot in cold blood when he was on his way to Zouala simply because he didn't have his voters registration card on him to show that he had voted for the president in the last presidential elections, which the president won by a magical 90 percent? Uh-huh, that man that was assassinated so savagely is my younger brother, and this is his wife who is now mine. You know what we say in our language. If a chicken cannot eat the corn, give it to the pheasant."

At the mention of her late husband, Ufei—looking haggard and wrenched by misery—exploded in sobs; and tears gushed down her eyes prodigiously like water rushing down the sides of a dam whose walls had suddenly collapsed.

While Ni Ngwed consoled her, some of the children laboured desperately to hold back the tears that had flooded their eyes. They still had vivid memories of the death of Ufei's husband and especially of the gruesome circumstances of his death. The wound was still too fresh to be stirred again.

Unable to blunt the sting of the pain that was racking him as he saw Ma Ufei sobbing, Pa Asaah ordered that she should return to her own house.

After Ma Ufei was taken out, Pa Asaah continued, "Reverend, something must be wrong with this country. Ever since that police officer slaughtered my brother in cold blood last year, nothing, I mean nothing, has been done to him. He was locked up briefly and then released clandestinely. No trial. No accountability. Passengers travelling along the Zouala highway say they sometimes see the same officer at checkpoints. And instead of mending his ways, he has become even more arrogant and terrifying because he knows he has protection from above. You know what I mean? He has protection from the powers that be in this country." Pa Asaah paused, glanced at the dio whose head was bowed, and added, "I can't blame him because if the law had taken its course, the fellow wouldn't be on the highway but in jail where he rightfully belongs. Anyway, you and I know how things are done in this country."

"But, Pa Asaah," the dio spoke as he raised his head laboriously, "how can a mere police officer receive protection from above, from the powers that be? I mean, eh, I mean, eh, what access does he have to the pinnacle of power in this country?"

"Dio, that's why we say that those of you who are in power don't know what is happening at the grassroots level. Who in this country doesn't know that he has always been fronting for the commissioner of police? Now, you know who the commissioner of police is, don't you? He is the nephew of the minister of state in the president's office. Do you know of any magistrate in this country that is bold enough to take the risk of imprisoning the guy? These are facts, and you people in power better come down to earth."

"Mr. Asaah, you know I too have also heard the story," the dio responded. "In fact, who in this country hasn't? Even though the government newspaper tried to hush up the news, everybody is aware of what happened."

"And has anybody protested? A few opposition papers reported the news very timidly, but since it involves the nephew of the commissioner of police who is close to the minister of state in the president's office, nobody wants to undertake a thorough investigation."

"But the Chuforba Torch newspaper is on the case."

"Granted, but the light from the Chuforba Torch doesn't seem to have revealed anything."

"I hear they received anonymous phone calls to stop any investigation into the case."

"And they did? You mean they bowed to threats and intimidation?"

"If you are in their place, what would you do? Expose yourself to blackmail, arrest, and detention on flimsy excuses?"

"C'mon, journalists should have the force of their convictions."

"I agree with you but not when their life is in danger. We've seen what happened to journalists who resisted. Their presses are burnt down, and their families sent death threats."

"That's true, but people should be prepared to die for their ideas."

"That is, if the rest of the people know why the others are dying. You know that the population needs to be educated about many things, especially as the government controls the media and dishes out daily doses of disinformation to discredit all those who do not toe its line. In this particular case, the police officer was made to appear as a patriot while Ufei's husband was the villain. How can you explain that? A police officer slaughters an innocent unarmed civilian in cold blood, and the victim is accused. You know there's honour among thieves. The police hierarchy protected one of its kind."

"And so what has the government done about it?" Pa Asaah probed.

"But I thought you said the fellow is back at checkpoints? Pa Asaah, you are older than me and have more experience in this country than most people I know. What can the government do in situations like this?" the dio wondered.

"Dio, let me tell you frankly. During the colonial times, we had a real police force made up of conscientious and law-abiding citizens. Now we don't know the difference between the police and the criminals. Now we don't know who does more killing of our people, the police or the bandits."

"I see you have a nostalgic desire for the colonial period."

"I know what you mean and your inference, but that's not what I mean. My point is that our forces of law were well trained, better disciplined, better equipped, nonpolitical, and more humane. Today they are ruthless. Their only aim is to protect the Oga in power and, if possible, take over the country themselves. Tell me, Dio, since you are the people in power, why have things deteriorated so badly since we achieved our independence."

"At least we are free. We have our own president, our own parliament, our own institutions, etcetera."

"I beg your pardon, Dio?"

"No, I said at least we now have our own president, our own parliament, our own institutions, etc."

"And you are proud of them? Do they work?"

"That's not the point, Pa Asaah. A mother doesn't run away from her child's faeces."

"You are right, Dio, and I see the analogy. But can't you, as the dio, do something about it?" Pa Asaah crowed.

"Mr. Asaah, I hope you don't mean me."

"Of course, I mean you. Aren't you the dio of this province? Or do you wish to run away from your responsibilities as everyone in power in this country is doing?"

"As you know, Pa Asaah, I was appointed to this position only recently after I had stayed at home doing nothing following my recall from my previous ambassadorial position. In any case, you know that there is nothing I can do about it," the dio answered apologetically.

"I don't understand you, Dio. What do you mean by you can't do anything about it, when you are the dio of this province? You are the highest authority in this province, and if you can't, who else can? This entire province is under your jurisdiction, no?" Pa Asaah asked somewhat ruffled.

"That's true, but the alleged crime took place before I became dio," the dio answered with reluctance.

"True, but you can, at least, request an enquiry into what happened."

"Please, Mr. Asaah, don't ask for my head," the dio pleaded. "You probably don't know how things are done in this country. Corporal Manpikin, the alleged murderer, is scot-free, and you think it is I who can bring him to book?"

"Of course, you're the dio."

"Granted, but you're giving me too many powers. I don't think you know that I don't have the powers to lock up anybody. I am not the police or gendarmerie."

"Please, Dio, don't tell me that you have no powers because everybody knows in this country that tracking down popular opposition leaders, outspoken journalists, and very vocal human rights advocates is the speciality of governors in this country. Moreover, as the president's representative in this province, all presidential powers are vested in you."

"Mr. Asaah, I'm afraid you don't fully understand how things are done in this country. If you did, you wouldn't be saying what you're saying now," the dio replied, a little anger showing in his voice. "Since I was appointed to this position I have not arrested anyone."

"Maybe not directly because you can't do the arresting yourself, but you cooperate with the forces to do so."

"Pa Asaah, I don't think you know me well."

"I don't believe you, Dio. I honestly don't believe you," Pa Asaah said shaking his head in utter disbelief. "The last dio we had, and I don't mean the caretaker dio you took over from who had been acting for eight months before your appointment. I mean Dio Akame. He was a real dio. Who in this province doesn't remember Dio Akame? He had the full powers of a real dio and did anything he wanted. I'm not sure he went through the hassle of obtaining permission from anybody in the capital to do anything he wanted. Under him, the students' association was banned, people were arrested and locked up for months for apparently no reason, the authority of the chiefs was curtailed, private land was expropriated, mammoth crowds were always out there to welcome him whenever he was returning from a trip to the capital, and so on and so forth. I remember that the people of this province sent petitions upon petitions to the president to remove him from office but to no avail. I understand he was only recalled eight months ago to be sent abroad for treatment because he was poisoned."

"Mr. Asaah, I'm happy that you have answered your own question. You say petitions upon petitions were sent to the capital for him to be recalled and nothing was done. That's just the point. Notwithstanding my predecessor's exactions, nothing came out of the petitions, and you think I'm the one who can change the way things are done in this country?"

"Why not? That's precisely what's wrong with us in this province. We don't know how to enjoy power. Here you are. A dio. Born and bred in this province even though we know your parents are not from here. However, instead of using your powers, you are afraid of I don't know what. Yet we consider you a son of this province. A son of the soil as some people say. That's exactly what some of us have been saying, namely, that we don't know what's wrong with our own people. We allow outsiders to come and rule us even in our own province. What are you afraid of, Dio? Someone of your calibre?"

"Please, Mr. Asaah, let's not get into this any more than we've already done. There are too many things that I don't want to be forced to say just to make you believe that I don't have any real powers."

"Dio, you surprise me because I used to have a lot of respect for you. I mean it."

"Well, Mr. Asaah, I don't think I should misuse my powers just to make it appear that I am enjoying power. Who doesn't enjoy power? My own view, and I may be wrong, is that I don't have to exercise power by misusing it. In fact, that's why we're not making any progress in this country. For my part, I'm not going to do like my predecessor just to please our people."

"You sound like all the people from this province who have power," Pa Asaah cut in with a raspy voice. "What are all of you afraid of? Look around you and see how other people are wielding power. Steal a leaf from your predecessor's book. Take a look at the branch manager of the Damenba Commercial Bank. Everybody knows that he owns the entire GRA (government residential area) and that he has majority shares in many of our large corporations. You also have the director of lands and surveys, the big Oga's nephew as well as the brother of . . . of . . . of . . . you know who. They constitute the axis of everything that is evil in this country. They have acquired all the choicest land in this country. Plus they wheel and deal, etcetera. You people in government don't think we have eyes. Our eyes are not closed. There is also the managing director of the country's telephone company. There are many more I can cite. But when it is our people, they are afraid to chop from this government as if government is not meant to be chopped. Dio, honestly speaking, I've lost confidence in all of you. I mean it. If our people cannot do something as simple as chopping, I don't see what else they'll be able to do."

"Mr. Asaah, I thank you for all the examples you've quoted," the dio answered somewhat querulously. "Everybody knows that everything you've said is true, but the day of reckoning will come someday."

"A day of reckoning my foot," Pa Asaah sneered. "That's what our people keep on saying. We've been hearing this since I was a boy. You Southern Merooonca boys are just not smart. In fact, you are stupid. Plain stupid. That's all. Has anyone ever told you that you shouldn't chop government, or that our leaders are against chopping? Do you know of any one that has ever been imprisoned for chopping in this country? Just name me one person if you think I'm lying."

"Oh Mr. Asaah. Many people have been imprisoned. In fact, countless. I'm sure you must have heard of Elias Ngu, Peter Nyamfukah, John Mbinetoh, and many others who are languishing in jail at this very moment because they were accused on the spurious charge of misuse of government funds."

"Please, Dio, you know better than that," Pa Asaah chuckled. "If you are going to quote examples, quote good ones. Who doesn't know that all the people you've referred to were not really jailed for misuse of government funds? You know it, and I know it too. Weren't they jailed on trumped-up political charges because they are supporters of the Southern Merooonca National Congress? It is common knowledge that they wrote a petition to the president of the republic calling for an enquiry into the mysterious death of Ekaney, the student leader allegedly bludgeoned to death by the forces of law and order during the student demonstration, calling for a national convention."

"Then you are indirectly admitting what I have been saying all along, namely, that you don't have to have committed a crime to be found guilty. Mind you, the justice of politicians is not the justice of the courts."

"I agree with you to some extent. But that's not the point. Why can't we do like others? Who asked them to write a petition? I am talking about chopping and not about petitions. Why must we try to be holier than the pope?" Pa Asaah retorted with a flickering of resentment in his voice.

"But, Mr. Asaah, that's not the way to develop this country—" The dio was about to expatiate, but Pa Asaah interrupted him.

"Dio, I'm getting sick and tired of this worn-out argument in this country. I asked you why our people are trying to be holier than the pope. When people from any ethnic group occupy a small position, it is their entire group that benefits; but when it is our turn, we put every other group first. What are we trying to prove? And who cares anywhere? Aren't we the losers? Go to some ministries and state-owned companies and you'd think you are in a foreign country. All you hear is the language of the ethnic group from which the minister or managing director comes. Please, Dio, don't try to justify the unjustifiable. My point is very simple. Why can't we also concentrate on chopping like other people are doing and stay out of politics?"

"Mr. Asaah," the dio murmured as he looked at his watch."You know chopping and politics go hand in hand. Now that time is against us, I think we don't have much time to enter into a detailed discussion of this delicate issue. But let me give you an idea of the problems we face even if we stay out of politics and just do our work. Do you know that the commissioner of police for this province, for example, is supposed to report to me? But do you know that in reality, he sends the results of his investigations directly to the president's office and not even to his minister?"

"That's preposterous, Dio," Pa Asaah shrieked. "But we're talking of a murderer, an assassin who is just a corporal."

"Please, Pa Asaah, never say just a corporal," the dio offered. "In this country, some corporals are more powerful than generals or, if you like, some corporals are generals."

"Dio, what you're saying is crazy."

"No, Mr. Asaah, let's please keep insults out of this. I don't want us to add fuel to the fire. I'm simply telling you the way things are done in this country. You think you and I can change the situation?"

"Lord, have mercy!" Pa Asaah exclaimed. "But, Dio, you think the president knows about all this? Have you ever brought this to the attention of the president?"

"Which president?"

"There you go again," Pa Asaah growled. "What do you mean by which president? Okay, I know everybody is saying that we have a very weak president, but how many presidents do we have in this country? Of course, I mean the president of the republic, unless you people in the opposition already have another one in mind."

"Please, Mr. Asaah."The dio sulked."You know that I'm not in the opposition."

"Maybe, but that's what all of you in government always say. Nobody in government ever officially acknowledges that they're in the opposition. If that, indeed, is true, how come the opposition knows exactly when the president farts?"

"Mr. Asaah, please, please. Let's keep the president out of farting. Since I was recalled from my previous position as ambassador eight months ago, I have not succeeded in obtaining an appointment to see the president. You can't imagine the incredible amount of time I have spent waiting to see him but to no avail."

"But isn't he the one who appointed you to your present position?" Pa Asaah asked somewhat ticked off.

"Sure," the dio answered wearily with a drawl. "But so too has he appointed many other people to positions of influence. You don't expect him to see everybody, do you? Or for him to know all those he appoints? You are talking about the president of this country, you know, Mr. Asaah? Maybe you really don't know it, but our president is extremely busy and does not have time to see everybody who wants to see him."

"Please, Dio, let's keep jokes aside. I'm not sure you mean what you're saying. I certainly don't expect the president to receive everybody who wants to see him, but you are the dio."

"Of course, I am the dio. But do you expect the president to know everybody he appoints?" the dio replied tartly. "I've said our president is an extremely busy man. He is probably the busiest man in the world. Have you ever heard that our president took leave? You think it is because he doesn't like to rest? Now you imagine someone working for so long without ever taking leave. I'm sure he'd have liked to go on leave, but he knows that in this country a president can't just go on leave like that. You know what I mean, right? Do you know of any president on this continent who takes leave?"

"Maybe it is because they don't have an official holiday resort of their own like presidents in other countries."

"C'mon, Mr. Asaah. That's precisely what I've been saying. You simply don't know this country and its institutions. Our president, for your information, has presidential mansions in every province, but he never visits the provinces. So it's not that he lacks a place to go to."

"Granted, but he spends much time abroad with broads than he does at home, right?" Pa Asaah asked with a mischievous smile spreading across his face.

"Right, but that's not leave. We're talking about leave and not about pleasure trips abroad on taxpayers' money," the dio explained wryly.

"Please, Mr. Asaah, the more this discussion unfolds, the more I realise that you don't really know much about our president. And if you don't, I'm sure most people in this country don't either."

"You are the one who thinks we don't know our president. We know him too well."

"I don't know about that, Mr. Asaah, but there is no doubt that you've been reading a lot of opposition papers."

"Anyway, Dio, come to think of it now that you're talking about it, I don't remember ever hearing that any of our presidents has ever taken leave. You really mean that our president has never taken leave?" Pa Asaah probed, intrigued.

"Well, I honestly cannot say. Not even ministers, and I know what I mean since I was one. None of us can take the risk of leaving our positions for even one day to say we're going on leave."

"But surely no one can work without going on leave. You need to rest."

"But, Mr. Asaah, who says we don't rest? I said we don't go on leave, but it doesn't mean that we don't rest. Who says a man can only rest when he is on leave? Of course, we rest when we want to, but we do not make the mistake of going on leave. Make that mistake, and before you come back somebody else has already taken your place."

"Now you're talking. I can understand that in the case of ministers. I know how things work in this country. But certainly not the president. He should have nothing to fear since the press is always singing about his popularity," Pa Asaah said with mortifying assurance.

"Then you don't really know how things work in this country, Mr. Asaah," the dio answered."That's what I've been telling you all along. You sincerely don't know how things work in this country. You know our soldiers. Ever since they learned that the gun can be used to shoot one's way to power . . . well, you know."

"So what, Dio? How did our own man come to power?"

"Well, Mr. Asaah, all I know is that if the president has not had the time to receive some of his ministers, you think I'm the one he will see? I speak from experience. Don't forget that I used to be the minister of state in the president's office."

"I know."

"Don't forget too that our president has six ministers of state, thirty-five ministers, eight deputy ministers, fourteen secretaries of state, eleven governors with the rank of full ministers, and twenty-one advisers. That's a lot of ministers for a small country like ours. In addition there are managing directors, party luminaries, etcetera, whom he has to see from time to time. How do you expect him to receive all these people?"

"But, Dio, you are not anybody. You are a former ambassador, and prior to that you used to be a minister of state and a member of the executive committee of the ruling party. Now you are the dio, and you want me to believe that you do not have access to the president?"

"Well, it is your view that I'm not anybody, and I thank you for it. But, Mr. Asaah, if you do not mind it, I'd rather we discontinue this discussion because I see that there are too many things that you do not quite understand about this country."

"But certainly this country can't be that different from other countries. You know I used to be the interpreter for the British governor general when the British were ruling us in Southern Merooonca," Pa Asaah said, straightening himself as if to release the overbearing wisp of arrogance clasping him.

"You've told me that before," the dio replied.

"That's the point. I don't recall anything similar to what you're telling me."

"But, Mr. Asaah, we're talking about access to the president of this country and not to some other president. Surely you don't mean that you had access to the British prime minister or the Queen."

"Of course, that's not what I mean, but I got to meet the British prime minister all the same when he visited our country in those days. I have never met our own president."

"But, Mr. Asaah, let's not exaggerate things. You cannot compare an African president to a mere prime minister or the Queen even if they are British. Do they have the power our president has, to do anything he wants and get away with it? Do you know an African president that is accountable to anyone?"

"Dio, what you are saying is sickening."

"Isn't everyone saying that the continent is sick? Yet we elect quack doctors to heal it."

"Hearing you, I feel like throwing up, Dio. Okay I see your point, but maybe it is because I do not know too much book that I'm showing great surprise at all the things you're telling me. I sincerely can't see how all the things you've been telling me can be real."

"But they are, although I'll leave it to you to believe what you want to believe."

"This is incredible, Dio. If the president doesn't listen to people like you, who then does he listen to? Who advises him?"

"I suppose he has his trusted aides."

"But then how does he get to know what is happening in this province which is your area of jurisdiction?"

"I suppose he has his own people planted in the various ministries and even in my office."

"You mean spies?"

"There you go again, Mr. Asaah. You are out to hear what you shouldn't hear from me. The people in question don't have to be spies. In fact, they may just be ordinary people in whom he has abiding trust. You know, these people may be people from his tribe and people like that. To give you an example, do you know that it is easier for me, whenever I have something that I believe would be of interest to the president, to float it as a rumour in the presence of my driver's wife since she is related to the cousin of the president's wife? Before you go to the toilet and return, the president has not only received the message but has responded to it immediately. As you know, many people don't believe anything you tell them unless you first float it as a rumour."

Pa Asaah half closed his eyes and breathed deeply.

"Please, please, Dio, please. Please," he entreated the dio. "Kindly spare me the agony because I have a bad heart. Please don't kill me."

Pa Asaah took in another deep breath and suddenly stopped, blipping from his mind the swear words he was about to pour out. After the pause, he continued, "I'm sorry, Dio, that we even got into this discussion. The more I reflect on what you've been telling me, the more I . . . well, let's forget it. Let's forget it and go to something else. I'm mad. Really mad. Please let's go back to where we were. I think I was introducing my wives to you."

"Yes."

"Let me now introduce you to Mombo, a princess from Mbey behind those hills over there. The Fon of Mbey was a good friend of mine, and in order to cement our relationship, he gave my father his daughter. When my father passed away, I inherited her. The newest arrival, the youngest of them all that I married last year is this one by my side, Agyen. She is still fresh as you can see. She is fourteen years old. As you can see, she is expecting a baby soon. Although I married her just last year, she has been my wife since she was born. I recall that the day I laid my eyes on her when she was just a few months old, I served notice to her family that she would be my future wife. From that day on, she was treated like a married woman until last year when she was brought to this compound. You see, when I look at all these my wives and the good harvest of children they have produced, I can only be thankful to God."

The women smiled radiantly and shook hands with the visitors briskly. Pa Asaah then ordered his wives to return to their own houses. Women must not sit down together with male strangers especially when an important discussion is taking place. The women strode out respectfully and obligingly. Ndi, Moma, and Tsek carried three calabashes of palm wine and followed the women to their houses.

Pa Asaah turned to the visitors and pointed to Achu.

"You see, Dio and Reverend, in fact, I had seven wives, but the mother of this troublesome one here passed away. She was called Ma Bong. Uh-huh, Ma Bong. An exceptionally obedient and respectful wife who was loved by all her mates or, as we call them, mbanyas. Ever since she left this world and went to the great beyond, the other women have adopted this boy here like their own child. In fact, she passed away when this little boy was still pulling on her breasts."

A certain feeling of anguish overpowered the visitors as they watched Achu tend the fire while his fingers grazed the hair on his father's legs. Pa Asaah hurled more firewood into the fire, and its blaze illuminated the house.

Chapter Five

It was fast slipping past four o'clock in the morning, and one could hear the cocks crowing and breaking the silence in which the village had been shrouded. The pastor glanced at his watch and then peered at it for a moment while sending furtive eye messages to Mrs. Ndefru. Yawning, scratching, and then stretching, he looked in the direction of Pa Asaah and caught his eye.

"Mr. Asaah," Pastor Ndumbe said inaudibly as he yawned. "I didn't know that the time had sped by so fast." Then straightening his rumpled tie, he added, nudging the dio with his elbow, "I think we should call this a day, or shall we call it a night? You know I have church service this morning. Today is Sunday, don't forget, and there will be communion service."

"I understand," Pa Asaah replied, yawning too, a little fatigue showing in his watery eyes.

Mrs. Ndefru zipped open the purse that had been sleeping on her laps, took out a bottle of perfume, and sprayed her underarms generously. After that, she flicked on some mascara and applied a gentle tone of red lipstick that restored to her face the same timeless elegance, beauty, and sensuousness it had conveyed when she strut in.

By now all the Asaah children had already succumbed to the anaesthetic effect of sleep, and only Achu was wide awake, keeping his father company as he entertained his guests.

Mrs. Ndefru glanced at the pastor, parted her lips to say something, but quickly withdrew the glance and pursed her lips.

"Yes, Akwen, you want to say something?" Pa Asaah enquired. She blinked to the pastor, pretending to ignore her brother.

"Reverend, did you bring your Land Rover?" she asked wistfully.

"Yes. Why? You want a lift?"

"Yes, Reverend, if you do not mind it," she answered promptly, cheerfully, switching on an alert, broad, and triumphant smile.

The dio looked in the direction of Mrs. Mokom, but she too had been overpowered by sleep. Her lappa had parted a little, exposing part of her beefy buttocks, folds of flesh around the stomach area, and her shapely legs.

"But, Reverend, if you want to leave now, you should at least lead us in a word of prayer," Pa Asaah entreated the pastor as he picked up his walking stick and poked the children who were sleeping to wake them up. They woke up listlessly with weary hearts and tired eyes.

"Sorry, Mr. Asaah," the pastor responded somewhat ruffled. "I had almost forgotten. In fact, I didn't think a prayer was necessary at this late hour; but since these children are already up, we might as well chat with our Lord. Let us bow down our heads and pray."

Heads bowed down as he led them in prayer.

"Our dear heavenly Father, we thank you for bringing us here together and making this evening a truly memorable occasion. Thank you for everything you've done for us. Guard world peace, oh Lord, and protect us, as does a hen to its chicks. In particular, Lord, please do not make us be like the chicken that gets drunk and forgets about the hawk. Amen."

"Amen," the entire house chimed in.

Reverend Pastor Ndumbe then took leave of the Asaah household and walked out followed by Mrs. Ndefru, who didn't bother to say anything.

The Asaahs soon heard the moaning and anguished screams of the Land Rover as it strained to climb the treacherous Nonji Hill. Mrs. Mokom, who hadn't quite woken up yet, stirred and fidgeted with her gold-plated necklace, her hands trembling as if some minor electrical charge was going through her.

The dio's eyes swept the room in one quick movement as he poured himself the last cup of palm wine.

"Drink to the bottom," Pa Asaah told him, drawing on his pipe. "There are other calabashes of palm wine in the cellar for those who will be coming for the family reunion."

Dio Mofor lifted his head slowly as if it was some heavy load and stared at the dregs sitting placidly at the bottom of his cup, his bulging eyes betraying his uneasiness. Just as he squinted and turned to say something to Mrs. Mokom, the door which had been unlocked since the reverend pastor and Mrs. Ndefru left, swung wide open unexpectedly. Mr. Ndefru marched in, wearing a pale countenance. He was perspiring profusely and breathing volubly as if he had been running a race with death. The log of eucalyptus that had been crackling cheerfully in the fire held its peace.

Mrs. Mokom craned her neck to be noticed; and when her eyes met Mr. Ndefru's, she gave him a curt smile, which he rejected, pretending not to have seen her.

"Papa, I'm looking for Akwen. Would she, by any chance, have come here? She left the house this morning and has since not returned," Mr. Ndefru said in a loud, booming voice.

"Ndefru, what is wrong with you?" Pa Asaah shot back angrily. "First, you come in without even knocking, then you do not greet, and as if that was not enough, you shout to me as if I'm your equal. What is this nonsense? Am I your equal?"

Mr. Ndefru forced a sheepish grin, but it was obvious from the way he looked that he was fighting stubbornly to subdue the raging anger that was taking hold of him. Beads of sweat rolled down his cheeks and dropped like hailstones.

"Papa, I'm sorry," he said in a trembling voice. "As I said, Akwen left the house this morning and has still not returned. I myself just returned home a few minutes ago and was told that she hadn't returned from wherever she had gone to. Look at the time of the day. It is morning."

"What is the time?" Pa Asaah asked turgidly.

Mr. Ndefru looked at his watch and raised his left hand to his ear to listen to the watch's heartbeat. Then he shook his hand wildly and stared at the watch sternly. It was 4:43 a.m.

The dio winked at Mrs. Mokom, who could not wink back because just then Mr. Ndefru's eyes caught hers.

"Why are you looking for Akwen at this time?" Pa Asaah asked calmly.

"Where were you all this time? Is this the time for a devoted husband to be looking for his devoted wife?" Without waiting for Mr. Ndefru to respond, he continued, "In any case, you have nothing to worry about because your wife left us a short while ago with Reverend Ndumbe. We had been expecting that you would join us much earlier and not this late."

"That's true, Papa. I should have been here earlier, but I had some business partners to entertain in the Garden of Eden Bar. We finished just about thirty minutes ago, and I rushed home to see if everything was okay. But where is Akwen, Papa? I went home, and she was not there."

"As I said, you need not worry. She is with Reverend Ndumbe and must be very safe. I'm sure she is in good hands and being taken good care of. I wouldn't worry if I were you."

Mr. Ndefru strutted back and forth disconcertingly, pounding on his chest as he talked to himself, his rudderless emotions adrift. Trying to digest what Pa Asaah had just told him, he blurted out, "I see, Nei, did I hear you say she is safe? In the pastor's hands? Nei, I hope you don't mean that catechist-turned-pastor, that one you call reverend. I mean that irrelevant and irreverent reverend if ever there was one. A playboy reverend. You mean he is the one who took my wife home? And you say she is in safe hands and being taken good care of? By that rascal of a pastor? Who doesn't know him? He better pray hard to his god because when I catch him, well . . ."

"Mr. Ndefru—" Mrs. Mokom opened her mouth to say something, but Mr. Ndefru cut her short.

"And you, whatever is your name, haven't I told you that I don't want to see you with my wife again?"

Mrs. Mokom chuckled implacably and looked straight at Mr. Ndefru with revolving eyes and said in measured tones, "Listen, Mr. Ndefru, I have told you countless times not to let your money go into your head. You must not drag me into your family squabbles because your wife is not a child that someone can take away without her consent. This is her family's house, not mine; and if you don't want her to visit her family, don't hold me responsible for it. I'm not responsible for her actions. Doesn't she have her own two feet?"

Mrs. Mokom's shrill voice was so sharp that it overshadowed the loud snore of Moma, who was sleeping soundly on the mat near her. Moma rolled over and went back to sleep.

Anger illuminated Mr. Ndefru's face. He fiddled with his horn-rimmed eyeglasses for a while, and still not able to control himself, he poured out his bile, "You shut up, blighted soul, and don't you ever dare talk to me like that again. I will not accept that from a woman, let alone from you. A woman who has never respected herself, a woman whose sole purpose in life is to go round like a bee, sucking nectar from every plant and stinging men in the process. Yet you call yourself a married woman. Married my foot. Don't let me ever catch you again with my wife. I know that you are the one who wears trousers in your house, but in my own house, I wear the trousers. You, therefore, better be careful how you talk to me."

So saying, he stormed out of the house in a defiant mood. He slammed the door and staggered to his car. Anger and jealousy competed to consume him and sap his energy.

Before Pa Asaah could say anything, Mr. Ndefru barged into the house, cursing and swearing, "What the hell is this nonsense? God forbid. A dirty woman like this one here is allowed to talk to me like this? And all of you just sit around without anyone saying anything? Anyway, before I go, let me warn all of you that you are all responsible for any mishap that may befall my darling wife."

No one paid attention to him, and he slipped out meekly like a dog with its tail between its legs. Many more cocks had by now joined the few who had initiated the crowing chorus earlier. At the same time, the first gong for the Sunday early morning worship service was also being played. Pa Asaah flung open the door, and fresh, invigorating air flushed into the house.

Shortly afterwards, the faint sound of a distant automobile could be heard. It grew louder and louder as the automobile drew closer and closer to the Asaah compound. When the Land Rover drew near the Asaah house and parked, Pastor Ndumbe and Mrs. Ndefru stepped out briskly and walked into the house.

There was an unusual silence when the couple marched in. The dio and Pa Asaah looked at the couple in utter disbelief as if they had just arrived from Mars.

The dying flames dimly showed the pastor's luminous face. Mrs. Ndefru played with the diamond ring on her little finger, turning it round several times. Pastor Ndumbe decided to break the studied silence.

"Mr. Asaah, as we left like that, uh huh, uh uh, terrible things can befall a man. It is true they say that anything contrived by human beings is not without imperfections. Mr. Asaah, when we left you, we had to pass through the mission because we needed petrol. I usually store some spare petrol in my house. After filling up the tank, the Land Rover wouldn't start. I did everything humanly possible. We even prayed. No way. I checked the battery terminals, the plugs, the points, and even the carburettor but nothing happened. The damn thing—I apologise for my language—the lemon wouldn't respond. In the end, I had to take the battery to be charged."

Pa Asaah shook his head and just stared at the pastor and Mrs. Ndefru for a while.

"Well, you better think of something better to say," the dio said, "Mr. Ndefru was here, and I'm sure he's all over the place looking for you."

"I know," Pastor Ndumbe responded, unruffled as he waved his hand negligently.

"How?" the dio asked, intrigued.

"Because he came to the mission and banged on the door, and we refused to open. We didn't want him to kill us."

The dio looked up at his friend and shook his head. Rising, the dio thanked Pa Asaah for a most pleasant night and gave his hand to Mrs. Mokom who grabbed it and clutched to it. With a slight pull from the dio, Mrs. Mokom was up. She and the dio bade good night to Pa Asaah and vanished into the early morning mist that had blanketed the village.

Achu jumped into his father's bed to catch a little sleep before the family reunion that would be taking place later that day. He was impatient for it to take place because he needed to return to college to prepare for his final examinations. He had been given only three days' permission.

Chapter Six

It was one of those very cold mornings in the middle of the dry season in the northwest province of Meroonca when the cold eats right deep into one's marrow after penetrating the skin and benumbing especially one's fingers and toes. That is the time of the year when lips crack as if in imitation of the cracked asphalt on the street. And as one breathes, one sees wisps of breath wafting frenetically in the air. Konman Town in Damenba was like that at that time of the year because of its high altitude.

The college bugle had just been sounded, and the echo could be heard at that time of the morning in neighbouring villages. In fact, the college's bugle served to wake up people in the neighbouring villages because whenever it was blown, usually at five thirty in the morning, the village men and women—ever so dutiful, ever so methodical—would wake up instantly and prepare for the day's chores.

Achu, like the rest of his dormitory mates, jumped out of bed startled. He rubbed his eyes and gazed at the geometric figures on the ceiling. Then he yawned irrepressibly and scratched himself generously. And as he scratched his back, the itch seemed to be eluding him, playing hide and seek, darting from one spot to another. He'd have been glad to have Ejuba, his neighbour, help him scratch his back because he always enjoyed Ejuba's hand scratching him. But then it was still too early, and Ejuba was still lying in his bed lazily.

Making for his window, Achu opened it reluctantly, and a gush of fresh, cold-laden air slapped him in the face. He closed back the window instantly. He looked at his watch as it ticked 5:37 a.m. As none of his dormitory mates had really woken up since they always waited for the second sound of the bugle at 5:45 a.m. Achu dived on his bed, pulled the blanket over his head, and stuck his cold hands between his thighs. He couldn't fall asleep anymore because he knew he would soon have to be up again.

Here it was again, another school day; and the morning, ever so impatient to take over from the night, had come too fast, depriving the students again of their sleep. And especially in the dry season, one had the feeling that left to the morning, there would be no night. Daybreak was always lurking stealthily, depriving young people of their party time and now of their sleep.

When the second sound of the bugle went off, the entire residents of Cohesa college stirred. The students got out of their beds lazily amidst sighs. Some even had eyes full of tears because it was very cold, and they would rather remain in their beds hugging their pillows snugly and sheltering themselves from the cares of the world.

Thursday wasn't Achu's favourite school day because apart from the general cleanup that the students had to undertake early in the morning, he had to take two courses he loathed with a vengeance because he had flunked them the term before and had thus lost his grip on the third place that he always clung to in his class. He had also come to hate Mr. Ngwa who taught these subjects because he believed it was he who had—with a translucent smile that betrayed an obstinately no-nonsense approach to teaching—forced Latin, a dead language, down their throats.

That particular Thursday morning, unlike other Thursday mornings though, was going to be exceedingly busy because in addition to their normal chores, the students had been informed just two days earlier by the principal, Brother Jakai, that the minister of education would be beginning a nationwide tour of colleges and other institutions of learning that weekend.

Considering that Cohesa College usually did exceedingly well among the colleges in Southern Meroonca through the students' brilliant performances in the General Certificate of Education examinations (GCE), the minister had decided to begin the tour with a visit to the college.

When the news had first filtered through to the students, they welcomed it with disbelief because any one who knew the minister of education knew that he wasn't one to abandon the high-rolling political crowd for a fleeting moment with students.

Hon. Jean-Pierre Paul-Bernard Mbarga Ndzana had always felt that students were kids, and that since they had nothing to do with his appointment, he didn't see why he should be accountable to them. On the face of it, the minister was right. It was, after all, the president who appointed and fired his ministers at will. And since they served at his pleasure, it was to him that they felt they owed their blind allegiance.

As one of the longest-serving ministers in the cabinet—he had been minister for eighteen unbroken years—Honourable Ndzana had become a household name in the country. Everyone knew that not only had he and the president been classmates, but they also came from the same village. As the president's close friend and confidante, he was therefore always certain to maintain his position in any cabinet reshuffle.

Honourable Ndzana had, in fact, served in some of the key troublesome ministries. When he was minister of internal affairs, he used the police and army to clamp down on restive provinces that were clamouring for development projects. One of his major accomplishments in that ministry was the construction of maximum-security prisons in several locations in the country to which political opponents were sent for indoctrination.

Furthermore, he had been the instrument used by the government to turn the Southern Meroonca provinces into garrison states under the pretext that they harboured so-called terrorists of the Southern Meroonca National Congress (SMNC), an internationally recognized movement established to fight for the Southern Meroocan cause and against their marginalisation.

Then as minister of education, Honourable Ndzana was the one who had sent armed troops to the university campus to quell the student demonstrations that had been organised to protest against the government's persistent refusal to nurture dialogue with the Southern Meroonca freedom movement. There were conflicting views about what had actually taken place. While the students claimed that the army and police had killed four students and raped some female students, Honourable Ndzana issued a statement challenging the allegations and refused to set up a commission of enquiry as the opposition coalition requested.

Given the charged political atmosphere in the country, when the principal of Cohesa College confirmed the news of the minister's visit, the students initially welcomed it with very subdued enthusiasm. Some militant students clung to the idea that the students should boycott the visit while others, especially the student government, counselled moderation arguing that the visit was an opportunity for them to face the minister with their litany of grievances.

Once the students agreed to the visit, they had a lot to do especially as they wanted it to be etched in the minister's memory as the most memorable visit he had ever made to any institution of learning in the Southern Meroonca provinces. And since it was generally known that Cohesa College produced some of the best student results in the country, the students wanted to live up to that billing.

In preparation for the minister's visit, the students had to cut the grass that was invading the entire campus, manicure the flowers and plants, whitewash the buildings, and erase the various forms of graffiti that were inscribed on the walls of the administration building. The dormitories too, which were in a sorry state, had to be cleaned and cleansed. There was, for example, the sordidly disturbing smell of shoes and unwashed laundry, the putrefied stench from rotten pears and other fruits hidden away in cartons in the storerooms, and the revolting odour of stale urine seeping through from the septic tank.

One could hear the students as they rushed uproariously to their bathrooms. Some defied the cold and took cold showers and others simply sprinkled water on their bodies and rubbed them dry. They called this dry cleaning. Others wiped themselves clean with wet towels.

At seven in the morning, with military precision, the students began drifting towards the refectory for breakfast. They were all ornately dressed in their school uniforms—white shirt tucked in white shorts, white socks, and white canvass shoes. Some, because of the biting cold, also wore the college's trademark red sweater with yellow stripes.

As the students flowed to the refectory from different directions—from their different houses named after popes, saints, and angels, not necessarily in that order of sanctity—they rubbed their hands together, imploring on friction to chase away the biting and disrespectful cold.

Some of the students chatted about their favourite tutors and prefects; others gossiped about schoolmates who were going out with girls from Our Lady of Love's College and the Presbyterian Secondary School on the other side of town. Others discussed the impending visit of the honourable minister. The sports meet that had been scheduled to take place that weekend between Cohesa College and Meroonca Presbyterian College, their legendary football nemesis, had to be postponed.

Achu was already standing at the entrance to the refectory with a notebook and ballpoint pen slung from his ear as carpenters always do with pencils. A row of pens decked the pocket of his shirt. He was ready to jot down the names of latecomers who would be punished that afternoon. Given the minister's visit and the fact that the student body had lots of cleaning to do, latecomers were going to be punished rather severely.

One after the other, the students trickled into the refectory and took their places. The first-year students, the Foxes, always sat down last after those in the senior classes had taken their seats. Honour to whom honour is due, or if you like, there is honour among thieves.

Breakfast was soon served. Unusually fast. It was also unusually copious and delicious. Two scrambled eggs; a slice of bacon; some tea—real tea, not the kind of yellowish water the students had been used to drinking; fried potatoes; and some toast. It was as if the college authorities had decided to fatten the students in one day because of the minister's visit.

From one corner of the refectory to the other, one could hear the clanging of cutlery and the voices of students calling for the teakettle, extra sugar, or butter. The students ate with relish and smacked their lips. Never before had they tasted of such a relishing breakfast. And, for once, they felt they were getting their parents' money's worth of food.

The students had often complained in the past about the quality of their meals, but nothing had been done about it because the contractor was the senior tutor himself. In fact, the students had even gone on strike several times, but the promises made by the principal that he would look into their grievances had never been kept.

There were two very important announcements to be made that morning. And it was Achu's responsibility to announce them since he was the discipline prefect. Achu strutted to the front of the refectory, mounted the dais, and beamed. Only a few students noticed him because all of them were engrossed in their breakfast.

"May I have your attention, please," he said, stifling a burp and wiping his mouth with the back of his palm. A few heads looked up, craning to see him. Eba shouted from his corner.

"The discipline prefect speaketh or wanteth to speak. Please lend him your ears."

Achu smiled, bit his lips tenderly, and waited for the noise to subside. He scanned the hall as if he was counting the students to detect those who hadn't showed up for breakfast yet.

"Well, fellow students," Achu began. "I have two announcements to make, two very important announcements. I hope you all pay attention. The first is that there will be no classes."

Even before he finished the last sentence, the students started bubbling with joy. Better the cleaning, some of them said, than classes that day. They yearned for a break because the brothers running the school were always pressurising them to outperform the other schools in the GCE exams. Not that the students did not appreciate this or that they did not like going to school, but they felt that they needed a break from the daily class routine. Thus they exploded in instantaneous jubilation, some clinking glasses while others in a mad fit of glee that only happiness can explain, were beating the dining tables with their cutlery.

Achu waited patiently as the roistering tapered off, retreating first from the front rows and then disappearing slowly at the back of the hall, leaving faint echoes that died down lazily.

"Thank you, guys, a lot. We don't have much time to waste so I'll try to rush through all the announcements. There will be no classes today as I have said, but that is because, as all of you already know, we'll have a lot of cleaning to do in preparation for the minister's visit."

"Uh uh uh uh uh uh uh," the students protested. Some of them felt that the college grounds should be left as untidy as they were so that the minister would see for himself that the college needed more labourers. Most students couldn't understand why it was the case that each time a minister or the president was visiting a region of the country, people would be hired overnight to do what should normally have been done much earlier such as repairing roads, painting houses, and the like. It seemed that no matter how difficult the economic times, money always became instantly available whenever there was an official visit to a given region.

"I haven't finished, please," Achu pleaded, raising the pitch of his voice above that of the students. "Please give me your time and undivided attention. More importantly, the executive committee of the student government will have to meet all morning to start drafting a speech that will be presented to the honourable minister. I'm sure you guys know we have a lot to tell the minister."

Once again, there was an outbreak of collective boisterousness as the students welcomed the idea of presenting the honourable minister with a speech. They saw in this a most welcome opportunity for them to air their grievances. There was the issue of their scholarships to resolve, the problem of job prospects after graduation, the banning of politics on campus, and the publication of their monthly newspaper, the Student Champion.

Of even more immediate concern to the students was the arrest and detention without trial of three of their colleagues who had tried to engineer a strike against the college because of the poor quality of the meals served. Thus, as far as the students were concerned, the visit of the minister couldn't have come at a better moment.

After the two brisk announcements, Achu wiggled his way past the crowded dining tables and returned to his seat. He bit hard into his toast, which was by now cold and hard. When he raised his head to sip his tea, he saw someone unconscionably filthy straying into the refectory. He was panting heavily and carried a long machete in his right hand. An old underwear hung precariously from his shoulders, and one could see tufts of hair pinned to his body through the wide gaping holes on the underwear.

The man wasn't much of a tall fellow though it would be wrong to suggest that he was short. Even though shaggy when one looked at him, one knew that he must have been a tantalisingly handsome man when he was much younger. But then, Jobajo, that trademark beer of which every trendy Meroocan lives to taste, had had its gnawing effects.

Mr. Chop Die, as he insisted the students should call him, kept on fondling an unkempt and shabby beard that he was raising. He darted from one corner of the refectory to the other with kindling glances flashing across the room. His face glistened with sweat.

Achu looked at Mr. Chop Die and blinked. Then he squinted and bit into his toast. Mr. Chop Die bent down to ask one of the students something, but just then he decided to mop the sweat that was dripping from his pimpled face with his ragged underwear. When he took the underwear to his face, he revealed a big, bulging navel and tattoos all over his body. It was obvious to anyone who saw the tattoos that a medicine man must have planted lots of medicines in Mr. Chop Die's body ostensibly to enable him to ward off evil spirits and protect him from any harm.

Mr. Chop Die's chameleonlike eyes caught one of the students, and he ran to him as the entire student body just looked on with some disgust. Agbor, the student to whom Mr. Chop Die was speaking, turned his head sideways away from Mr. Chop Die to avoid picking up the foul smell of alcohol and sweat that Mr. Chop Die was giving out freely.

Mr. Chop Die peered at the assembled students and then burst out in a husky voice that matched his rugged self.

"I am looking for the discipline prefect. Can't you people see? And no one can point him out to me?"

While every student knew Mr. Chop Die and he too knew them well by name, it was difficult for him to sort out the discipline prefect from that student crowd, especially as all the students were dressed in uniform.

When at last someone pointed in the direction of Achu's table, Mr. Chop Die wobbled to it as if he was nursing a sore toe. When he reached Achu's table, he wiped his drenched face and whispered into Achu's ear.

"The principal wants to see you, Mr. Achu Asaah. It is very urgent, and he says you should drop whatever you're doing and come over immediately."

"As you can see, I'm still eating breakfast," Achu responded. "Breakfast will soon be over, and I'll be there in a jiffy."

Mr. Chop Die looked at Achu ruefully and scratched himself. Achu could see that Chop Die's eyes were lingering convulsively on his breakfast.

"Well, thank you, Mr. Chop Die," Achu said casually. "Please tell the principal I'll be there immediately after breakfast."

"But the principal says it is urgent," Mr. Chop Die pleaded.

"I've heard you," Achu responded.

As Mr. Chop Die turned to leave, Achu called him back. "By the way, Mr. Chop Die, do you know why the principal wants to see me?"

"No, Mr. Asaah, I'm sorry I don't know. All I know is that he says it is very urgent. You know I can't know what big people like you and the principal are always discussing," Mr. Chop Die answered with a shrug and walked out.

Achu sipped his tea leisurely, letting his mind and thoughts rivet on the minister's visit. That, after all, he thought, was all the students were discussing. And no doubt, he surmised, the principal wanted to see him to perhaps give further instructions as to how the day should proceed.

As Achu was about to call to the next table for some more sugar, one of the cooks, Mr. Mbah, ran across to his table. He was clutching a folded newspaper that he dropped with reckless abandon on Achu's table. It was the Chuforba Torch, the local Chuforba newspaper and voice of its people.

"Mr. Mbah, is this today's issue?" Achu asked.

"No, Mr. Asaah, it is yesterday's," Mr. Mbah answered as he stalked to the next table to clean the mess left behind by two foxes. "But newspaper news no dey old."

Achu flipped the pages until he got to his favourite column, "Sister Ngwe Whispers," a column for lovers and the broken hearted who want consolation in despair. After he had finished perusing the column, he beckoned to Mr. Mbah to take back his paper.

"Mr. Asaah, you must be joking," Mr. Mbah said in a grim voice. "Don't tell me that you have read the entire paper."

Seizing the newspaper, Mr. Mbah turned to the front page. Where his thumb rested was the headline news "Chuforbas Lose Warrior."

Achu summoned his eyes to scan through the article swiftly, intempestuously, as there was no time to finish the paper. Half smiling to himself, he read it once; and as the smile began to retreat, he read it all over, then a third and a fourth time. It didn't make much sense to him. He read it all over again and still could not make much sense of it, but then his heart began to pound heavily.

Achu pushed away his teacup and turned towards Wirbah, one of his tablemates. Wirbah had left, but Achu's eyes caught those of Ngom who was peeping at him furtively.

Achu pored over the article again, but for some reason he still could not fathom what it was all about. His body began to quaver as a lethal chill went up his spine and set forth a numbing feeling he had never before experienced. He turned left and then right. No one seemed to be looking at him directly. The students had bowed their heads.

There was unusual gravelike silence in the refectory, which was usually a boisterous and quarrelsome place, but one sensed its utter vulnerability because it wasn't normal for the refectory to be so quiet.

Achu wiped the few beads of sweat that had formed on his forehead and read the article all over again, this time following each line with his finger. His heart continued to pound away inexorably, and as he read through the article, he shifted uncontrollably in his seat.

He beckoned to Mbelem, who was sitting at the next table. Mbelem approached him and stared at the article as the rest of the students looked on incredulously. Mbelem took a deep breath, stared at Achu, but avoided his eyes and said nothing. Mbelem's eyes drooped, and his mouth remained gaping. He nudged Arrey and showed him the article. Arrey glanced at it and then fixed his eyes on Achu.

Achu suddenly found himself powerless to say anything. He tried to speak, but no words could come out. The students too were at a loss for words as some of them shook their heads in abject disbelief.

For one fleeting instant, Achu's eyes caught his breakfast staring at him from the plate. He immediately started to beat his chest and a terrible foreboding feeling began to descend upon him, ganging up to assault his senses. He got up slowly and tried to pace up and down, but the harsh pounding of his heart seemed to be sucking away all the energy he had. He staggered and flopped into his chair.

By now a few students had gathered round Achu to prop him up. Mbelem stood by his side, comforting him, calming him, and urging him to be a man.

Achu buried his head in his hands and then slowly allowed his fingers to walk through his hair. Tears invaded his eyes, and when he blinked, they rolled down his cheeks like boulders rushing down the steep Chabga Hill. A few students, trying very hard not to be noticed by him, took out handkerchiefs from their pockets and wiped the tears that had formed in their own eyes. The boulders rushing down Achu's eyes with extreme velocity had hit them with indescribable force.

Achu's mind began to wander and stray. He looked back at his past and recalled the many tears that had been shed in the family. Tears for his mother whom he hardly knew; tears for the twins he was told his mother had given birth to but who died just weeks after birth; tears for Ma Shiri, his mother's sister who had been taking care of him after his mother's death but who passed away when he was ten years old. And now tears for his father. Why all these tears, and why him?

Furthermore, Achu recalled that just the week before, he had been with his father and that they had prepared for the family reunion together. But he had had to leave to return to college because most family members had not arrived by the time his three-day permission was up.

In any case, as far as he was concerned, Achu could not understand why the Chuforba Torch would announce under bold headlines that Chuforba had lost a warrior whose name resembled that of his father. As far as he knew, there was no other person in the village with such a name except his father. Could the newspaper, therefore, actually be referring to his own father, whom he had left just the week before?

Achu couldn't understand the contents of the newspaper. He read it again carefully and closed his eyes to contemplate what he was reading. The form and substance of the article slowly began to take shape in his mind, unveiling a striking sculpture of death. Just as slowly, it began to dawn on him that the article might indeed be referring to his father, given the details it contained.

Achu started to ask himself, searching and agonizing questions. Why his own and not somebody else's father? He couldn't understand it nor could he explain why. Nor could he believe that Papa would so suddenly, without notice, and especially without informing him, decide to pass away. He felt that other people might choose to do so if it pleased them, but certainly not his father whom he knew wasn't one to give in so easily to anyone or anything, be it death. How come then, Achu asked himself, could the newspaper carry such an untrue story? Achu wringed his hands in utter disbelief. A throbbing headache dropped its payload of wrenching pain on him, and he paused. He felt his heart beating harshly.

With his hand to his chest, he began to wonder. Didn't his father love everyone, and didn't the entire village think the world of him? Didn't Pa Asaah know everyone that mattered in the whole Chuforba? Didn't budding politicians go to him to benefit from his wise counsel? And wasn't he respected as one of the elders in the province? How then could death be so disrespectful? Achu shuddered all over despairingly as his mind went blank.

Achu was filled with trauma. He shook his head and bit his lips. He looked in the middle distance; and as his mind wandered, anger and resentment gripped him, and a certain feeling of choking overwhelmed him. It was as if a certain force was pinning him down under water, making it impossible for him to rise to the surface and breathe some life-sustaining oxygen. He passed out momentarily.

At that very moment, the bell rang; but before the students could disperse, Achu, still dazed, made an effort to fight down the emotions that were besieging him. Trying to put aside his misery that was irrepressible, he moved forward nonchalantly with sorrow visibly inscribed on his face.

There was one last major announcement to be made, something to the effect that since there wasn't much time left, considering all the work that the students had to do before the minister's visit, the students should wash their own dishes and cutlery. As Achu made his way to the dais, one could hear the audibly perceptive silence. Even the flies, which usually sparred with the students for some of their food, showed graceful reverence and kept their distance.

Achu stood before the students, transfixed like a post. What he had gone out there to say abandoned him. His voice, normally resonant, was transformed into a whisper inaudible even to himself. He felt tightness in his throat. Struggling not to bow to the pangs of remorse that were surging though his entire body, he raised his hand and with a pantomime of mindless and incomprehensible gestures, he motioned that he had something to say. The students held their breath.

Achu looked at them as if his eyes were tracking them down, but in reality, his wide eyes were not focusing on any of them. Rambling thoughts landed on his mind and clouded his thinking. He paced forward and backwards, clasping his hands tightly together and kicking a little piece of paper that lay on the dais, somehow venting his anger on it.

Heaving a heavy sigh and shaking his head, he looked up and tried to say something. Some inner force within him would not let him open his mouth. He tried again to say something but his mouth remained ajar as his mind again went blank.

Suddenly, unannounced, in a state of permissive despondency, his body began to shake while his eyes started to spew out tears. Achu struck his head with his fist and beat his chest. Then he staggered out of the refectory and wobbled in the direction of the principal's office.

The students watched as he hobbled along, his hands trembling as he shivered.

Achu limped along laboriously, dragging his feet gingerly as excruciating pain bound them. Grief, anguish, and despair had chained him.

Chapter Seven

As Achu's overcrowded mind teemed with ideas, it suddenly dawned on him that that morning, when the students had been cleaning the yard, a vividly beaming rainbow had appeared in the sky, looking down in a snooty condescending manner at the students.

No one had paid attention to it because the minister of education's visit had overshadowed everything. Then, also, the normally loquacious birds that congregated every morning on the pine trees behind the dormitories had postponed their chirping conference. Again the students had not paid any attention to such telltale signs.

Even more significantly ominous was the appearance on the roof of the St. Thomas's House of an owl just when the students were going to take their bath. Achu had, like all the students, not thought much of it. They had simply driven it away without using wood ash forgetting that according to the Chuforbas, owls are messengers of evil.

Achu's mind flashed back, and he started to ask himself if these telling signs were not proof enough that someone important in Chuforba had passed away. But then he just, as quickly, shook his head again in disbelief. Yes, death could take someone important in Chuforba but not his own father, the hoary old man whom all Chuforba people venerated. Death, at least, had to venerate age and wisdom, he thought, beating his breast.

When Achu arrived in front of the principal's office, he hesitated for a while, not knowing what to do. All students knew that they couldn't just walk into the principal's office even if they had an appointment with him. The principal had made that clear several times by suspending a few students who had stormed into his office without an appropriate appointment.

Achu wiped his eyes that were full to capacity with tears. The stubborn fact that the Chuforba Torch had reported the death of someone whose name was exactly like that of his father continued to torment him. Trying to disguise his feelings, he dredged up whatever little strength he had left and knocked on the door and entered. He did not wait for an answer.

The principal was not in, but Mr. Benedict Kome, the senior tutor, was sitting in a chair, chatting cheerfully on the phone. Achu's eyes cast about the room unreflectively and casually met those of a man sitting in the corner forlornly, distant from himself. Mr. Kome motioned absentmindedly to Achu to sit down as he continued to chat on the phone.

The principal's office was a cosy large room full of exuberance. A giant-size mahogany table sat in the middle of the office. On it were three wooden trays with the inscriptions In, Out, and Pending. An electric heater that lay near the leg of the table generated comfortable heartwarming heat.

The walls of the principal's office were splattered with certificates of all kinds as well as with pictures of the Virgin Mary and Jesus, just as Achu had seen in some of the churches he used to attend.

Mr. Kome, for his part, was a robust, balding man with a ginger beard. As he spoke on the phone, he would occasionally play with the ballpoint pen he held between his fingers and fidget with some old files that were lying in one of the trays.

The man who was hived up in the corner, looking withdrawn and unapproachable, followed Achu from head to toe but said nothing. He looked like someone in his late forties. He had sunken jaws and his eyes, which were somewhat subdued, showed that he had been crying because tears had washed his face from all evidence.

With the ballpoint pen between his teeth, Mr. Kome put down the receiver of the phone and began to search for something in the drawers. He pulled out files, rifled through them, sighed, stood up, paced up and down, sat down, and put the files back.

Mr. Kome then cupped his chin in his hand, glanced about, and said nothing.

The phone began to ring. Mr. Kome picked up the receiver and leaned back in his rollicking chair. As he spoke, his eyes twinkled, his face radiating a smile. The conversation continued for about ten minutes, and then he dropped the receiver suddenly and continued to search in the files.

"These wenches are the same," he said. "What does that one think I am? That I look like someone who can just throw his money out like that? Some women just don't have any imagination. How can someone call me so early in the morning to narrate her problems to me as if I don't have mine. They think we have money to throw away just like that?"

Neither Achu nor the gentleman said anything.

After lingering for a while over the files and still not finding what he was supposedly looking for, Mr. Kome raised his head and saw the vacuous stare from the balding gentleman sitting on the chair in the corner. The man smiled in the direction of Mr. Kome, exposing tobacco-stained teeth.

"I'm sorry, but this is the way this office operates in the morning," Mr. Kome managed as he bent down his head. "We don't have time for ourselves, and from the time we come to work, it is headache all the way. You don't know what it is like to teach students. When they are not the ones humbugging you, it is their parents. The lady who just called is the mother of one of the students whom we expelled because his fees haven't been paid. Now instead of paying the poor chap's fees, the mother has a thousand and one excuses. I don't know where parents got the funny impression that because we are a mission school, it means we should accept their children for free. It's ridiculous, and they know it, but it doesn't stop them from trying."

The gentleman in the corner just peered at Mr. Kome blankly, unconcerned, unmoving. It was obvious that he was not paying attention to what the senior tutor was saying. In fact, even though he was staring at the senior tutor, he showed no sign that he was listening to him.

Mr. Kome then started to dial the phone again while speaking to the gentleman.

"Oga, you see, the principal sent for this boy; but before he came, the principal had to run to town to see the bishop at the Catholic Mission across town. That's why I am here. You know, this is not my own office. Anyway, this is a very difficult situation. Of course, no one likes death, not even those of us who are Christians. We are all sorry this happened although the Good Lord knows why he did it. Holy Mary, please pray for the soul of the departed."

As he spoke, he noted that both the gentleman and Achu were not listening even though their eyes were fixed on him. Both of them just sat in their places frozen, withdrawn, and lost. Melancholy had overwhelmed them.

The senior tutor pushed aside the phone, wiped his face, and then shoved his middle finger in his nostrils to clean them. Clearing his throat, he glanced at Achu and said, "Yes, Achu, I know how you feel. Believe me I do. Losing someone is an unbearable burden, and I can understand your feelings, your agony. The principal has asked me to convey to you the school's heartfelt condolences. Your relative, Mrs. Ndefru, called this morning and asked the principal to grant you permission to attend the funeral. I'm sure you know the gentleman sitting next to you. He is your uncle, and he came this morning to fetch you. You may go. You have four days."

The gentleman by Achu's side blew his nose, and Achu looked at him cryptically. His eyes were full of tears. He wanted to say something but suppressed it. Achu took in a long deep breath and shook his head. Then he looked up. The gentleman looked at him. Both of them stared at each other like two cocks spoiling for a fight. The man looked familiar to Achu, but Achu could not say for sure who he was or where they had met. The man's looks, even though stern, seemed to be kind, gentle, and loving. He tapped Achu on the shoulder and then ejected a scream.

"Achu, is this you or somebody else?"

Achu took a closer look at the man. The man's voice was broken but familiar. Achu wiped his eyes and looked intently at the man who had been peering at him all this while. It was, to his utmost surprise, his uncle, his father's brother, Pa Ngwed. Sorrow had wreaked him tremendous havoc, transforming him into an unrecognisable person.

Before Achu could say anything, his uncle broke down sobbing nervously.

"Oh, Achu, Papa is gone. Oh Pa Asaah, papa Asaah, why did you have to do this to us? Why, Papa, when you know we love you? Why Nei, why, please, why? Why you, Nei? Why us? Why us, Nei, why us?"

Pa Ngwed had, as tradition demanded, shaved his head; and to conceal the tears, he had worn a pair of square-rimmed eyeglasses. His all-black outfit, coupled with his disconcertingly doleful looks, indicated quite clearly that he was in a state of mournful anguish.

Achu, already drenched in tears, stared at his uncle, gasping for something to say but no words came forth. He couldn't believe that the gentleman who had just spoken to him was his own uncle. He had appeared so unrecognisable, transformed as he was by sorrow.

Pa Ngwed stretched out his hands, and Achu jumped up and clung to him, grabbing his neck and putting his arms round it as he sobbed.

"Oh, there lies Papa somewhere alone, lonely. My own father; he who yesterday laughed and joked, but today is no more. Oh Papa, my own papa who has left me alone in this life. Why must you do this to us, Papa, when you know that I had only you? Papa, why must you? Papa, please Papa, tell me, who did you leave me with?"

Pa Ngwed took Achu and held him close to his chest, removed a dirty handkerchief from his pocket, and ran it across his face to dry his tears. Achu's heart skipped aimlessly, and his wide eyes focused on something his mind could not really settle on. He closed his eyes tightly trying desperately and unsuccessfully to shut out from his mind the continued intrusion of the misery and total dejection he was feeling.

Pa Ngwed put his arms round Achu; but his rough, tangled beard rubbed on Achu's jaws, and he winced.

"Achu, why? Dry your tears. You don't have to wail, you honestly don't have to," his uncle tried to comfort him. "Your father lived a rich and full life. In actual fact, he died a very old man, and we should even impose a fine on all of you for allowing him do so much overtime."

Achu stepped back a little, shook his head, and fixed his wide-open eyes questioningly on his uncle. It was a deadly stare that bespoke the utter contempt he had for his uncle for such macabre humour. He ran his hands to his face to shade the tears that had accumulated in his eyes, ready to spill over.

Achu trembled and shivered all over at the thought of what his uncle, his father's own junior brother, had just said.

Pa Ngwed stood up and gave Achu his hand, and both of them took leave of the senior tutor. When they opened the door, they walked straight into the fierce cold outside as it battered their face and made their eyes water.

Achu could hardly find his normally nimble feet to run. He walked heavily, gagged by shackles of pain. Sorrow was weighing him down with its heavy might.

When Achu arrived in the dormitory to pick up a few belongings, there was no soul around. This was surprising to him because usually when there were no classes the students would, if they were not toiling outside cutting the grass or working in the college's farm, transform their dormitories into chirping nests.

Achu ran to the toilets. There was nobody in sight. However, he could smell the repulsive odour coming out from the toilets. As he got closer, he heard someone farting behind the closed toilet door and the sound of faeces dropping in the toilet bowl. Twat twat twat twa—like the crackle of a blacksmith's den gun. Achu stepped back.

When Achu heard the faint chorus of the college choir as it sang some religious songs in the chapel, he immediately made the connection that the students had obviously assembled to sing a requiem mass for the repose of his beloved father's soul. In the midst of his sorrow and gloom, he realised that there is no greater satisfaction and peace of mind than when, in one's most trying hours, one receives comfort and consolation from one's friends. That gesture by his friends helped him overcome, at least temporarily, his grief and despondency.

After all, the burden of sorrow is lighter when shared. Achu rummaged through his belongings carelessly and chose what he would be taking home meticulously. He took his worn-out clothes and shoes and arranged them in his small metal box since those were the ones he would be taking home for the funeral. As was customary when anyone died, tradition required Achu to look shabby and haggard for the villagers to be convinced that he was in a mournful mood since one was not expected to look clean at a funeral.

Chapter Eight

Achu and his uncle were soon on their way to Chuforba, the small rugged postage-stamp village wedged among the famous Boza, Fomusongma, and Wumu hills. The Chuforba population was just about two thousand people although when you heard any Chuforba person talk, you'd think the Chuforba people outnumbered every other village in the country. They were a relatively boastful people because they had produced some well-known politicians, including a vice president of the country, a prime minister, two ministers, top national and international civil servants, managing directors, writers, artists, and, for good measure, loud-mouthed stubborn women. Not surprisingly, people alluded to them as the Chuforba Mafia because they just couldn't explain how such a small village could have so many prominent sons and daughters.

Achu was perched precariously on the carriage of his uncle's rickety bicycle, his small metal box tied to his back. As his uncle pedalled strenuously, the bicycle galloped along, roughly responding stubbornly to each turn of the pedal. On occasion, Achu and his uncle would alight from the bicycle to push it uphill or to inflate the tyres.

As they approached Mebankwe, Pa Ngwed started to complain that he was hungry and threatened that unless he had a bite, he wasn't going to continue to Chuforba immediately. Achu looked up at the sun, which was about to hide its face behind the clouds. Then he looked down and saw his fading shadow. When he raised his right foot and tried to stamp it on the reflection of his head on the ground and couldn't, he knew it wasn't yet noon. Since he had, in his mad haste to leave the college, forgotten to take his watch when he had gone to take his box, he couldn't tell the exact time. All that mattered to him in any case was how to reach Chuforba as soon as possible.

They trudged along, and when they got to a point where the road branches off to the home of Pa Ngang, a well-known hunter, they entered the One in Town Restaurant by the side of the road and sat down beside some rude flies that were playing fearlessly with some meat that lay across from them. It seemed that the restaurant's proprietor, Ma Florence, was preparing to cook that meat for dinner.

At the far end of the table were two big plastic bowls with dirty water. Pa Ngwed sat down on a bench and immediately ordered a bowl of garri and okra soup and a bottle of beer to wash down the food. Achu did not order anything because he was not hungry. Death had robbed him of his father and also of the joy of eating. His only concern was to reach Chuforba as soon as possible to see his father's body before it could be buried. Since the Chuforba people did not keep corpses for more than a day, unless they decided to use the mortuary, he was afraid that if he did not hurry home, he wouldn't be able to see his father again.

Achu's mind teemed with obstinate thoughts that instead of going away jarred though him. In his unsettled state, he tried to look at the future to see if it had anything in store for him. All he saw was cold misery sneaking up to him and bracing itself to tear him apart. He winced with a sudden jerk, looked back, and recalled the day before the family reunion when he had been clutching to his father's legs by the fireside. He choked on a lump that had been forming in his throat and tears streamed down his rumpled face.

His thoughts next landed briefly on his stay at Cohesa College. Anger sped through his body with compelling speed at the baffling and incomprehensible loss of his father at a time when he most needed him. He didn't know if he would be able to continue with his schooling, but while that persistent thought kept on assailing him, he brushed it aside for the moment and turned his rambling thoughts to the funeral.

Pa Ngwed ate his food with relish and drank his beer leisurely as if he was on a picnic. Achu eyed him evasively and restlessly as he took his own time. Achu grew increasingly impatient as Pa Ngwed dillydallied with his food and drink. But Achu couldn't dare rush him. That's not something you do to your father's brother, who is in fact your junior father, or to any adult for that matter.

The thought of his father's death kept on jabbing at Achu and nagging him. For the next five minutes or so, although to him it seemed like an eternity, he was lost in a world more remote and isolated from the real world. He still couldn't believe that he was going to Chuforba to attend his father's funeral because there was no departing from his father, the man he loved most. Why, he asked himself, is it that only those we usually love and cherish are usually taken away from us?

Realising that Achu was completely smothered by excessive grief, Pa Ngwed belched and turned in Achu's direction, mumbling through a mouthful of garri.

"Achu, what is the matter with you? Because Papa has died then you too must die? What's all this? You are not happy that he made you his chop chair, his successor?"

A feeling of devastating anger consumed Achu. He was appalled that his uncle should be saying such things when he, Achu, had not even seen his father's body. How in the world, he thought, could his uncle, his father's own brother from the same womb, be saying such things?

Okay, it is true, Achu ruminated, that when his father had been alive, he hadn't really seen eye to eye with his brother, Pa Ngwed, but that was only because Pa Ngwed had wanted to covet the title of successor and next of kin to their father. The family had unanimously elected Achu's father, and Pa Ngwed had challenged that decision and rebelled against the family. But granted that the two brothers had, as a result of this succession palaver, not pulled along well, Achu couldn't understand why Pa Ngwed was not showing any special concern that his brother had passed away.

No matter how angry Pa Ngwed was over the chop chair palaver which had been festering for over thirty-five years, Achu felt that it was wrong of his father's brother to be thinking of the succession and purely material things when his father hadn't even been buried.

As all these thoughts flashed in Achu's mind, Pa Ngwed carved out the last lump of garri with his fingers, dug his thumb into it, scooped up the okra soup, and swallowed it. It landed down his stomach with a thud.

Pa Ngwed must have noticed that his nephew was growing weary from impatience because he refused to let his eyes meet Achu's.

Achu, in a bid to attract his uncle's attention, blew his nose and coughed restlessly. Pa Ngwed raised his head slowly and looked at Achu.

"Achu, what's wrong?"

"Papa, please let us leave now. I'd like us to reach the village before the funeral." Achu pleaded, somewhat helplessly.

"But you know that we do not keep dead bodies," Pa Ngwed responded. "Pa Asaah died yesterday, and I'm sure he has been buried by now."

"But I thought they might keep the body until Doctor, our eldest brother, arrives from the United States," Achu responded testily. "I don't think they'll bury Papa just like that. They should know that we the children would like to see him before he is buried."

"Achu, stop arguing with me," Pa Ngwed hollored."Who are you calling they? Don't you know that things in that compound can only be done in keeping with my instructions? I say he has been buried, and you are arguing with me. What is this nonsense? So because somebody has died nobody should live again? Don't you know that man no die man no rotten?"

Pa Ngwed spoke testily working himself into a tidal rage while Achu was so taken with the desolation he was reeling under that he felt like crashing the dishes from which his uncle had just eaten as a way of letting off steam. But then he held his peace, not letting his uncle's utterances goad him to violence. He looked at his uncle scornfully as his face was vacant of any emotion.

"Papa, I am sorry. You did not understand me," Achu set out to explain. "When I said they—"

"Shut up, Achu, shut up," Pa Ngwed cut in harshly. "Shut up for the millionth time. You are still saying 'they' even after I have spoken."

The blood in Achu's veins turned cold as a feeling of desperation tore him apart. He did not recall when, in blessed memory, anyone he had known reacted so uncouthly when death had struck. Each word that leapt from his uncle's mouth drove a tormenting dagger in his heart. Yet death, like life, must be respected.

Achu knew his uncle was considered selfish in the village, but little did he know that he was also stingy with compassion.

Achu bit his lips, balled his fist, and then tried to calm down a bit. He glanced at his uncle and wished he could strangle him.

What a mean person, Achu thought to himself, one who only thinks of money and estates when someone dies, as if wealth is all that matters in life.

Achu's mind flashed back to what his uncle had earlier said, namely that his father had, before dying, anointed him as his successor. Achu dismissed the errant thought. He cared less for the succession because it would be the beginning of more problems in the family. What was of paramount concern to him was for him to reach the village on time before the burial so he could take a last longing look at his father resting comfortably in Abraham's bosom.

Achu knew that as long as he relied on his uncle, chances were that they would be getting to the village fairly late, maybe even after the funeral. After watching his uncle sipping his beer leisurely, Achu stood up briskly without permission, grabbed his metal box, and ran out of the restaurant leaving his uncle behind in the company of the smoke from the pipe he was pulling on.

Achu forced a passage behind the restaurant through a small, narrow meandering footpath that led to the motor park. He still had some of the money his father had given him the week before when he was returning to college. He intended to use it to pay his way to the village. He brushed aside the dew and moved on very fast.

Achu arrived at the motor park amid all the noise and commotion. The snoring of engines and the hooting of cars, the shrill voices of park collectors as well as the chiming of the bells of the truck pushers were deafening. Achu clung to his metal box like a partner in a tug-of-war game to avoid it being snatched by the ubiquitous thieves that roamed the park and thrived on the innocence of unsuspecting passengers.

Talking about thieves, who in the province didn't know that motor park operators and especially Chakara and his gang ran the most notorious crime syndicate? Who also didn't know that even though Chakara and company had been caught many times, they had never really been brought to justice because they had succeeded in establishing for themselves their own laws by which everyone else was governed?

Yes, who didn't know Chakara and company? Wasn't it rumoured that they had every police officer and most judges and magistrates in their pocket, and that nothing could be done to them? Barely three weeks earlier, Chakara and his gang had turned the entire police force into ridicule by breaking into the safe in the senior police inspector's office in broad daylight. To add insult to injury, they had left a note stating that they expected the senior inspector of police to leave them more money the next time around otherwise he would be killed. That message had sent the entire police force on alert. They cowardly put some money in the safe but claimed to the press that it was to be used as a bait to nap Chakara and his gang. Chakara and company wiped the whole safe clean again and have still not been caught even though everyone knows them and sees them embedded in their theatres of operation.

Achu looked at all the taxis and buses carefully. There were three buses and four taxis each of them going in a different direction. Save Me Oh God was going to Bavut, Go and Return to Chuforba, Charity Brothers Transport to Zambui, Vox Populi Vox Dei to Wali, the Family Crown to Katibo, Money Hard to Yanta, and the Pilgrim's Progress to Ganso.

Park collectors beckoned avidly to Achu. Achu approached each vehicle to find out if it was going in his direction. One husky gruff-looking park collector motioned authoritatively to Achu.

"Pikin, come here. Where you dey go?" he enquired.

"I dey go for Chuforba," Achu responded in a tremulous voice.

"Enter here quick. This bus go soon flop. Na only two more passengers we dey lookam." So saying, he immediately grabbed Achu's metal box and tossed it into the bus. Achu flinched. The man then stretched out his hand instantly.

"Your fare, oga. You go pay one thousand. Na so every passenger dey pay from here to Chuforba."

Achu looked at him with apprehension.

"But from here to Chuforba na five hundred. Na five hundred we dey usually pay from here. I mean, uh, I mean, we dey usually pay five hundred francs," Achu muttered.

"Who tell you say from here to Chuforba na five hundred francs?" the park collector gnarled. "You want travel or you no want travel? No waste my time. I no get time for the big big grammar wey you dey brokam. You no know sey die dey for Chuforba and say when die dey we dey get plenty passengers?"

By now the horrendous noise the park collector was making had attracted the other park collectors. Even a few passengers gathered round to see what the noise was all about. There are always people sniffing around for news. Achu bristled with anger, his hair standing on edge like the quills of an angry porcupine. He shrugged off the anger to simmer down because he could not win any fight against that park collector because solid bonds of solidarity bound park collectors, making it impossible for anyone to challenge them and win.

Besides, even though fares were set by the ministry of transport and ought to be respected, the Park Collector's Union didn't care a hoot. It charged its own fares, and passengers had no choice but to pay them. And again, like in the case of Chakara and company, no one could do anything about it.

Achu thought about the fare and mulled over it for a few seconds. As much as he did not want to spend almost all the money he had on him to pay his way home, he had no other choice. He tried to beseech the park collector to let him pay five hundred francs, but the fellow wouldn't listen. In fact, he had already left the scene to look for other passengers. Somehow the nagging misery and throbbing pain that had left Achu returned with driving force. Tears welled in his eyes.

Achu fought back the emotions, wiped his face, and pretended to put on a bold, daring front. He ran after the park collector and confronted him.

"Oga, I don come again. I really want go for Chuforba. Immediately if possible. Please help me. I dey go for cry die."

The park collector looked at Achu with evasive eyes and cast an unappreciative glance at him.

"I don tell you say make you no waste my time. The bus don almost flop. I don tell you say na one thousand francs. I beg you no waste my time if you no get the money."

Achu strained to invite a smile to part his lips a little, but the overpowering agony that had overwhelmed him stood guard over his lips and chased the smile away.

"Okay, my brother, I beg you take six hundred. Na only six hundred I get am. I beg you. You no see say I no dey work. I be student."

The park collector ran a hand through his hair and scratched his head. Then he drove his finger into his ear to clean it and scooped up some wax that he crushed between his fingers. He bit his lips and looked at Achu languorously.

"Okay, I go help you because you be student and also because you dey go for cry die. Na who die?"

"Na my papa," Achu responded as he began to sob hysterically, hiding his face in his handkerchief.

The park collector looked at Achu with compassion, moved closer to him, and tapped him on the shoulders.

"Young man, na weti you dey do so? Man pikin like you dey cry like this for public? I beg no bring shame for man pikin their head. You no get for cry for public like this."

Achu raised his tear-filled eyes in the man's direction. The park collector turned his face away for an instant and then smiled wanly.

"Okay, since na your papa, and any papa na papa for we all, I go take only two hundred fifty. Give me two hundred fifty francs."

Achu cheered up and summoned a quavering smile, and it hovered over his lips and lingered on it for a while. Then he slogged his hand into his bag and took out a dirty piece of cloth in which he had tied the money. He untied it and handed the two hundred fifty francs to the park collector. When the man received the money, Achu raised his hands to heaven and thanked him heartily.

The man entered his name in the logbook, gave him an official receipt for two hundred francs, and moved on.

Achu watched the park collector as he strode to the other buses and taxis, announcing that Go and Return was ready to leave immediately. Achu couldn't believe his luck. Here was a guy who minutes before had appeared so heartless and now had become so understanding and thoughtful.

Achu clambered into the bus without wasting any time. Some of the passengers were already seated. In front of him was a vacant seat beside an elderly woman who looked out of place in her dazzlingly swanky outfit. In his mad haste, Achu accidentally stepped on the woman's foot. She jerked and snarled. Achu immediately pulled back his leg jumpily. He must have stepped on the woman's toes on which some warts were growing because she'd been walking waveringly as if she had jiggers on her feet.

"Use your eyes, you bastard," she screamed even before Achu had time to apologise. "You walk without seeing? What do you think your eyes are made for?"

"I'm sorry, ma," Achu apologised.

"Don't ma me. I'm not your ma," she blurted out.

Achu didn't say anything. He simply sat down by her and tried to look straight, avoiding her eyes as much as possible. The other passengers, about seven of them, were stealing quick glances at the surreally sophisticated woman. Quite apart from the coat of cosmetics that she had smeared on her face, it would seem that she had just done her curls. The infamous Damenba dust that never lacked a thing to settle on had landed on the curls and her eyelids, adding some belittling glamour to her.

The lady tilted her head slightly and stared at Achu watchfully as if she was inspecting him. It was the kind of impassioned stare that eloquently depicted how she was feeling. Achu was aware that her eyes were focused on him, and so he continued, quite uneasily, to look straight ahead in the middle distance.

Suddenly, as if she had been pricked, the lady started to laugh lightly to herself and then stopped abruptly when Achu mistakenly turned to see why she was bubbling so effusively.

"Turn away your face from me, you rat," she barked. "Don't look at me. I don't like dirty children. You mean you cannot take a bath? A big boy like you? Or you want to do like many white people who don't like to take a bath?"

"Ma, sorry, oh madam, sorry. I—"

"Shut up, you mean miss. I'm not your madam," she interjected.

"Sorry, miss, Sorry. My uncle and I were cycling all morning, and the dust woken up by passing vehicles landed on us. I am rushing to the village to attend my father's funeral. My father just died yesterday," Achu explained expansively.

To his utmost surprise, the lady almost split her sides laughing. She laughed and laughed and laughed, showing her dust-coated teeth. Her eyes watered, but she continued to laugh. At this point all the passengers, usually very boisterous, pursed their lips and turned towards the lady. She continued to laugh, and then some of the passengers too started to laugh, not so much because they knew why she was laughing, but because of the funny way in which she was laughing.

Achu had initially felt anger slicing his flesh; but then on seeing some of the passengers laughing so drearily, he too smiled, dulling in the process, at least momentarily, the pangs of remorse he was feeling.

Unexpectedly, the lady stopped laughing abruptly. Her face tightened, and she commanded her eyes to focus on Achu steadily. "My pikin," she growled. "I do not blame you. You mean you are dirty like this because you are going to cry die? And what will that change? You will wake up the dead? Mourning as far as I know never did bring back the dead. This is one thing I do not understand in this country. When someone dies, it is as if everyone else should die with them."

Achu glued his lips and threw up his hands in the air dejectedly. He looked at the lady sullenly, the stare bespeaking the wisp of anger that ran across his face. Just then the driver hoisted himself up into the driver's seat. The motor boy, the bus attendant, counted the number of passengers and passed on the number to the driver. The driver, a tall drooping man with thick broad-rimmed lips and a deep tattoo gash across his cheeks, fixed his seat and the rearview mirror in position and started the engine. Before pulling off, he told the passengers that if the police should ask them how much each of them had paid, they should all say five hundred francs each instead of one thousand francs.

The bus sped on trundling its passengers and their load and raising the dust from the earth that had been baked dry by the scorching heat. Inside, the passengers sweated uncontrollably because of the furnacelike suffocating heat generated because the windows had had to be closed to shut out the throat-irritating dust.

Just about two kilometres from the motor park, the driver screeched to a halt to buy some fruits by the side of the road. A weary-looking and consummated man approached the bus and beat his emaciated stomach.

"Please, sah, please, sah, I beg for ten francs."

The driver brushed him aside. But the man blubbered on. Out of anger rather than compassion, the driver fumbled in his shirt pocket, pulled out a few coins, and flung them at the beggar. Achu peeked at the sloppy, ungainly man as he stirred the dust with his jigger-infested toes, looking for the coins. After he found them, he picked them up and approached the bus again. Achu watched him as he stretched out his hand to the passengers imploring them to give him some money.

"Please, sah, please, mami, I beg for five francs for buy something chop."

Achu looked at the beggar with a solemn expression. Sympathy rose from within him, and he half smiled to himself impersonally. He knew he didn't have much for himself, much less for any beggar. But then here was a guy who, from all appearances, probably hadn't eaten since morning although he reeked of the repellent odour of alcohol that early in the day. Achu rushed his hand into his pocket, took out a twenty-five francs coin, and gave it to the man. The beggar strolled to the next window.

The lady sitting by Achu's side was restless and looked nettled. It was obvious that her brittle patience was going to snap at any moment. She looked at her watch several times and took out a pocket calendar to check out something best known to her alone. No one paid attention. The male passengers were animatedly poking fun at the female passengers and teasing them. When the lady's eyes fell on the beggar whose hands were still outstretched at the next window, she frowned and drove him away.

"Get away from here, you miserable wretch. Away from here. You should have relatives to take care of you, or your own parents for that matter. Get away from here. An able-bodied man like you who refuses to work because you want the easy way out."

Before she finished screaming, the beggar, terrified, walked away. The passengers who up to that point had either intentionally neglected her or were simply oblivious of her presence, stopped their generous chatter and looked in her direction. She flicked on a smile that lit her face in self-contentment. Everybody just looked at her with no one daring to say anything. The way the lady looked, she could have been a big man's wife or girlfriend, or as they call them in the province njumba or deuxieme bureau. But then what could any big man's wife or njumba be doing in a bus? After all, buses like that one were not meant for well-to-do people. But then also the way she was spitting fire, no one could tell. Even the way she sounded. It was possible that she had just returned from white man's country. The passengers continued to look at her and to make eyes to each other.

"Another miss don come o, another nyango," one of the passengers said in a derisive tone that brought down the bus.

When the driver returned, the lady eyed him flippantly. Before he could sit down, she burst out, "You this mere driver, what is wrong with you drivers in this country? All you know is how to go on strike. You're all the same. No respect for your passengers. You think you can just leave us like that and go about your own business without our permission? What right did you have to stop and do your shopping without telling us? That your foolishness in this country must stop."

"Sorry, madam," the driver was about to apologise, but she cut him short.

"You shut up. I am not your madam. Can you madam me? A mere driver like you?"

"But, madam, you no get for broke that big grammar for me," the driver yelled, retorting sharply. "You think say driver too no be person? Why you dey talk for me like that as if me I be your pikin? I beg you, you go keep that wina thing for other driver, not for me eh?

"You know me? You know who I be?" the lady asked, raising the tone of her raspy voice. "I no care who you be. Even if you be who i wife or njumba, that one no be my problem. I no know, I no want know and I no care."

The passengers roared vicariously. The lady allowed a smile to appear on her face and just as immediately withdrew it as the passengers continued to titter.

Content with himself, the driver slammed shut the door and once again the bus was on its way. It swept past a village bristling with tall elephant grass that was competing with the corn in the fields. A few goats whose owners hadn't bothered to tether them were roaming about and sampling the maize.

From the snorting of the exhaust pipe which was sending out an aching drone as the bus revved uphill, Achu guessed that it was already climbing the treacherous Mebah Hill which leads to the market. He looked out of the window and saw thatched houses dotted here and there.

The lady continued to speak but this time, softly to herself in a drawl. The passengers too continued to whip up a steady crescendo of provocatively derisive laughter. She maintained stony silence and buried her head in her hands. The faintly perceptible jabber that came from her direction was the rowdy redolence of the cologne she had splashed on her body.

Suddenly, Go and Return started to crawl by fits and starts instead of cruising normally. It jerked for a while and then stopped. The motor boy skipped out nimbly and wedged the bus with consummate dexterity to prevent it from rolling backwards. The driver turned off the engine immediately, and the passengers held their breath. It was as if by turning off the engine the driver had quenched the light chatter that had been going on in the bus.

There was an unbelievably palpable silence. The decorated lady by Achu's side held his hand tightly. Achu yanked the hand from her control. Then she clung to her seat, holding it tightly, her eyes hermetically closed.

The driver started the engine and stepped on the accelerator harshly. The bus groaned and moaned as it surged forward. The passengers applauded.

Cresting the steep Nap Hill, especially in the rainy season, had never been easy particularly if a bus was loaded. After going about midway up the hill, Go and Return started to emit ululating gasps. The driver sensed trouble and ordered everyone to disembark instantly.

There was, surprisingly, an orderly stampede as the younger passengers allowed the older ones to disembark first. The only ruffled feathers came from the lady sitting near Achu. She had, in a mad haste to flee from what she saw as certain death, tried to rush out before everyone else, but her dress had been caught in the door, exposing her visibly oversized buttocks. The male passengers turned their faces away as the female ones struggled to disentangle the dress.

When she disembarked, she rummaged in her purse for a handkerchief, took a deep breath, and mopped her sweat-drenched face.

When the driver realised that the belching bus wouldn't go any farther on its own steam, he requested the passengers to help push it up the hill. Just then the Brotherhood of Man approached. It was on its way to Zaounde through the secondary ring road that goes through Chuforba. As soon as the driver of the Brotherhood of Man saw Go and Return moaning and groaning, he parked at the bottom of the hill just after the Ndo bridge. He and his passengers alighted and ran towards the hapless Go and Return.

While all the male passengers joined forces to push the bus up the hill, the female passengers moved to one side of the road and climbed up the embankment. Some of them took the opportunity to respond obediently, without any fuss, to nature's call in the neighbouring bush.

As the passengers pushed and pushed, Go and Return revved strenuously. The ladies poked fun at the men who, accordingly to them, claimed they had all the strength in the world; but when it came to a simple thing like pushing a bus uphill, they couldn't do it. That somehow got to the men, and they vowed to prove to the women that they were indeed men. After all, men are men.

A fairly heavyset man in flowing robes swallowed the ladies' sneers hard. He anointed himself the leader of the group and ordered all the male passengers to put their shoulder to the bus. Then he bellowed, "Rejei."

"Hey," the male passengers responded in unison.

"Rejei."

"Hey."

"Rejei."

"Hey."

"Woman fit piss for bottle?" he asked derisively.

"No, unless she use funnel," they responded in a chorus.

"Then push, push, push, push, push, push, push." So saying, the men pushed and pushed until the bus reached the top of the hill. The women applauded and congratulated them. The driver of Go and Return thanked the passengers of the Brotherhood of Man without whom Go and Return might not have gone, let alone return.

The passengers of the two buses exchanged pleasantries affably and then entered their respective buses. Once again they were on their way. And they had nothing more to worry about because that Nap Hill was really the last major hurdle that buses plying that way had to clear. The Brotherhood of Man for its part had no problem climbing the hill as it was a much-newer bus and had a four-wheel drive.

Go and Return drove through wide-open fields in which cattle were grazing. Occasionally it would slow down when approaching the few villages that dotted the road. Little boys and girls in tattered loincloths waved bye-bye as the bus sped by while some of the older children quickly dismounted from their locally manufactured wooden bicycles and pelted the bus with stones.

Chapter Nine

Go and Return soon approached the Ngumba Junction. It slowed down and on seeing no approaching vehicle, sped off. Just then, from nowhere, the driver and passengers heard the blast of a whistle, the by-now familiar irritating sound that gendarmes take pleasure in making and that drivers and passengers had come to resent.

The driver stepped on the brakes abruptly, and the bus skidded to a stop. The driver looked in the rearview mirror and saw the silhouette of a man standing on the embankment in the middle of some tall drooping corn plants. The driver was about to reverse when the man approached the bus. He wore a well-trimmed blue khaki uniform and carried a baton under his armpit. A pistol jutted from the holster he had round his waist.

Before the driver could get down, the man was already near the bus. "Driver, you disrespected a gendarme's whistle," he scowled.

"Oga, how now? Na you?" the driver asked disarmingly since he knew the officer very well.

"My friend, who are you calling oga?" the officer asked with a vicious look on his face. "I say you disrespected a gendarme's whistle."

"But, Officer, you no know me today again? Weti happen?" the driver asked apologetically.

"My friend, listen. Today no be yesterday eh. Ne t'amuse pas avec moi. I don't know you, and I repeat that you disrespected a gendarme's whistle."

The driver looked at the officer and couldn't understand what was happening. While he didn't really know the officer's name, he knew that all the drivers plying that road always called him Oga to which he took no offence. In fact, they had become so close that whenever Oga was the officer on the road, the driver had nothing to fear.

"No, sah, I no disrespect you. I break when I hear the whistle," the driver explained, his lips trembling with fright. He had started to think about how much the gendarme would ask him to pay. If it was the standard rate, there would be no problem because after all that was what each driver always gave. But then some wicked gendarmes bent on extorting more than the usual amount sometimes accused the drivers falsely of violating the Highway Code.

"Don't lie, my friend, don't lie," the gendarme asserted authoritatively. "You heard the whistle and didn't stop immediately which is a crime punishable under our national Highway Code."

"That's not true, sah. You fit even ask my passengers. I break when I hear the whistle. You know I no fit lie for you. Na today you know me, oga?"

"Don't oga me. Where do I know you from? You're saying I'm a liar, right?"

"No, be so I talk, sah. I no say you dey lie."

"You are arguing with an officer, do you know that?"

"No, sah, I no dey argue. I dey explain."

"Explaining what? What do you have to explain? Didn't you see the junction? And don't you know that we have control here?" the officer thundered.

"I know, sah, but I no be see any officer," the driver explained.

"You are supposed to stop at a junction whether or not there is an officer. You didn't. You've violated the law, and I'm sure you know the penalty."

"I no understand you, sah," the driver said, somewhat terrified.

"I say you have violated the law, and you know the penalty," the officer deadpanned.

At that point, one of the passengers decided to intercede on behalf of the driver.

"Officer, please leave the driver alone. He didn't do anything wrong. He stopped immediately when he heard your whistle, and had he in fact not been a good driver, this bus would have somersaulted."

The gendarme writhed with anger and took a few steps towards the back of the bus. That was an indirect way of summoning the driver to meet him there. A few passengers urged the driver to go to the back of the bus to negotiate with the officer since that is the way deals were made. Some of the passengers speculated that the officer might have been pretending not to know the driver because his boss might be around.

Before the driver could alight from the bus to go towards the officer, the officer returned. One could see from the curve of his lips and the contour on his face that he was swelling with rage and indignation although he was trying to conceal it.

"Driver," he called out dismissively. "I see that you brought a lawyer with you. We'll see who is a better lawyer." So saying, the officer scrutinised the passenger that had just spoken and looked at his watch. Just then Save Me O God roared past with its passengers singing and waving.

The driver of Go and Return disembarked and walked towards the officer who had conveniently moved towards the back of the bus. That is the way the gendarmes and police officers operated. They would berate a driver in front of his passengers to make it seem that they were doing their work when in reality they were expecting the driver to meet them behind the bus.

The passengers overheard them discussing something merrily in hushed tones. Then they glided into the hut by the side of the road where the officers usually sat to wait for oncoming vehicles. Two officers were quaffing beer and playing Jambo while two others were involved in an intense game of draughts.

In the absence of the driver and the officer, the passengers began to discuss the wheeling and dealing that usually took place in the small hut. It was there that the greatest traffic deals were struck.

The passengers were chatting among themselves when the officer returned, waving his baton and dangling a whistle from his lips. A benign smile hovered over his face. The passengers toned down their inconsequential chatter and looked in his direction.

When the officer realised that the passengers were shooting at him with bullets of disdain from their eyes, he drove away the evanescent smile and tightened his already taut mouth. Achu's eyes filled with tears when he looked up and saw the retreating sun lurking behind curdling clouds. He knew the night was not far. He dug his finger into his nostril and sneezed.

The officer approached the bus in short, precision-like measured steps. He seemed to be a man too taken with his own power. He nodded to a few passengers and then yawned.

"All of you come down. This is control. Make it quick please. We do not want to sleep here. Everyone should have his papers ready. National identity card, tax receipts, voting card."

The passengers obeyed mindlessly and alighted from the bus with obliging dispatch. They formed a single line behind the motor boy.

"I say everybody get your documents ready—national identity card, tax receipts for the past five years, voting card. Add your party card," he snarled.

One after the other the passengers showed him their documents. The officer scrutinised them and snapped, "Okay pass."

It was next the turn of a glamorous young man who was dressed in a tight-fitting sports suit and baseball hat.

"Young man, your papers," the officer crowed as he looked at the young man with a glance that could wither anybody.

The young man handed him his passport.

"Oga, I said your papers, not your passport. We want your identity papers," the officer shouted.

"But my passport can identify me," answered the young man reassuringly.

"That's what you think."The officer shot back drearily as he flipped through the pages mechanically. The passengers looked on. The officer licked his finger and went over the pages two more times, shaking his head bleakly.

"Young man, when did you enter this country?"

"Two weeks ago, sir."

"I can see that, but where is the stamp to show that you left this country years ago? When did you leave this country?"

"Thirteen years ago."

"Thirteen years ago?" the officer rasped and then laughed nervously. "That's a pretty long time ago. You mean you are one of those who go abroad and refuse to come back home eh?"

"Of course not," the young man responded guardedly. "After I finished studying I started working in America. This is the first time I am coming home after so many years."

"Okay, mister, know all from America, are you aware that you don't have a Meroonca stamp in your passport?"

"That's true but then if you look at my passport, you'll see that it was issued by our embassy in Washington. The first passport had the stamp when I was leaving the country for the first time thirteen years ago. It expired after ten years, and this one was issued in Washington."

"The law says you need a stamp to leave this country, and I see that you have been out of the country with this passport without a stamp."

"No, Officer, this is the first time I'm coming home on this passport. Obviously, I shall obtain a stamp when I'm leaving next week. Surely you don't expect me to have a stamp in a passport issued in Washington, do you?"

"Young man, you don't ask an officer questions. You answer his questions. I'm the officer, not you, and I know what I'm talking about. You can't teach me my job, and you don't have the right to interrogate an officer," the officer said firmly. "Please do not waste the time of the other passengers. The law says you must have a stamp in your passport when leaving the country. I see that you don't have one. Please move aside and don't argue."

"Officer, Officer, but I'm not leaving the country now," the young man pleaded.

"Don't officer me, my friend," the officer interrupted him. "The law is the law. Move over there. Next."

"I don't think you are being fair to me", the young man protested.

"Okay, since . . . d'accord, puisque you think you connais my job more than me, let me see your tax receipts."

"But I don't have tax receipts for Meroonca. If I don't live here how do you expect me to pay tax?" screamed the young man.

"As long as you a Merooncan you are supposed to pay tax. Point final."

"What you are saying doesn't make sense, Officer. I can't be expected to pay tax when I don't live in this country even though I am still Merooncan. The people who should be paying tax don't, and it is innocent passengers that you are holding to ransom."

A few impatient passengers called the young man to the side and asked him to give the officer a thousand francs bribe because that is what they said they were certain the officer wanted.

"On my dead body," the young man vowed. "This is what is wrong with this country. Nobody is willing to stand up for their rights. Everybody is afraid. Everybody goes round giving bribes for service to which they are entitled. I will not give that officer a franc."

"Then you'll sleep here," they predicted.

"I won't because I'm sure there must be someone in the gendarmerie that is honest and knows the law." They laughed him to scorn and said he was being very naïve. Meroonca had not won the much-coveted world cup for corruption a number of times for nothing.

The officer who had questioned about twenty passengers now came face to-face with a missy girl whom the passengers had been jeering all along. She looked lost and just kept on staring at the officer.

"Woman or little girl," the officer screamed. "I said I want to see your documents."

The girl fidgeted a bit, somewhat nervously, but didn't respond. She just looked at the officer.

"Il ne faut pas me perdre le temps eh. Don't waste my time eh, you girl, because I know you Damenba people. You are very stubborn."

The officer must have been quite bilingual because he spoke in French and English. The English-speaking officers who were generally more bilingual than their French-speaking colleagues systematically refused to speak any English whenever they were dealing with English-speaking passengers. This was because if they spoke English, they would be forced to show compassion and thus not extort much money.

The girl chuckled and then began to shell out irresistible peals of laughter. The other passengers too began to laugh as if they were snitching on the girl. A sour-sweet smile zoomed past the officer's face and then rage spilled out of his eyes. In a fit of wrath, the officer called one of his companions who was in the hut cross-examining other passengers and extorting from them whatever little money they had left to take them to their destination.

The officer who was in the hut responded smartly and walked to the bus briskly. From all appearances, even though he was dressed quite splashily, he must have been a much-junior officer judging from the way he greeted the officer and stood at attention.

"Oui, Chef " he answered promptly.

"Come and see another one. This young squirt here. She has no papers," the senior officer snapped, pointing to the girl and still fuming with rage.

"Mademoiselle, tu t'appelles comment?" the young officer asked the girl.

"I don't understand French," the girl shot back spadishly.

"Iz not my problem. You suppose to speak French. Are you not a Merooncan?" the officer sniffed.

"I am. So what? Where is it written that every Merooncan must speak French?"

"Iz your problem not my own. Meroonca iz bilingual country. Vous devrez parler les deux langues," responded the junior officer as he nodded in the direction of the senior officer unctuously.

The girl paused for a second and then, as if recollecting herself, yelled. "I know that Meroonca is a bilingual country, but there is no law that states that all Merooncans must speak French."

The other passengers seemed to be happy with the girl's response. Some of them began to cock a snook at the two officer's backs and snoot at them, making signs to her to hold her ground.

The two officers looked flabbergasted. They took a few steps away from the passengers who divined that they were going to hang heads together to determine what line of action to take.

While their backs were turned, the passengers began to murmur and complain aloud within earshot of the officers that they wanted to be allowed to continue their journey because the girl had done nothing wrong.

When the officers strode back to the bus, the passengers snickered at them.

The senior officer looked at the girl intently and asked, "You have a vaccination card?"

"What for?" the girl asked astonished.

"What do you mean by what for? I mean your vaccination card, you know. I presume you are a . . . you know, I mean you must be that kind of a woman, not so?"

"Officer," the girl chuckled, "are you a medical officer or a veterinarian or for

that matter an immigration officer?"

The passengers broke out laughing. "Do me I do you," some of them said tauntingly. "Book don meet book."

"You, Mrs. Big Mouth, move over there," the senior officer said as he pushed the girl aside without asking her any more questions. "We'll return to you after we've finished with the other passengers."

The girl giggled nonplussed, and the passengers continued to blather. After inspecting the documents of a few more passengers, the officer came face-to-face with Achu, who grimaced and raised his dilated eyes towards him. At close range, Achu felt a certain feeling of bitterness that made him want to break the officer's neck for wasting so much time, but he held himself in check. The bitterness he felt seemed to have given him so much strength that he was certain he could beat the two officers to pulp.

"Your documents, my boy. Your documents," the officer commanded.

"I am a student, sir," Achu responded, trying to be cheerful.

"Yes, wisdom. I say your documents," the officer replied.

"But, sir, I just said I'm a student. You know we students do not—"

Before he could finish the sentence, the officer started to laugh disparagingly. "We students my foot," he gasped. "We don't know students here. Anybody who takes public transportation should have valid travel documents. We're doing our job, you know. So your documents please."

Achu showed the officer his school identity card. The officer plumed his jaws and plucked Achu by the shoulders harshly, "Hey, my friend, don't waste our time," he muffled. "I've told you I want to see your documents. We don't have time for students. This country educates you free, and all of you go round saying the vilest things about the government. We cannot tolerate lawlessness and lack of discipline. Your documents or else. You fellows are the ones who are always telling us that we do not respect the law. And now what about you? Your documents, my friend. Please don't waste my time."

By this time, the passengers had started to make faces at the officers. The junior officer who was following what the senior officer was saying obsequiously careered round the hut to respond to nature's distress call. So poignantly urgent was the call that even before he glided out of sight behind the hut, he had started to unzip his pants.

"Move over there," the officer shouted. "Move over there and stay with that small whore, that akwara."

Achu stepped aside. A maelstrom of thoughts whirled in his head, niggled him and then seemed to vanish, abandoning him in a state of nothingness. He made efforts to prime his attention on the unfolding scene before his eyes, but he just couldn't sort out the magpie variety of thoughts that buzzed around in his mind.

The officer approached the next passenger.

"What is your name?" he questioned menacingly pronouncing each word with authority.

"Ebai, sir," the passenger answered timidly as he recoiled in fear.

"Your documents. I don't care if you are Ebai the proprietor of Ets Ebai or Ebai the barrister in Konman Town. I don't care. I'm only interested in your documents."

Ebai bent down to search for his documents in his brief case. The officer dragged him by the collar of his shirt and ranted at him.

"Move over there, my friend, and don't waste my time. You were supposed to have your documents in your hands."

Just then a Land Rover put-putted by kicking dust in the air, and the passengers dashed for cover in disarray as if the dust was some form of tear gas that had been sprayed into their midst.

Ever since the last student and popular demonstration that had been repressed with intimidating force, Damenba people had come to dread anything vaguely reminiscent of tear gas.

Achu's blood boiled, and he tried, quite unsuccessfully, to undo the thoughts that seemed to have bound him. The river of tears that took its source from his flooded eyes rushed down his puckered face prodigiously.

The evening had slipped by somewhat cheerlessly, and now darkness was descending a little too flamboyantly, romping down the countryside and cuddling it snugly.

Achu and the other passengers who had been unable to produce their papers were bundled together in a squalid, shaggy room not too far from the checkpoint. They were told that they would have to spend the night there and then be transferred the following day to the notorious BMH at the government station.

The BMH, the Brigade Mixte Hostile, was a police cell into which citizens arrested on the flimsiest of excuses were dumped and tortured on government's characteristically trumped-up charges without the benefit of a trial. When Achu heard that they would graduate from the small detention hut by the side of the road to the BMH, he knew death couldn't be far. Hadn't countless and innocent sons and daughters of Damenba, especially patriots of the Southern Merooncа National Congress lost their life in that liar's den?

Chapter Ten

The cell measured in all just about sixteen square meters, and had, for purposes of ventilation, only one big window that was closed. The little light that gleamed through the window lit it very dimly. And with over eighty detainees, it was redolent of the foul and pungent stench of urine and sweat. There was virtually no standing room; and when Achu and his fellow passengers were hurriedly huddled into it, the older detainees broke out into a distressingly instantaneous outburst of squalling, which they claimed was their own civilised way of welcoming the newly inducted detainees into their fold.

A succession of eerie thoughts swept past Achu as he trembled, with ripples of rancour surging through his entire body. He pictured his father being lowered down in the grave, and just as slowly, tears, like raindrops, pearled down his glum swarthy face. He then tried to bestir himself and looked around morosely at the physically and emotionally battered detainees straggling along the wall. More roily tears streamed down his cheeks.

Achu thought desolately about the father of one of his closest friends, Pa Kongmu, who had recently been released from the infamous Ndinguinkol underground prison after twenty years of hard labour just because he had dared to publish an article calling on the authorities to open up certain inconsequential political positions like that of president of the republic to open competition. Pa Kongmu had held firmly that the incumbent president had no particular qualities to occupy that position considering his background. The one party government in power had arrested him, subjected him to the most ignominious treatment possible, and dumped him in that dungeon.

Pa Kongmu had been released only because Harmless International and other human rights organisations had made a lot of noise about the wanton suffering to which he had been subjected.

Even then, he returned home blind after losing his sight in that underground dungeon. Achu shuddered at the sickening thought that he too, like his codetainees, could be visited by such wry criminal malevolence.

After all, Achu knew that in a court of chickens, the cockroach could never be expected to win a case. Achu looked about himself, but it was difficult because of the darkness to make out any of the detainees. The detainees were sweltering profusely and jabbering with prolixity, each one giving vent to their emotions and explaining away why they thought they should not have been detained at all in the first place.

A pale-looking slim man with a nappy hairdo slowly wangled his way to the front of the cell and sputtered out something. The older detainees, to the bemused astonishment of the new ones, broke out in a frenzy of rapturous applause and feet stomping.

Suddenly, an officer burst into the cell with a flashlight in his hand and squalled.

"Do I hear that noise again and all of you will live to regret it. What are all of you proud of? That this is your country? And that you have done what for it? I won my medals in battle. You are all criminals. You criticise the government and yet cannot make it better. You claim to be good citizens yet cannot respect the law. You say we are old and should be retired, yet you are not fit to take over. Let me just hear that commotion again."

Then turning to the fellow who was the object of the madhouse, he first rammed his pipe with his index finger, puffed heavily, and then railed. "And you this mangy-looking zombie who wants to spend the rest of his life in detention. I saved you from the gallows, and you know it. Haven't I told you repeatedly that unless you change, there is no way you'll ever be released? First you were accused of leading an insurrection in the university; now you want again to be the ringleader of this, this, uh, misguided group. Let me just hear the commotion again, and you'll not live to tell the story."

He immediately stormed out of the room in disgust, lumbering along laboriously. Achu struggled to digest what the officer had just said, and it seemed to him that it was all a kind of a joke, and a cruel one at that. But then, one could readily discern manifest seriousness in the forthright manner in which the officer had bellowed. And that's what got on Achu's nerves.

How, Achu wondered, could the officer be heaping such scorn on them when he ought to know better?

Not sure whether the officer was still lurking around or not, the detainees spoke in whispered, worn-out voices among themselves. They huddled together, some of them rubbing their hands to feel a little warmth because the bare cemented floor was becoming intolerably cold and the wind that made the trees swagger tremulously as if they were tipsy infiltrated the cell and prowled about aimlessly.

Achu reflected impulsively and compulsively on the thought of spending the night in that foul cell, and it sent a chill up his spine. He tried to dislodge the thought, but it strayed to the village. In the fertile recesses of his mind, he saw contour lines of agony that had burrowed the glum transfigured faces of the villagers as they sobbed together at the loss of his father. He was seized by a spasm of pain that wrenched him. He winced, and a certain emptiness filed him, overwhelming him in the process.

Just then the door swung wide-open and armed columns of spine-chilling air broke into the cell and expelled some of the stench instantly. Behind the phalanx of cold air marched in another officer swaddling himself in a woolen blanket. His flashlight was dim and his voice dishevelled.

The officer who had just entered gave the distinct impression that he had been aroused from sleep and that he very likely had been cursing the person who had woken him up. He shone the wan light round the cell as if he was looking for someone in particular. By this time hearts were leaping.

No detainee wanted to be identified by any of those officers because one never knew. Stories abounded of detainees who had been selected at random at night and who were thereafter never heard from.

As the light from the flashlight darted from one part of the cell to the other, Achu's heart continued to pound away restlessly. The light tarried for a while on the guy who had earlier wangled his way to the front of the cell to speak. Since Achu wasn't far from him, some of the light had shone on him. Achu clenched his heart in awe and bowed his head, not wanting the officer to see his tear-torn face. All the detainees looked sideways not allowing their eyes to meet those of the officer.

The officer rubbed his hands together and then dipped his right hand into his pocket. He jostled for a while with whatever was in the pocket and then took out a little piece of paper that he scrutinised carefully with the dim light from the flashlight. The detainees raised their heads subtly. Some even tried to crane their necks to see what was on the paper.

The officer cleared his nose and throat and cast about the cell. A dithering spell of suspense bound the cell for a fragmentary second and then was broken by the rustling of the wind rattling the zinc roof.

Crinkling his eyes as the cold wind rushed into the cell, the officer lifted his head and asked in a deep voice, "Who among you is called, uh . . . who of you is called . . . shit, I can't even see the thing clearly, okay, okay, who among you is called Asaah?"

The detainees looked round, each one's eyes revolving like those of a chameleon to see who would respond. Since no one knew if it was for good or evil, they held their breath. Could it be that they were choosing one more person for the slaughterhouse?

No one came forward. The officer's eyes skipped from one detainee to the other.

"Who of you—I just asked—is called Asaah?" he asked with ramrod authority.

Achu looked round askance at his fellow detainees and then focused his attention on the officer who by now was wearing his patience very thinly.

Achu lifted a finger feebly and answered in a faint and frightened voice.

"I, I, I, I am Asaah, sir." Before he finished, a ramshackle man with a tangled beard ambled to the front, grinning sheepishly and flashing tobacco-stained teeth. Achu took one step backwards and gazed at the man. The officer glowered at both of them and yelled, "I asked whether there is Asaah among you. What are you two doing up here? Making fun of an officer of the armed forces of this country? You don't know that that is an offence under our law?"

"But I'm Asaah, sir," Achu and the ramshackle man responded in unison as if they had been rehearsing for a play. Excitement and laughter rippled through the detainees. The officer couldn't help smiling even though the anger and disdain anchored to his face was unshakeable.

While all this was going on, Achu and the ramshackle man kept on looking at each other questioningly, but the light from the flashlight was so dim that they couldn't readily recognise each other.

The officer stroked his luxurious beard and grinned deprecatingly. Achu shivered and shuddered as the cold wind spat on his face. He felt a devastating sense of sadness and hopelessness. For how long was he going to be detained? Would he really be transferred to the BMH? What chances were there that he would see his father?

Achu decided not to allow himself to be pushed into the abyss of deadly depression. Somehow he maintained the faith that come what may he would be able to see his father before the final separation.

He knew though that there was pretty little he could do to convince the officers to let him go. For one thing, he did not have the money to bribe them. For another, it was already getting very dark, and he was sure that he wouldn't be allowed to leave at that time of the day. Nevertheless, as far spent as the night was, he was prepared, if he was released, to go home. But then the thought of trekking to the village at that late hour, in the dead of night, sent a streak of fear through him.

Achu thought about the telltale story parents usually narrated to their children about witches roving around at night, looking for unsuspecting victims. Then there were the owls, those messengers of evil who, with crinkled eyes and wrinkled contours on their faces, flew about defiantly at night. The thought of owls, in particular, sent a wave of chilling fear that tore at him with raging brutality. Achu winced, straightened himself, and stared at the officer.

The officer pinned his attention on Achu and the ramshackle man. Because of the dim light, he really couldn't make out who was who of the two. He called a junior officer and commanded him to bring the big kerosene lamp that was in the office. Within a few minutes, the junior officer marched in with a soot-stained glass lamp.

The officer raised the lamp above his shoulders and peered at Achu and the ramshackle man. Achu took the opportunity to scan the room to see who the other detainees were.

It was all very fast. He saw, though not quite distinctly, ten or eleven bodies hugging each other on the cold and bare cemented floor. Over ten others were leaning against the wall. His eyes caught what seemed to him like a pregnant girl of about sixteen years or so who was sleeping away her sorrow in the far corner. Again, it was all very fast because just then the officer blurted out, "Hey you, my friend, look here."

Achu pretended that he didn't know the officer was addressing him.

"I say, pickin, look here," the officer squawked with military bellicosity. "I'm looking at you, and you're looking somewhere else? You want me to call you twice before you know I'm calling you?"

Achu immediately dragged his eyes away from the unfolding scene around him and turned towards the officer who had pinned a sardonic stare at him.

"Sorry, sir," Achu mumbled.

"Yes, you better be sorry," the officer responded benignly, hunching his shoulders. "You prisoners think we don't have better things to do, eh. You are even lucky that we're in a good mood today. All of you would have gone to the BMH today. Bless your stars."

Achu jerked. His heart bounced roughly, and he instinctively squeezed his own hands tightly together as if he was recharging himself with some life-sustaining tonic. He tried to slog through the muddled thoughts that were clogging his mind, but it was difficult. It was as if by trying so desperately to divest himself of the thought that he might be made a prisoner, he was instead becoming increasingly aware that, to all intents and purposes, he was already a prisoner. After all, being a prisoner is not restricted to being in physical bondage.

Achu took a deep breath, blinked, and his eyes squirted tears. The officer could see that he was draped in abject misery. The other detainees looked on in total silence because they didn't understand what was happening nor did Achu.

Normally in the dry season, at that time of the night, the crickets would come out of their abode and chirp the night away; but for some strange reason, they had held their peace as if they were commiserating with the hapless detainees.

The officer lifted the lamp closer to the dishevelled man standing near Achu. Achu turned his head blithely towards the man and scrutinised him. The man in return examined Achu. Both of them gasped at the same time and exchanged stares for a while until Achu withdrew his and bowed his head in deference to the man. It was of course improper of him, he told himself, to look straight into the eyes of an older person without blinking.

Just then a vehicle screeched to a halt, and the officer strode outside to see if it was another load of detainees that had arrived. Something in Achu nudged him to strike a conversation with the bearded man. To get the man's attention, Achu prodded the man's foot with his toe. The man moved his foot away and turned round to see who was kicking him. Achu gave him a broad smile, and the man smiled back congenially.

"Excuse me, sir, I think I know you," Achu ventured.

"You do? Really?"

"I think so, sir."

"Where?"

"I'm not quite sure, sir, but I believe I have seen you around. You probably will recognise me when the light returns and you look at me carefully."

"Maybe," the man responded with another big smile wreathing his face.

"But whose son are you, and what for heaven's sake are you doing in a place like this at your age and at this time of the day?" he questioned Achu.

Some sharp pain burrowed its way up into Achu, distorting his face in the process. His voice echoed with the agonising sound of muffled sobs.

"My name is Achu, sir, the son of Pa Asaah of Chuforba, and I was on my way to the village when—"

Before he finished the sentence, the bearded man thrust his hand into his pocket and brought out a handkerchief. Then he put his arms around Achu and clasped him tenderly as both of them broke out into distraught sobs to the utter bewilderment of the other detainees. In between sobs, the bearded man informed Achu that he was Pa Ngwed.

Achu and his uncle continued to sob on each other's shoulders with rivulets of tears flowing down their cheeks. The two of them were still clasped in each other's embrace when the officer returned. They immediately stopped sobbing.

The officer looked down at them with a trenchant stare that seemed to rip through them. The nauseating silence that descended on the cell overpowering the usually boisterous and garrulous detainees overcame the officer. He stood motionless and speechless as the kerosene lamp he was holding spewed out a steady stream of smoke that wafted in the air with hysterical frenzy. The unusual silence, the still of the night, and the incredibly tamed and subdued wind all made Achu's heart beat quicker. And again, errant thoughts on the loose, roaming at large, cluttered his mind like flies attracted to stale meat.

Achu's uncle, Pa Ngwed, no longer able to contain his anger, looked straight into the eyes of the officer and bristled.

"Officer, let me remind you that moments ago you asked for Asaah. We are here. The two of us. The two Asaahs." A few hoarse voices rose from the back of the room amidst contemptuous giggling.

The officer turned the wick, and the lamp sprayed its light on the detainees. Achu could see that the officer's eyes wielded tremendous power.

"Look here, my friend," the officer shouted cheerlessly. "I'm not here to be made a fool of by the two of you. I asked for Asaah, and both of you came forward. Surely both of you can't be Asaah."

"That's just the point, Officer," Pa Ngwed answered. "Both of us are Asaah. Okay, which Asaah do you want?"

The officer thrust his hand into his pocket, took out a piece of paper, and looked at it. He squinted, and his eyes flashed from side to side.

"Ecoutez mon ami," he blurted out. "This paper simply says Asaah. It doesn't say which one. How am I to know which one of you is the real one?"

"But then that's your problem, Officer, not ours," Pa Ngwed answered. "All we know is that we are Asaah. You better tell us what that paper says. Are we next on the firing squad since that is your speciality?"

"Ecoutez cher ami, je n'y suis pour rien. My friend, I'm not responsible for this mistake. Am the one who arrested you?" the officer asked.

"How am I to know? What difference does it make?" Pa Ngwed shot back.

"That's not the point. Am the one who stopped you at the junction and asked for your papers?"

"No."

"So that's what I mean. I didn't arrest you. I am simply executing orders. The paper just says Asaah. It does not say two Asaahs. So I can't say who of you it refers to."

"Sure you can, Officer, if you want. Sure you can. You don't because you don't want to. You guys here can do anything and get away with it. Nothing can happen to you. So don't tell me that." Pa Ngwed was becoming heated up again.

"Sorry I can't say who of you is Asaah. And since I can't, I'll have to wait for the officer to come and solve his own problem. You want me to be court marshalled?"

"Use your discretion, Officer."

"Oh, no no no no no. Pas question. No way. Can't talk about discretion in this kind of case. You are dealing here with sabotage, you know. According to our laws, what you guys have done is tantamount to sabotage. You know it, and I know it. No, I'm sorry, I can't. Uh-uh. No. Sorry. Not in cases of this kind."

"This is what?" Pa Ngwed screamed, gnashing his teeth as he lunged forward to punch the officer. "This is what? Sabotage? Sabotage of what? Is there anything left to be sabotaged in this country? You guys have ruined the economy of this country and mortgaged our political future, and you are telling me that this is sabotage? Sabotage of what?"

Pa Ngwed was boiling with rage, and one could see disdain and contempt emerging from the dark pit of his eyes. The other detainees held him back from punching the officer.

Achu who had been following the exchange closely struggled to hold back the tears that were washing his face. The officer, may be out of shame, smiled very faintly and then let his tongue lap his upper lip.

"My friend, you don't have to shout at me, an officer. I know how you feel, but let me tell you that you have worsened your case. You have insulted an officer on duty. Again that is an offence punishable under our law. I was going to take your case up with the captain on duty, but you have spoiled your chances. We'll see who of the two of us is powerful in this country."

Pa Ngwed again lunged forward, but his hand couldn't reach the officer. His eyes were by now brim with tears and rage was written all over his face. The officer marched out and slammed the door. Achu's heart swelled, and a certain pain rose from the bottom of his stomach, crawled upwards, and dulled his senses. His temper too began to rise.

Pa Ngwed was beside himself with resentment. He bit his lips, threw up his hands in the air, and wagged his head in utter disbelief. How in the world, he muttered to himself, could anyone act so unreasonably? Here was a bunch of fellows who had decided to interpret the law the way they saw fit to suit their own whims. How, he tried to imagine, could the officers be so uncaring? How could they arrest so many innocent people and lock them up in such squalid conditions without giving them the option to defend themselves? The more he thought about this, the more he thought he was having memories of a bad dream. The adrenaline swished more and more in his veins.

Smarting under the weight of the contempt that was stifling him, Pa Ngwed tried to slowly unravel the tangled web of impenetrable thoughts that fettered him. It galled him that the officer would dawdle their time and indulge in such unnecessary dalliance with their freedom of movement.

Pa Ngwed couldn't believe that this was indeed happening to him. It had always seemed to him that such things happened to other people. And now he was not only a witness but also a victim and spectator in a macabre play being staged by the officers. It beat his imagination that the forces of law and order in the country always succeeded in turning an inconsequential event into a well-crafted piece of theatre.

As he shuddered because the feeling of anger was about to rise again in him, he said involuntarily that a spider usually dies in its own web.

Achu, who had been so clobbered by misery that he didn't have the strength to say anything, looked up at his uncle; and when their eyes met, he flopped into his hands, the breath moaning in him. The heavy silence that had dropped on the rest of the detainees smothered them and held them down gasping out their lives.

While all this was going on, a melancholy wind sighed past at cannon ball speed. Pa Ngwed shook off Achu lightly, trying to free him from his grasp. Achu took one step backwards as the feeling of helplessness consumed him. He staggered backwards, and his uncle grabbed him while two detainees who had been witnessing the scene rushed forward to give him a hand. They propped Achu up.

Outside the cell, the moon peered down peevishly from behind the parting clouds.

After Achu had recollected himself, his uncle, with a strain of sorrow pathetically evident on his face, took him close to his chest and wiped the rivulets of sweat that were running down his cheeks. Achu's glazed eyes stole quick glances left and right to see if his codetainees had noticed what was happening to him. His uncle gazed about the room, and realising that most of the frazzled detainees had bowed submissively to the overpowering influence of sleep, that great leveller, he decided he and Achu should talk and plan a strategy.

"Achu, Achu," Pa Ngwed called out as he shook Achu by the shoulder. "Achu, are you awake?" Achu stretched and yawned.

"Yes, Papa."

"Okay. Let's talk. But first, Achu, what are you doing here? How did you get here?"

"Papa, the gendarmes stopped us at the Ngumba Three Corners and arrested me because they said I didn't have my papers."

"What papers are you talking about?"

"You know, tax receipts, voting card, national identity card."

"But you're a student. Didn't you explain to them? Students don't pay taxes in this country, and you're not even of voting age yet."

"I know, Papa, but they wouldn't listen. They said they had instructions to request every passenger to show his or her papers."

"But surely something must be wrong with this country. How can anyone expect you to pay taxes, at your age, when you're still a student? As far as the voting nonsense is concerned, that's equally crazy. I don't understand how things are done in this country."

"Papa, I sincerely don't either. They even refused that pa sitting down there in the corner from continuing on the trip," Achu said, pointing in the direction of a feeble old man sagging in the corner under the weight of devastating grief.

Pa Ngwed turned in the direction of the man and beheld him brooding over his misfortune. Pa Ngwed walked across intrepidly towards the old man with compassion glinting in his eyes. When the old man saw Pa Ngwed approach, he recoiled in fear, thinking that Pa Ngwed was an officer probably sent to fetch him.

"No fear, papa, no fear. I be your pikin," Pa Ngwed assuaged the old man while the other detainees looked on. They couldn't believe what they were witnessing. The old man was rough-hewn and had large earlobes. Since it seemed that age had, notwithstanding all its craftiness, failed to alter him much, one couldn't readily guess his age. The beauty in him seemed to have begun to retire, although he still maintained a somewhat youthful figure.

Pa Ngwed bent down and studied the old man intently to see if he would recognise him. The old man bowed his head, not daring to look straight at Pa Ngwed. Pa Ngwed tapped him on the shoulder.

"Papa, you know me?" Pa Ngwed asked. The old man looked up. A few teardrops hung precariously from his eyes.

"No, I so sabi you," he answered in a hoarse voice, eyes half closed.

"No palaver, papa. I be your pikin. Weti you dey do for here?"

"Ma pikin, leave me oh. Me sef sef I no know why I dey here. They say I no get tax receipt for the last five years. But I'm a retired civil servant on pension. I even showed them my pension card, but they no want listen. Ma pikin, na all this oh."

Tears sprang from the old man's eyes, and he wiped them.

"Where you dey go?" Pa Ngwed asked him.

"Ma pikin, leave me. I dey go Nzoundere. My pikin dey work there, and i send message say make I come see ye for some family palaver. Na my first time for go dey."

Pa Ngwed wanted to respond, but the clicking of the heels of the officer's boots across the cemented corridor announced his arrival. Pa Ngwed rushed back to his place. Achu was sobbing.

Chapter Eleven

When the officer walked in, he didn't have the blanket. He rubbed his hands together and smiled broadly, exposing two curtains of white teeth. None of the detainees could surmise why he was smiling, and Achu turned his face away from him.

Achu thought dismally that maybe the officer was gloating over their arrest and detention since they were his prisoners.

The officer fixed his gaze on Achu and his uncle, and even though he wasn't saying anything, the unmistakable impression he gave was that he was very happy that so many people could so easily surrender their lives to him. He smiled sparklingly to himself as his head bobbed.

"Hey, the two of you looking at me as if I'm some strange creature. C'est quoi là même? Look at me good," he said with sardonic glee.

Achu and his uncle looked up instantly.

"Follow me," he ordered, pointing to the two of them as he marched out of the cell. Pa Ngwed and Achu tarried for a while, and when they were sure he had left, they waved to their cellmates and then put their hands in their pockets to shield them from the blistering cold outside.

They walked past a few offices and met the officer knocking furiously on the door of one office and screaming for whoever was inside to open it. A wave of anger blew across his face with tremendous force as he grabbed the doorknob. The door resisted him with buoyant force. The officer took two steps backwards, rushed towards it, and yanked it open with a punch. Then he entered and sank into a chair behind a fat wooden table and signalled to Achu and his uncle to enter.

In the far corner, a heavyset man with medals on his battle fatigues slugged in the quietude of slumber, his outstretched left hand clasping a whistle and his right hand clutching a pistol. A mighty larger-than-life picture of the country's president grinning ruefully hung from the wall behind him.

The eyes of the officer who had just entered the office reached out for his companion who lay there snugly in sleep's bosom as if in death, severed from this world and oblivious of the angry and tearful screams of the anguished detainees next door.

As if caught in the dragnet of the officer's stare, the officer with medals stirred, even though still profoundly asleep, and turned. Achu couldn't help but see that the man's rumpled shirt was dissimulating not quite so genially, a paunch that he believed was undoubtedly nourished by money squeezed out of drivers plying that road.

Achu and his uncle stood feverishly in front of the officer, their hearts pounding away. They did not know if they had been called to anticipate their freedom or death. Life in Southern Merooncа was like that. People always walked the thin razor's edge between life and death.

The officer was going to arrange some documents on his desk when the phone began to jingle. He let it ring twice and then picked up the receiver.

"Oui," he answered as he turned the receiver over to his left hand. Apparently either he couldn't hear the speaker well or the speaker had simply hung up.

"Oui, yes, allo, who's speaking? Hello, allo, yes, allo, allo, mais c'est qui à l'appareil? Hello, who's speaking?" He put his hand across the mouth of the receiver, turned to Pa Ngwed and Achu, and said, "I don't understand how these phones work. One jerk calls and then refuses to speak. Maybe it was a wrong number, but he should have had the decency to apologise instead of just hanging up."

Then he blew into the phone and began all over again. "Allo, hello, can I help you? I'm sorry I can't hear you. Allo, hello. Qui est à l'appareil?"

Achu and his uncle just kept on watching as anger slowly draped the officer's countenance. He shook the phone with ferocious force and then decided to pump insults too rude and bordering on the obscene into it. Having let off steam, he slammed the receiver on the phone, took one quick look at Achu and his uncle, and said nothing.

Achu glanced at the frumpy officer and almost asked him if he knew anything about decency, but he decided to hold his tongue in check.

Achu and his uncle were hoping the officer would tell them immediately why he had called them to his office. When they saw that he seemed rather interested in his desk, the facade of poised respect that they had maintained looked as if it would crack.

Achu's uncle trained his eyes on the officer who kept on playing with the papers and files that cluttered his desk. Anger surged in Achu and his uncle suddenly belched out.

"Officer, this nonsense must stop. First, you arrest us for nothing, then you detain us, and then, to make matters worse, you give us a glimpse of freedom, and then blindfold us. Either you are prepared to set us free, or you send us back to that stinking cell to meet our friends. It is usually said that what cannot be cured must be endured, but I think that does not apply to us. We don't need to endure you since we know the time will come when we'll someday cure you."

Achu who all along had been drenched in sorrow managed to force a smile. The vicious anger that the officer's eyes contained was irrepressible. The officer jumped out of his seat and scuttled up and down in the room pounding on his chest. For a while, he didn't say anything because Pa Ngwed Asaah's statement had come unannounced and stunned him.

"No one talks to an officer like that, and I wouldn't have you hurl insults at me," the officer blared, waxing his hand contemptuously. "You can't talk to the president of this country like that."

"But you are not the president," Pa Ngwed countered coolly. "Plus you can't even say we have a president. The one we have spends all his time abroad with broads."

"Who says you should speak about our esteemed and revered president like this, especially after seeing all the good things he has done for this country? I know I'm not the president, but when I'm in uniform I represent the president of this republic," he exclaimed, eyes red shot with anger.

"In that case, you're a servant of the people."

"Who? Me? Servant? You must be joking. You call me a servant? A servant of the people? That's how it all starts eh? You'll soon reduce the head of state to a servant of the people. You are the people who go around and ask our people to consider our revered president as a servant, right? How dare you call the president of this country a servant? Who is he serving? A servant of which people? What do the people have to do with my appointment? How can you equate the president with a servant? Eh? What's wrong in this country? Because presidents in white man's country are considered to be servants of the people, you opposition people think you can just do the same thing in this country? White men presidents may be servants because they are weak but definitely not our own. Our presidents are very strong. They know how to handle their people. Better tell those who like you are misguided that they're wasting their time trying to compare our presidents with white man's president."

So saying, he sat down on the edge of his seat and pointed dangerous glances at Achu and his uncle as if he was looking in a magnifying glass to discern some hidden speck of thought roving helplessly on their forehead. Achu and his uncle just stood in front of him impassively.

"You here," he ordered rankled, pointing to Achu's uncle, "Since you think you can talk to an officer, the president's representative anyhow, since you say I'm a servant of the people, you will go back to that cell and let the people whom you say are my bosses release you."

Pa Ngwed looked as cool as a cucumber. He grinned and didn't say anything. The officer walked to the door, turned to Pa Ngwed, and showed him the way out. Pa Ngwed walked out pliantly, and the officer accompanied him back to the cell.

When the officer returned, Achu stood up in mock imitation of a junior officer standing at attention. The officer beamed, his livid face radiating satisfaction.

"That man there, whoever he is to you, will learn that he cannot talk to any officer anyhow," he chortled. "We are here to protect the peace of this country, and no one can breach it with impunity and get away with it."

"I agree with you, Officer, but that shouldn't apply to my uncle," Achu pleaded.

"I don't think you can say he breached the peace. I mean . . . how can you say he breached the peace? That's a scurrilous accusation."

"That's what? Scurry what? I see you too want to be insulting, eh? Anyway that's your opinion," the officer shrugged."Do you know that he was riding a bicycle without a licence? And that he was not carrying a national identity card either? These are the kind of people who threaten the peace of our peace-loving country."

"How, Officer?"

"You too want to argue with an officer when he is doing his duty?"

"Not so, Officer. I'm not arguing. I'm asking for an explanation. How can you say that because my uncle was riding a bicycle he was threatening the peace?"

"My friend, listen and shut up. I don't owe you an explanation. You are not my boss. In any case, did you say that he is your uncle."

"Yes, Officer."

"Okay, let me tell you the truth. That your uncle was not just riding a bicycle. His bicycle has no licence, and then to make matters worse, he himself does not have a national identity card."

"So how does all that threaten the peace of our country, Officer?"

"Are you his lawyer?" the officer snapped.

"No, Officer."

"Then shut up, otherwise you'll worsen your own case. Look here, my boy, we do not derive any pleasure from arresting people, but just for one moment imagine what this country will be like if we allowed everyone to do as they please."

"I agree with you, Officer, but isn't there something called discretion? There is the law and there is the law. The same law you're referring to gives you the right to use your discretion in certain cases," Achu tried to reason with him.

"Young man, I can only agree with you. Mais la loi là dont vous parlez, vous savez même que, you know, you're right, but the licence and national identity card are not something to joke with, you know eh?"

"That's true, Officer, but I have my school identity card, and that didn't prevent me from being arrested."

"That's another matter, my friend. Your own case is different. You were not riding a bicycle, were you?"

"No, sir," Achu answered a little hoarsely, his voice almost cracking.

"Then what's your problem?"

"I myself don't know, Officer. I really don't know."

"Who arrested you?"

"That short officer with a bulging stomach," Achu replied and pointed to the officer.

"You mean Corporal Nemangue?

"I don't know his name, sir. Maybe he is the one."

"What did he arrest you for?"

"I don't know, sir."

"My friend, don't waste my time. How can you say you don't know why? Corporal Nemangue cannot just arrest you like that. We're not like that in the force. You are the kind of people who go round spoiling our name for nothing, saying the meanest things about us. You think we are stupid to just arrest people like that? For nothing? Who do you take us for?"

Achu paused briefly so that the encompassing disdain that was choking him could loosen its grip. The officer rummaged in a jacket that hung on the wall behind him, took out a pack of cigarettes, and laid it on the table with force.

"Quel est ton nom là même?" the officer asked as he rubbed his nose and gawked at Achu, an intimidating stare etched on his face.

"My name?" Achu asked, quavering nervously.

"Yes, your name, that's what I asked for. What else do you think you have that I can ask for?" the officer thundered.

"Achu, sir."

"Achu? Achu who? Is that your first or last name?"

"It is my first name, sir."

"Then that's not a name. Don't you know that your family name is more important? What is your father's name?"

"Asaah, sir."

"Asaah, Asaah, did you say? Which Asaah?"

"Asaah, sir. Pa Asaah of Chuforba."

The officer chuckled to himself halfheartedly and looked at Achu and shook his head.

"I'm sure you don't mean Mr. Asaah, well-known interpreter. You must be from Damenba, right, with a name like that?"

"Yes, sir, I am from Damenba and from Chuforba to be precise. My father is Pa Asaah, and we are from Kembene, or, if you like, Ndzahma in Chuforba."

"You mean Pa Mission Asaah?"

"Yes, sir."

"Now don't tell me that you're Pa Mission Asaah's son."

"I am, sir."

"Jesus wept, the shortest verse in the Bible," the officer exclaimed. He paused as if to listen to the resonance of his own voice. "I know Pa Mission very well. Isn't he the one who used to be the interpreter to the British governor, and after that he helped to translate the Bible into some Damenba languages?"

"He is the one, sir."

"Of course, I know him. He is a traditional wordsmith. Who doesn't know Pa Mission Asaah, a man blessed with immortal happiness. A very nice man who considers every child his own. I know your father very well. He is called Pa Mission because he is a very religious man. He used to sometimes pass here on his way to town, but then I haven't seen him for quite some time now—"

"Papa is now gone forever, oh Papa is now gone forever," Achu sobbed. When the officer looked up, Achu's eyes were flooded with tears, his nose moist, and face covered with grief.

The officer drew a deep, heavy breath and looked at Achu blank eyed. He couldn't understand why Achu was crying. As he rolled up the sleeves of his fatigues carelessly with his rough hands, Achu saw a number of tattoos chiselled with ill grace on his arm.

Hunching his back and chewing coarsely on his lower lip, the officer glared defiantly into the distance and then looked in the direction of Achu, hunting him down with his haunting eyes. Achu, feeling the piercing pain of anguish, jerked in a spasm of savage agony.

The officer's forehead gathered sweat, and he twiddled his thumb and summoned himself to push back the marauding tears that had invaded his eyes. But then even the bravest soldier, no matter how inured to death, sometimes succumbs to the torture of remorse.

The officer put his hands to his face, shutting out from view the sight of his watery eyes.

Achu cast a baleful glance at the officer who had made him his captive. The officer, not wanting to be seen surrendering to remorse, straightened himself and let his roving eyes dart here and there. Achu's head, which was seeding with ideas, spun like a reel of pictures.

"Officer, if you say you know my father," Achu implored the officer, "why can't you let me go?"

"My friend, it is true I know Pa Mission," the officer answered, his voice trailing away. "But you must understand that I can't just let you go like that. Things don't work like that when we are dealing with sensitive security matters. Even if I let you go now, there is no guarantee that you wouldn't be held up by another control. You know that we have lots of control now because of the great number of criminals and terrorists."

"But it's always been like this, Officer. One can't travel in peace in this country."

"Young man, I'm not supposed to discuss our security apparatus with you, you know that, don't you?"

"What do you mean, Officer?"

"Am I the one who arrested you? Am not the commandant, non? Am I the one who brought you here?"

"No."

"That's what I mean. I don't have the authority to release any person arrested by a superior officer. Only a dog owner can remove a bone from his dog's mouth."

Achu gasped for breath and stared at the officer vacantly, unable to verbalise the shards of broken thoughts he had managed to piece together. What on earth, he asked himself, was he doing in a police post at such an ungodly hour, and why had the officers, unbeknownst to his family and school, arrested him when they should know better? The more he thought about this, the more he realised how easy it was for anyone to cross the unguarded and very porous frontier between life and death.

In everything the officers did, Achu began to see insouciant similarities with death. Just as death had so arrogantly snatched his father without permission, so too had the officers so arrogantly arrested him, depriving him of his freedom without authorisation And just as death, ever so wanton in its greed, plucks us when we are full of sap and in full bloom, so too had the officers, in their blind allegiance to power, dragged him uncannily from the light of freedom into the darkness of captivity.

Achu broke down and cried.

Chapter Twelve

Achu's mind was full of thoughts that jabbed at him from all sides. An officer walked in, placed her purse on the table, and eyed Achu up and down. Without a word, she beamed radiating happiness.

Achu put down his head and watched the newly arrived officer from the corner of his right eye. She had a stubborn kind of sophisticated ugliness that did not go well with her engaging courteousness. Achu wondered why any woman would allow herself in this age of cover-up cosmetics to be so resistantly ugly.

The officer looked at Achu again and then turned to her colleague.

"Emah, what is this little boy doing here?"

"Captain, he was arrested yesterday for vagrancy. He does not have his tax receipts."

"I beg your pardon," the female officer said, raising the tone of her voice. "He was what?"

"But I was not the one, Captain," Corporal Emah responded, his lips trembling.

"Who arrested him then?" she queried.

There was stony silence. The female officer looked daggers at her male colleague and worked herself into a rage, sloughing off her mask of congeniality. "Granted that you're not the one, you could, at least, have used your discretion. You know that a child like this should not be in a cell, especially at this time of the day."

"But, Captain, the law is the law, and all we were doing was implementing it."

"The law my foot. Emah, you know as well as I do that the law is an ass. Proof is that your president doesn't go by the constitution. You in particular have been in the force long enough to know that even though in the rules and regulations on the payment of taxes the law is silent on children and students, the general provisions of the laws of this country state that no person under the age of eighteen may be locked up in a cell, let alone allowed to spend the night there. I don't know the law you guys say you are implementing."

Corporal Emah clasped his hands and bowed his head and threw furtive glances at Achu.

Captain Nana walked across the room to a locker in the far corner and hung her cotton sweater. Then she looked around the room as if she was inspecting it and sat down behind the huge cluttered table.

"My friend, come here," she said, pointing to Achu.

Achu got up slowly because the weight of emptiness was holding him down. He couldn't look straight at the officer whose prying eyes were fixed on him.

"Yes, small boy, what's your problem?" she asked twisting her mouth.

"I want to go home, Officer."

"Home where?"

"Chuforba, madam."

"Why were you arrested?"

"I don't know, madam."

"You mean you don't know why you were arrested?"

"Well, madam, you see, they asked for my tax receipts; and when I showed them my school identity card, they refused to accept it." Achu paused to mop the rush of tears flowing down his cheeks.

Captain Nana shook her head in utter disbelief and allowed her ire to be sublimated in a pathetically sardonic smile. Achu continued to mop up the seemingly endless stream of tears.

"Small boy," Captain Nana said, turning to Achu. "You shouldn't be here in the first place. Dry your tears and be a man." So saying, she threw quick glances at Corporal Emah.

"Emah, make sure that this boy leaves this place first thing in the morning before the colonel comes. You know how he is. I won't be surprised if he too reasons like all of you. We're someday going to get into trouble in this office because of the way we are enforcing the law. I have always been against the arrest of people on some flimsy statute that should normally be repealed. You yourself know how the colonel is."

"Yes, Captain," Corporal Emah answered as if he was about to lose his voice.

Achu was lost for words. The idea flitted across his mind that his nightmare of misery might soon be over. Inwardly he began to gloat over his eventual release, anticipating the freedom he would enjoy celebrating his father's death. It was a moment of great happiness to him, a moment for the kind of happiness that is born of despondency. Instead of being overwhelmed by disdain for those who arrested him and being ready to unload on them the explosive pent-up anger he was carrying, he was rather full of bounce and buoyancy about his freedom. It was as if Captain Nana was about to release an animal that had been in captivity.

Achu did not have time to harbour any ill feelings or malice towards those who had arrested him. All he wanted to do was to leave immediately so as to be in Chuforba before daybreak. Even the eerie thoughts he had harboured from childhood about travelling in the dead of night did not bother him. The death of his father had steeled him and given him rare courage.

It wasn't long before Corporal Emah beckoned to Achu to leave. Achu ran out of the police post with his small metal box into the cold crisp night. Some nighttime revellers could be heard in the distance singing and dancing. They sounded boozed up, but that wasn't Achu's concern. In fact, he thought dismally that those people too might be celebrating the loss of a dearly departed one.

Achu clattered over the cobblestones in the yard and bounced onto the main road leading to Chuforba. There was no soul in sight. The moon had retired for the night, and the stars were no longer visible because the arrogant clouds moving intrepidly in columns across the sky had blocked them.

Achu held his hand to his heart and trudged on accompanied by the boisterous echo of his movement. He walked very briskly, fearlessly, with his chest out as if he was challenging those unseen nighttime wandering spirits to dare approach him. In normal times, many adults, let alone kids like Achu, wouldn't dare take on that road alone at that time of the night. But then death had, it would seem, transformed the fear in Achu into valour.

Achu covered distances without realising it. Before long, he was toiling up the last hill in Daba village before Chuforba. When he got to the top, he looked down below and couldn't see much. The kola nut trees had hidden everything. He looked in the direction of his father's compound and saw some faint light. His heartbeat quickened, and he shivered. Then he turned round to see the long stretch of road he had covered, but he couldn't see far because of the pitch darkness. Yes, the darkness he had been taught from childhood to fear because it was at that time that evil spirits blundered about.

Achu couldn't believe that he had travelled so many miles at that hour alone. He kept on repeating to himself that nothing could be more dangerous and unpredictable than life itself. "After all, life," he said to himself out loud, "is a road mined with death."

As he reeled down the Botsug Hill and passed the schoolyard, he thought he heard voices and footsteps. He stopped and looked round, but there was nobody. His hair stood on edge. How was he going to pass near the huge kola nut and mahogany trees behind which some witch could be lurking before reaching the compound? For a few split seconds, fear bound and gagged him as he thought somberly of some mischievous spirit overpowering him.

"No," he burst out, shattering the placid atmosphere. The echo resounded in the kola nut bush."No, no, nothing can happen to me. Nothing. Not in Chuforba. I've done nothing wrong to anybody nor did my father or for that matter anybody in my family. No, Papa is watching me."

Having exorcised the fear that was in him, Achu turned round quickly in one movement, his heart beating very fast. The resentment that spilled from his eyes must have instilled fear into the heart of whomever or whatever spirit it was that had been tiptoeing behind him. The footsteps and voices he thought he had heard died down instantly. At that very moment, a big bird, very likely an owl, flapped its wings, flew overhead, and landed on a kola nut tree as if it wanted a staging post from which to watch Achu.

Achu drew in a deep breath and quickened his pace.

As he approached the compound, he saw the silhouette of two men coming in his direction. They had been chatting animatedly, but then they hushed their voices when they suspected someone was approaching them. Achu felt like ducking behind the nearest kola nut tree by the roadside, but he was afraid he might step on the faeces that kola nut pickers usually dropped on their trail. He decided to brave it and just moved on.

When Achu came upon the two men, he tried to dodge them. "Good morning, papas," he greeted them meekly, trying to conceal his real voice.

"Whose son are you, and what are you doing out here at this time of the night?" one of the old men enquired.

"I'm Achu, papa, the son of Pa Asaah."

"You say you're who? Whose son?" the second papa asked.

"Achu, papa, I'm Pa Asaah's son."

"You mean Achu? Nei's son? Achu himself? But you are our father. Achu, is this you like this, or I'm seeing somebody else?"

"I'm the one, papa."

"And why are you travelling at this late hour?"

"Because I heard of papa's death late. Plus those gendarmes at Ngumba Junction detained me for no reason."

"Oh, Achu, my son, thank God you came safely. Do you know who we are?"

"Of course, papa. How can you ask a question like that? You are Pa Eborobot and you are Pa Muyaka."

"That's good, my son," Pa Eborobot responded. "That's why we like intelligent children. Children who go to school in Abakwa but come to the village regularly to see us. Not like others who leave the village, and when they return they cannot make us out again. You're welcome, my son, and God will bestow his blessings on you. As you move about in life, no evil spirit shall ever befall you. Let your eyes always remain open, and if you hit your foot against a stone, the stone will break, not your foot."

"Thank you, Nei," Achu answered. "So where are both of you going, Nei?"

"We're not going far. We're just going to the bush to ease ourselves."

"And how is the death ceremony going on in the compound?"

"Very well, very well," Pa Muyaka responded. "It has drained people from the neighbouring villages. Everybody is there. You know your father and how popular he was. You know that Pa Asaah's death is the major event that this village has had in a long time. People have come all the way from Ngyen, Muwah, Nanjah, Mambei, Dabah, Botiba, Ngwimbe, Kumfoba, and so many other villages. Can you believe it? A high-level delegation has come from Babli with their own juju. If Babli is represented, you can be sure it is a great funeral. My child, you know God is a kind God. He gave us scabies and also fingers with which to scratch them. So don't let this thing bother you so much. God alone knows why he gives and takes back."

"Thank you, Nei," Achu said sobbing. "I'll precede you to the compound. We'll see you in the compound."

The two old men glided out of sight and dived under some cassava plants and squatted. Achu could hear the roar of the farting of one of the old men as they dropped their payload of stinking body waste. At the same time, he heard some voices coming from the compound and thought wistfully of the scene that would unfold when he got there.

As Achu drew closer to the compound, he saw that a huge tarpaulin tent had been planted where the coffee plants used to grow behind papa's house. That must be the house for the male mourners to sit in and drink palm wine and narrate stories. Smoke was pouring out of it.

Farther down was Abu's house, Grandmother's, where the women would normally be quartered. They must certainly be tired and be resting at that late hour, otherwise how come no one was dancing longe and mbaya? Achu walked slowly, not wanting to be seen by anybody who would recognise him. His presence, if detected even at that late hour, would set the village on fire.

Achu decided to bid his time, hoping to make his way anonymously to where the girls and boys his age were sleeping so that he would just lie down till daybreak.

As he walked slowly, he beheld a woman sprawling on banana leaves outside one of the houses. Her hair was understandably long and unkempt, and her breasts had fallen and were hanging loosely, dejectedly. Two babies about the same age, very likely twins, were pulling strenuously on them. Sorrow, that great mischievous artistic sculptor, had chiselled the woman's face. She was mourning, and from where Achu stood, he could hear her telling the babies between sobs that their father had gone away on a long journey from which he would never return.

"Oh, that death were but a passing eclipse after which shineth the sun," the woman wailed, tears washing down her face.

The thought flashed through Achu's mind that the woman must be Ma Bei whom he had heard so much about. The family reunion that had taken place two years earlier had degenerated into a shouting match because one of Achu's mothers that had accused Pa Asaah of having made twins with another woman.

Could this be the woman? Achu wasn't sure. He felt temptation creeping up his body and nudging him to walk over to the woman to find out if she was indeed Ma Bei and if those innocent twins were his brothers.

Just as the thought galloped past in his mind, two women emerged from the house to go and urinate behind the house. When they saw the woman with the two babies sobbing, they cast a baleful eye at her and burst out laughing mockingly. They made a few snide comments that Achu couldn't hear perceptibly, but it was obvious that they were bludgeoning the woman with insults.

Achu stood in the same place trembling from the merciless disdain he felt for the two ladies. He realised how true it is that ceremonies are fertile grounds on which seeds of the most slanderous gossips sowed in the morning blossom into thriving plants by nightfall.

Achu continued to look in the direction of the lady with the two children trying to make out who that mother might be and figuring out what to do next. Zillion thoughts surrounded him buzzing around with the blind fury of a swarm of bees.

Achu next turned in the direction of the tent where the men, the papas of the village, were sitting by the fireside drinking palm wine and chatting volubly. Something prodded him to break out into mourning as is usually done whenever someone arrives at a death ceremony. He was being pulled in every direction, and while his head teemed with thoughts, his mind was full of emptiness.

Confused as he was, Achu forgot that he was holding his metal box. He raised his hands to his head, laced his fingers, and began to sob.

The box fell with a thud. Two elderly men who had heard the noise rushed out of the tent to see if someone had slipped and fallen. They came closer to Achu who stood there as pale as a ghost and as still as a post unaware of anything that was happening around him.

The two men didn't recognise him. They ran back into the tent hastily to get a splinter of firewood. The haste with which they ran into the tent aroused the curiosity of the other men who were sitting by the huge fireside. All of them thronged out and approached Achu, who was still planted there oblivious of everything.

The men looked at Achu closely, and when one of them recognised him, he burst out in tears.

"Achu! Achu! Oh Achu! Achu! Achu is here himself. May that all the people of this village should come out and see who is here. Our father Pa Asaah is back. Pa Asaah himself is back. The successor and next of kin is here. Oh people of Chuforba, come out in all your numbers and see who is here. Pa Asaah is back. May that all of you should come outside and behold Pa Asaah himself. Pa Asaah, oh Pa Asaah, welcome back."

The others joined him on cue and within minutes, the whole compound had broken into frenzied mourning and wailing as the villagers poured out from various houses in the compound and moved towards the mourning grounds.

They carried Achu shoulder high and danced in a circle. Then they carried him behind the main house in the compound where his father was resting.

Just then Achu stirred and looked round. When he saw the fresh mound of earth that covered his father's grave and beheld that this was the work that Death, the Almighty Chaos, had wrought, he blacked out.

At the same time, a fierce wind howled past, and rain started bickering over the zinc roofs in the compound. A pall of sorrow spread its tentacles over the desolate fog-ridden village, wrapping up the villagers in its chilling blanket of anguish.

Chapter Thirteen

The sun had just rubbed its yellowish eyes and peeped from behind the slightly parted curtain of clouds that draped the horizon as if it needed assurance that it was time to come out on stage. Then suddenly, looking ashamed like an actor who had flubbed his lines and who was being booed, it tried to retreat hurriedly as the curtain of clouds began to flap.

Achu gazed at it with some unease and ambled along hastily for fear that the threatening skies might give vent to their anger and disgorge a heavy downpour. His pace quickened when a wild wind whistling obnoxiously howled past with rapacious rage, lashing against his face with unencumbered force. The trees and tall grasses, in a moment of togetherness that only their common fate could explain, huddled together and embraced each other in awesome fear, nodding submissively as the wind breezed by.

Achu was elated as he marched home triumphantly with his chest out while humming with good cheer the latest hit by the nation's top musical group, The Imitators. And just to be sure that his school transcripts were still on him, he would from time to time touch his side pocket to be certain that the transcripts were where he had tucked them.

Achu's heartbeat raced fast as he burned with desire to reach home as soon as possible. The warm and bright smile that bedecked his face bespoke the exuberant joy that filled him. To him, there could be no better and fitting tribute to his father than the excellent results he had obtained at the end of the school year for it was his father after all who had nurtured in him the persistent determination to outperform his classmates in everything he did. Achu beamed and strode home with hilarity in his every limb. He couldn't wait for he was rushing home to his aunt, his father's sister, who was his mother, Ma Akwen, Mrs. Akwen Ndefru. He had to share the good news with her and the rest of the family because good news like that wasn't the kind of thing one kept to oneself even if one was like Achu, who didn't particularly cherish the idea of always unbosoming his feelings.

As Achu hurried down the road, a flurry of thoughts settled on his mind. He wished his father was still alive to savour with him the success he had achieved in his end-of-the-year examination so as to bestow on him yet more blessings. Achu's father, Pa Asaah, had drummed it into his son's ears so many times before his death that Achu's future lay in his books. Accordingly, Achu had, unlike children his age, shied away from dilettantish indulgence in pleasures of the flesh and concentrated on his schoolwork.

The instant thought of his father sent a chilling sensation of despair and frustration through Achu's entire body because it brought back to his mind the thought of death. But then he just as quickly swiped the thought away because he knew that even though his father was no longer alive, he must be watching over him from wherever he was and interceding to God on his behalf so that he could succeed in life.

Achu looked into his mind's eye and saw a clear and well-defined picture of his ecstatic father jubilating over the brilliant results he had achieved. Achu smiled inwardly knowing that it must have been the countless blessings that his father had bestowed on him that instilled in him the love for his schoolwork. The comforting thought of his finishing high school and going abroad to continue with his education much like his father had always wished snuggled up to him, and they clasped each other momentarily. Going abroad to white man's country to further his education was all Achu was now living for in keeping with the wishes of his father.

Achu skelped down the road jauntily piggybacking his folded bag. He had to reach home as soon as possible to see his family members because the good news had to be shared since good news is no news if it isn't shared. And with the nimbus clouds dangling desperately in the horizon, suspended from the threatening sky by light woolly threads, Achu's heart ticked faster and faster and pounded harder and harder. The good news was too heavy a load for him to be carrying alone.

Achu advanced quickly, his pace becoming more briskly as he thought of reaching home. After crossing the Martyrs' Bridge, so named by the population after hundreds of defenceless Southern

Merooncans were massacred in cold blood on the false and spurious charge that they were terrorists and sympathisers of the Independence Party, he reached the People's Garage. He took the footpath that cut through the Ndongwefor market that usually met once a week on Friday evenings. Since it wasn't a market day, there wasn't the milling crowd that usually gathered there late in the evenings to drink and exchange gossips. Achu increased his speed.

As Achu passed near the empty stalls where secondhand clothes were usually sold on market days, he saw a group of mud-splattered schoolboys playing football in the area of the market where the market women from far-away villages usually sat to sell their wares. The boys had converted the area into a football pitch and were playing a tournament. Achu slowed down his pace and took off a few moments to watch the boys sloshing in grime and poaching in the pools of dirty rainwater that had flooded that part of the market. He was so absorbed in the game that when he turned away to saunter down the road, he squelched in the dirty water and wetted his tennis shoes. Achu blurted out a few harmless swear words to himself and hurried down the hill.

Farther down the road as he trudged on, Achu saw the empty huts to which palm wine tappers from Konman, Botiba, Futba, Nekwe, and Kwemedan brought their calabashes of palm wine on fully laden bicycles to sell. The thought of palm wine brought back to his mind the thought of the doddering old men of the village who liked to spend market days staggering from hut to hut, breathing fumes of alcohol. It also reminded him of all those palm wine buyers who came from different parts of the province to buy the white aromatic stuff for their traditional ceremonies since a traditional ceremony without palm wine was no ceremony.

Achu's anxiety to reach home before the menacing rain could catch up with him soared with each pace. He rushed past the few coagulated shops and stores that lined the road cheek by jowl and brushed aside the numerous hawkers peddling stolen items of all kinds. As he was about to skip over one of the many cavernous potholes in the middle of the road, he almost stepped on the rotten remains of a dog that had been crushed to death two days earlier by a car. Passersby had thrown some withering tree branches and leaves over the dead body, thus paying in their own way their last respects to the errant, straying dog. Society, after all, had to take care of its own.

Achu soon reached Death Bend, the treacherous steep bend that was well known for the high number of accidents that usually took place there. No one, not even the country's most prominent witch doctors, had succeeded in reducing the number of accidents at Death Bend. Achu turned round mechanically and saw by the roadside an unscalable mountain of garbage that the neighbourhood had allowed to pile up. It served as a fabulous abode for the awe-inspiring rats that were terrorising the entire town. Achu ran holding his breath to avoid inhaling the nauseating odour that was about to suffocate him.

Achu was racing down hill when he heard the hooting of an automobile. He turned to see from which direction the vehicle was coming and saw a rickety bus up the road. It was obviously from a football match and was speeding dementedly towards him with its full load of passengers singing and waving the flag of the Damenba Rangers Football Team. As the inebriated bus veered from one side of the road to the other trying to dodge the pocks in the road, it almost ran into Achu who leapt into the bush instantly for his dear life. But for his vigilance, Achu would have been crushed to death mercilessly and instantly like the dog he had just seen.

The passengers roared triumphantly, waving their flags as if their team had just scored a goal. The bus continued on its erratic course, and Achu watched it speeding down the hill tipsily, sending unsuspecting pedestrians scurrying for their lives. The pigs and goats that had been bound, gagged, and thrown unto the carriage squealed and bleated as if they had a premonition that they were being taken to the altar of slaughter. No one paid attention to them as they screeched and shrieked even though they were hoisting in their own way screaming banners depicting man's inhumanity to animals.

Achu was shaken and dazed. He stood in the same place trembling feverishly, his mouth flaring. He couldn't believe how close he had come to tasting of death, and it left a bitter taste in his mouth. On his mind's flashcard, he scored himself very high marks for having been vigilant enough to see the oncoming bus and for having stepped aside on time. He laughed softly inwardly for he had seen death's outstretched hand ready to grab his own, but he had been bold enough to refuse to take it. Achu shuddered at the wrenching thought that death could be so maliciously near and that it could beckon guilelessly to anyone at any time.

He saw in his mind's eye how in the twinkle of an eye he could have been in another world. That thought filled him with disorienting fear because he had seen at very close range how transient life could be. Achu took in a deep breath for he had come a long way. Visible warts of gloom and hopelessness grew on his mind, and he wondered if they would ever drain out. His eyes dimmed with tears, and he raised his shirt and mopped the beads of sweat rolling down his cheeks freely. Why, he asked himself, should death be so irrationally unfair and always lurking where it shouldn't, ready to pounce on innocent victims? And why, for God's sake, was it that the bad guys always seem to live long so they may have time to mend their ways while the good guys die young so they don't have time to commit any folly? Achu shrugged, nodded his head, and sighed. He didn't understand why death always seems to spare the bad guys, thus favouring them. Memories of his father came to his mind in a rush, and residues of his past misery nagged him sharply.

Achu recalled the unrecognisable dog he had just seen and its gratuitous death. Again he took a deep breath and gritted his teeth for had it been his appointed day with death, he too would have been lying down somewhere like the unlucky dog, lifeless, naked, and exposed to the entire world. A miserable feeling overpowered him, and he grimaced in despair.

With a heavy heart and twinges of pain all over his body and with the harassing thought of his brush with death twirling around him, Achu managed to remember what the preacher had said in church a few weeks earlier. He raised his hands upward towards the sky and towards heaven and muttered a prayer. Slowly the besieging fear in him began to retreat as if he needed the hair of the dog to vanquish his fear of death.

The courage that the prayer had helped him muster was now his escort. Achu lumbered along painfully as his mind raced past countless images in his subconscious. He saw his mother, father, and classmates; and he pictured himself in white man's country holding the hand of a white man's woman.

As the courage took over from the diffidence, Achu caught a glimpse of the Ndefru home very clearly in the distance. People who had been in the Ndefru compound described it as a home of extravagant taste. At any rate, it was a sprawling mansion set in the midst of a pleasantly blooming orchard. To hear the villagers describe Mr. Ndefru, he was a man who loved to cling to his colonial past with crude tenacity. It was therefore not surprising to anyone that apart from the mansion itself, he had added a gymnasium for his family and friends, a solarium, swimming pool, sauna, tennis court, and a large parking lot to accommodate all the cars that usually streamed to his estate whenever he was celebrating some occasion.

There was also a beautiful walkway through the well-manicured garden. Rows of flowering plants were always standing gallantly at attention in uniformed elegance and with flirtatiously flourishing smiles on their petals. Inside the cosy exuberant mansion itself, the Ndefru furniture and household mingled well. The marble tiles were so well polished that the villagers who were chanced to visit the mansion walked with extreme caution as if they were walking on eggs. Pa Ndekwe had once slipped and broken his leg because he had been paying too much attention to his shadow being reflected on the tiles.

On the walls of the Ndefru home were souvenirs and mementoes of all kinds that Mr. Ndefru had collected over the years from his travels throughout the world. The most prized, as far as he was concerned, was the artwork, especially the carvings from Côte d'Ivoire, the paintings from South Africa, and the brass work from North Africa.

In the four corners of the huge living room, Mr. Ndefru artfully displayed antics and heirlooms handed down from the time of his great grandfather, Nei Tafor, a well-known warrior for whom hunting had been a great diversion.

The day Achu went to the Ndefrus was a Country Sunday. Mbon as it was called. It was the day on which all villagers were expected by tradition to take a deserved respite from their normal daily activities, especially farming. On such days, the men would wake up with the chickens and visit the traps they had set the day before or go palm wine tapping. The women stayed at home, resting their tired and weary bones from the daily skulduggery to which their life as women had gotten them accustomed to.

A woman's typical day normally started around four in the morning when the boisterous roosters in the compound crowed in unison from their roost to summon every woman to her early morning duties just like a chief does from his palace when there is something of import that he wants to impart to his citizens. If the crowing failed to wake up the women, the roosters would remind the stubborn women at fairly regular intervals by stretching, flapping their wings, and blurting out a cacophonous chorus of squawking. The women would then immediately wake up dutifully to prepare food for the entire family before leaving for their farms two hours later to return in the evening when the sun had bidden the firmament good night. A woman's place wasn't only in the home; it was also in the farm and in the market.

Achu arrived at the gate of the Ndefru home panting heavily. He had had to be quick because the weather wore an authoritatively sullen and threatening face. Thunder too had begun to roll and rumble deafeningly while lightning cut sharp swaths across the countryside.

If there was any one thing Damenba people held in absolute awe, lightning was it, because it was unforgiving in its wickedness. Quite a good many Damenba people had sacrificed a relative to lightning. Usually people went to traditional doctors to send lightning to their enemies as a warning of worse retribution to follow. Initially, the lightning might be instructed to simply singe the hair on the enemy's private parts or armpits as a warning to him to desist from whatever evil thought and designs he might have been harbouring against the sender. Sometimes it was to settle scores. If, for example, someone suspected that you were sleeping with his wife or girlfriend, he might send the lightning to you to teach you a lesson. Things like that.

The first person to notice that there was someone at the Ndefru gate was deep-mouthed Lion, the savage Ndefru dog with a sullied reputation for uncautioned barbarism. Mr. Ndefru had bought the adult German shepherd from a departing American Peace Corps volunteer who had trained it to be a perfect watchdog. Lion carried out his daily chores with the meticulous care of a devoted housewife and with unapologetic vindictiveness. The only problem was that he couldn't distinguish between welcome and not-so-welcome guests.

Prior to Lion's arrival in the Ndefru home, thieves of all persuasions had made a fool of Mr. Ndefru and his family. They would, nobody knows how they did it, break into the Ndefru home at will under the nose of the entire household as it slept and cart away television sets, stereos, clothes, and valuables even though the compound was ringed with state-of-the-art electronic security gear. Somehow, as it always happened, the thieves would return when they knew Mr. Ndefru had replaced the stolen goods and skim the home of the newly acquired goods.

Achu hadn't rung the bell. Either he hadn't seen it, or seeing it, he probably didn't know how to use it. He had therefore spent about fifteen minutes at the gate trying to peep into the yard to see if anyone would notice him. When he realised that no one had taken notice of his presence, he finally decided to look for a piece of iron rod to bang on the gate.

Any noise, especially a pinging sound, round the fence surrounding the Ndefru property invited Lion's fury. When Lion heard the noise, he sprang forward and started barking, emitting endless reverberations of ear-splitting howls. At first, no one paid attention to its barking because the neighbourhood children who loved to pass near the Ndefru home regularly took great delight in teasing the dog.

Fri who had been playing behind the house came running with knots of tousled hair skipping and bouncing on her head. "Who is it?" Fri enquired breathlessly above Lion's sonorous barking.

"Please open the gate," responded Achu inaudibly, switching on a luminous smile to paper over the plastered cracks of fear on his face.

"Who is it, please?" Fri asked with earnest anxiety.

"I won't tell you who I am. Just open the gate," replied Achu with deliberate obstinacy, refusing to say who he was.

"But this must be Ni Achu," Fri broke out cheerfully. "I recognise your voice. Ni Achu! Ni Achu is here. Ni, welcome." So saying, Fri unlocked the huge and heavy metal gate to let in Achu, and the gate swung wide open with a loud clanking sound. Before Fri realised it, Lion had surged forward to attack Achu who froze in the same position.

"Lion, Lion," Fri screamed stridently. Lion turned back hesitantly for a brief moment and returned to Achu, smelling and sniffing him several times. Fri beckoned to it, and it came wagging its tail in self-contentment like a traffic police officer that has cornered an unsuspecting driver from whom he knows he'll be able to wrest some money. Fri stroked Lion's head, and he moved away distractedly.

Achu's heart had almost ceased to beat as he reached dizzying heights of fear. The shock of what might have happened had he openly manifested fear and try to run away from Lion brought tears to his eyes. Achu was flayed of all energy. He reeled off in his mind the incredible number of problems he had had in his life, and while he could hear the old ones receding slowly into the backroom of his imagination, what had just happened to him dug deeply into his flesh. First, the long trek from school to the Ndefru home was exacting physically. Then there was the near-fatal accident at Death Bend when the snorting bus almost ran into him. And now there was this brush with Lion right at home after he had reached his destination. Achu bit his upper lip and fixed his gaze on Lion, the son of a bitch.

You mean death can be everywhere like this? Achu pondered. And why me? he asked tearfully. This time his heart started emitting hard and harsh beats in an erratic manner. He winced and tried to shrug off his fear of the omnipresent death that he felt was stalking him all over the place.

Achu tried to put a bold face on the gloom that had flung itself on him. He stretched out his arms, and Fri jumped into them. They hugged each other, exchanged smiles, and giggled. Fri gasped for what to say.

"Ni Achu, welcome," Fri burst out excitedly. "We'd been wondering when you'd come home since most of the colleges closed a few days ago."

"That's true," Achu responded in a crushed voice. "We the senior students had to wait for the junior students to leave the campus. Don't forget that your brother is the senior prefect."

"Trust," Fri replied happily. "I knew I could trust you to assume your responsibilities." So saying, Fri took hold of Achu's bag and led him through the corridor to the back of the house where the family usually sits in the evening to listen to stories and riddles. As they passed near the big hall where visiting villagers usually sat, Achu heard some music.

"Fri, what's going on?" Achu asked with curiosity."I hear the sound of music."

"You know today is Country Sunday, and as usual the people from the village have come to see Daddy."

"I should've known that," Achu replied knowingly. "Where is Mummy? I'm impatient to tell her my results."

"But start with me, brother, please," Fri pleaded. "I'm also interested in knowing your results." While Achu wondered if he should tell her or not, Fri announced triumphantly, "Ni Achu, I was fourth in my class, and Ni Cho was forty-fifth."

Achu lifted his brows and swept Fri in his arms in one quick movement and held her close to himself warmly. A smile that had been hiding behind the halo of fear emerged suddenly and switched on the floodlights that illuminated his face. The face reflected brotherhood.

Achu followed Fri into Cho's elegant room that had its own private entrance from the other side of the garage. Apparently Cho had just left the room because as Fri explained it, the room wouldn't normally be so cluttered with dirty clothes lying here and there, especially dirty shoes, socks, and underpants. Ngwah, the houseboy, had a duty to clean Cho's room first thing in the morning and to return to it every few hours to ensure that it was spick and span.

Achu looked round the gorgeous room and held his heart in utter astonishment because of its extravagance. The crystal chandelier beamed from the ceiling with undiluted light and the teak wardrobe dominated the corner of the room, almost hiding from view the exquisite drapes trimmed with laces. The sensuous waterbed sprawling in the middle of the room laid back invitingly, waiting in suffused innocence to be mounted.

Fri, the only daughter of the Ndefrus and one of two children, was very excited to see her brother Achu. She paced up and down restlessly. The last time they'd seen each other was at the Friends International Clinic where Fri had been hospitalised for malaria. Achu had obtained permission from the principal to go and see her, and Fri had felt much better after the visit. But that was weeks back.

Achu recalls that it was during that visit that he had entered into a very spirited argument with an American doctor at the clinic, Dr. Peter John, on the viciousness of malaria. Achu couldn't understand why the Western world did not care about finding a cure for malaria even though it is the cause of millions of deaths in Africa and the tropical world. He had, much to the supreme anger of Dr. Peter John, accused the Western world of not doing enough to find a cure for malaria because malaria is not prevalent in their countries. And oh, supreme sacrilege, in an age in which everyone is supposed to believe that discrimination on the basis of colour is a thing of the past, Achu had insinuated that had AIDS been discriminatory in its attacks, attacking only black people, the Western world would not have cared.

Achu closed the door, and Fri helped him peel off the sweat-drenched shirt that was stuck to his body. He slipped on a black cotton T-shirt, and Fri led him through the corridor to the mammoth Ndefru living room that was so big it could host the annual mbaglum dance. Fri raced out of the room to inform her mother that her brother Achu was home at last. It was great relief to all of them because they'd been very worried that Achu hadn't arrived since the college closed on vacation.

On seeing Achu, Ma Akwen opened her arms wide, and Achu ran into them. She hugged Achu snugly and caressed him. She looked at him steadily and gripped him firmly with her usually stern stare. The stare slowly turned into a soft maternal glow. Achu dissolved in her arms.

"So, Achu, this is you?" Mrs. Ndefru asked cheerfully. "Don't do what you just did again. We were very worried because you hadn't come home. All your friends had reached their own homes."

"Mummy, don't blame me," Achu said apologetically."You know as the senior prefect, I have to hang around until all the students have left the campus."

"I understand," Mrs. Ndefru responded with a gleam in her eyes and a hint of anger in her voice. "But you should have sent us word through your friend Cornelius, who visited us just yesterday."

"You're right, Mummy, sorry. You know your son is the senior prefect."

"That is no excuse, and I don't want you to repeat it in the future," Mrs. Ndefru said, cradling Achu and running her hand in his hair. "And what of your results?"

"Mummy, I was first in my class out of sixty-three," Achu answered with excitement, proudly fixing his shirt. "I have been promoted to class five."

Ma Akwen didn't say anything. Fri was overcome with joy. She beamed expansively and stepped back to take a second, third, and fourth look at her elder brother Achu, whom she called with respect, Ni Achu. She clasped Achu in her tender embrace and half closed her eyes, letting herself to be wrapped up in the warm feeling being distilled by the moment.

"Wonderful. Wonderful. I mean wonderful," Fri mused, chuckling radiantly. "Trust. I knew we could count on you as usual. Congratulations, because you're always doing the family proud. I don't know if I have told you, but I was fourth in my class out of thirty-two girls, two of whom are nursing mothers."

Achu smiled. When Fri recalled that her mother hadn't said anything, she turned towards her. "Mummy, Ni Achu says he was first in his class, and you haven't said anything."

"Why?" Mrs Ndefru quipped. "I should blow the trumpet and summon the village to come and celebrate. Is he the first to be first?"

"Hey, Mummy," Fri pursued, "Surely this calls for a celebration. My brother is first in his class, and you don't think it is an achievement?"

"Why were you not first, and why was Cho just forty-fifth in a class of fifty-one?"

"But, Mummy, that has nothing to do with Ni Achu. So because Ni Cho and I were not first, you wouldn't congratulate Ni Achu?"

"I didn't say that."

"But your silence is obvious, Mum. I'll never understand you, Mum. Never."

Fri eyed his mother with contempt and tried to drag Achu away from her presence. Achu resisted.

"What of Ni Cho, Mummy?" Achu enquired about his brother.

"Ask for that one, well . . . I don't know what else we are supposed to do again," Mrs. Ndefru said, throwing her hands up in the air in despair. "We sent him to one of the best schools; I mean the best school in the hope that he would succeed, but he hasn't changed. We are thinking of sending him to a boarding school in white man's country. It seems that all the children who fail here succeed there." The smile that had been on Mrs. Ndefru's face faded.

"Mummy, I'm sure Ni Cho will pick up later," Achu predicted confidently.

"Well, he better do so in his own interest," she replied with detachment. "We've done what we're supposed to do as parents. The rest is left to him." She squeezed Achu's hand lightly. "Where are your things?" she asked.

Fri who was standing near Achu enjoying the moment answered immediately before Achu could say anything.

"Mummy, I have taken them to Ni Cho's room."

Mrs. Ndefru shrugged and looked at Fri evasively from the corner of her eye but didn't say anything. Fri danced round joyously and held Achu's hand, pulling on it gently so they could dance round together. Achu carried her up shoulder high and threw her in the air and caught her. Fri giggled brightly and clung to Achu, who cuddled her lovingly. She continued to latch on to him tenaciously, inhaling the haze of fraternity that was in the air.

"You must be hungry," Fri suggested as she took Achu by the right hand. She called out to Ngwah and gave him instructions to serve Achu something to eat.

Achu wolfed down the luscious meal avidly. He could hear Lion slurping down his own food outside. It was rice glopped up with some thick brown sauce.

After Achu had eaten, he wiped his mouth with the back of his hand. Mrs. Ndefru took him by the hand followed by Fri. She was going to introduce him to the old men of the village who were in the living room having a blast.

When Mrs. Ndefru entered the room with Achu moored to her, all eyes rolled and roamed them. Achu's eyes swept the room, and he saw the old men roosting on benches to which they were solidly anchored to avoid being tipped over by the blustering odour of the palm wine and beer they were drinking. They had been at the Ndefru home tippling since morning. That's the way they spent their Country Sunday.

"Papa them," Mrs. Ndefru called out, her face radiating happiness. "I'm sure all of you know who this is." She stepped aside and nudged Achu to move forward to be seen by the doddering old men who were squinting to make him out. "This is Achu, my son, my brother Pa Asaah's son. He is my brother's next of kin, our successor."

The old men gazed at Achu, grasping him with their questioning stares. Achu bowed his head in reverence while his eyelids dipped and rose with chastened timidity. Some of the old men began to whisper among themselves. Achu heard one of them say in an imperceptible whisper that he was a splitting image of his father.

As the old men schooled their eyes to recognise Achu, one of them gnarled, his voice carrying a gravel of anger.

"Achu, or whatever I hear your name is, come here and greet your fathers instead of just standing there looking at us. You think we're carved of stone? Your father was a thorough gentleman whom we all respected, and you better take after him, especially if as I hear you are his successor."

Achu shuddered, strode forward, and tendered his right hand to him respectfully, the left hand holding the wrist of the right hand. Then he bowed his head. The old man grabbed the hand gruffly and gave back a leering grin. The man's slender hand matched his slim pale figure.

The old man held on to Achu's hand firmly as if it were a bough to which he was ballasting his life. With the other hand, he wiped the dribble of palm wine that was at the corner of his mouth. Some dregs had been caught in the filter of his bushy moustache. The man raised his tired eyes and peered at Achu.

"Achu, do you know me?" he enquired.

"N-n-n-n-n-o, Papa," Achu responded, lips shivering.

The old man chuckled lightly, his rumpled face delineating anger. He pinned a vicarious stare on Achu that penetrated him and reached his heart. Achu visualised pain crawling up on him.

"You mean you don't know me?" he persisted.

Achu shuffled as his lips shuddered with fear.

"I'm asking you a question, and you better answer me," the old man intoned. "You mean you don't know me?" The heat of anger was burning him, and Achu could see its fumes lingering on his face.

Achu's lips quivered and a slight whisper of a headache went through him. Achu was speechless because he knew that if he answered in the negative he would be inviting great trouble. He fidgeted nervously and scratched his head.

"Okay," the old man pursued the interrogation with relentless zeal. "You mean you've never heard of Nei Ngubot?"

"Yyyyes, Nei," Achu answered stiffly. His eyeballs danced lazily, and his tired muscles were about to go to sleep.

Achu looked at Nei Ngubot but didn't recognise him. He, however, dare not show it. Even though the air conditioner in its grunting was fanning cold air directly on Achu, he was perspiring profusely. He stirred his imagination and foraged his thoughts and still couldn't remember his late father ever telling him about Nei Ngubot. Achu couldn't understand why he was being grilled so roughly.

Nei Ngubot rubbed his smarting eyes and signalled to Mrs. Ndefru. "Akwen," he exploded. "Look at me. This little thing here, he says he doesn't know me." He burst out laughing coarsely.

Mrs. Ndefru looked surprised and turned towards Achu and growled. "Achu, don't tell me that you don't know your father."

Turning to Nei Ngubot, she apologised effusively, "Nei, don't mind today's children. They don't know anything. Not even our traditions. It's a pity."

"Yes," Nei Ngubot protested vigorously."Don't blame the children alone. You the parents are responsible because if you had wanted this boy here to know us, he would have." Nei Ngubot paused to sip his palm wine. "Today's children are no good. I mean no good. Especially the ones born in town." He then dismissed Achu irritatingly. "Please move away from my face. They say you are Asaah's successor. What kind of a successor are you if you do not know us your fathers?"

Out of deference to the old men, Mrs. Ndefru couldn't say anything more. She was embarrassed that Achu hadn't recognised his fathers, especially as the old men would hold it against her for not teaching her children the dictates of their traditions. Mrs. Ndefru frowned, and, in a voice lacking in determination, she introduced the old man who had just spoken.

"Achu, this is your father Nei Ngubot, the one Papa always talked about. I'm surprised that you don't know him because Papa used to call him fondly as Pa German. I hope you'll recognise and remember him the next time you see him."

"Oh, now I remember. I remember Pa German. That's the name Papa used to call him." Achu smiled at Nei Ngubot. "Nei, I'm really sorry," Achu said in a hoarse voice. "I didn't know that you're the one Papa had always been talking about. I remember that Papa always talked about the time both of you served in World War II, and how you people helped crush Hitler."

"You mean Asaah told you all that?" Nei Ngubot asked, surprised.

"Oh yes, Nei. Papa spent evenings upon evenings recounting to us the exploits of the allies."

"That's correct, my son," Nei Ngubot replied with controlled anger. "We can say we played our part in history since we helped rid the world of that scoundrel called Hitler. But what has that given us? No money. No fame. You know what I'm talking about. What did Asaah, your own father, have when he died? What had he? Look at Pa Asaah. He rose to the rank of corporal, and see the wretched life he lived. Please don't remind me of that war because other people are enjoying from our victory more than us." Nei Ngubot stroked his beard and wiped his eyes.

Achu moved on to the other fathers and shook their hands, nodding reverently to them. There were eight of them. Achu knew Pa Ngusung well because he was well-known to every Chuforba boy for his jokes and riddles. Pa Ngusung was chewing on kola nuts when Achu walked over to greet him. His mouth was full, and when he opened it to speak, he sputtered some kola nuts on Achu's outstretched hand.

"Yes, my pikin," he said, shaking Achu's hand. "How you dey?" Before Achu could respond, he continued using the big grammar children had come to associate him with. "You say you have born how many children again?"

Achu, surprised and embarrassed, grunted some imperceptible guttural sounds. He could see quite clearly that Pa Ngusung was in a state of degenerative fuddle after sousing alcohol all day. The other old men, their memory equally fogged with fumes of alcohol, laughed abundantly.

Mrs. Ndefru looked embarrassed. Pa Ngusung who was drinking straight from the bottle guzzled his beer clumsily. It gurgled down his throat noisily. By the time he placed the bottle back on the table, Achu had slipped away from the clutch of his stares and moved on to shake hands with the other old men.

Pa Tanjim was in the far corner pulling on his pipe. His youngest son who always accompanied him everywhere stood behind him, serving him palm wine from the ewer near him. Pa Tanjim was known to be the village's most feared medicine man. Rumours swirled round the entire village that he was a member of the dreaded Ngamen secret society to whom it was alleged he had given his eldest son and third wife to be eaten. It was also claimed that had his family not taken the remaining members of the family to another tough medicine man in far-away Njinleka to be inoculated with an antiwitchcraft medicine, they too would have been eaten by Pa Tanjim's witchcraft.

Pa Achiri, whose withered face showed furrows of wrinkles, was a well-known member of the Ndzingyi juju clan. He was a quarter head from a prominent family in the village, and as such he was one of the chief 's most trusted councillors. Since councillors were, in fact, the veritable power behind the throne, they wheeled and dealt in the village and manipulated the chief to do as they pleased. The alcohol had sedated Pa Achiri, and he lay outstretched on the bench, snoring like a car with a broken exhaust pipe.

Lastly, Achu recognised Nei Fon, so called because of the dextrous manual ease with which he played the xylophone. A village traditional ceremony was incomplete without the xylophone. And a xylophone wasn't a xylophone if Nei Fon and his two elder boys didn't play it. The Fon's had attracted a lot of attention to themselves in part because of the way they handled the xylophone. Nei Fon in particular would twirl on his stool while playing, and the ungainly loincloth tied loosely around his waist would flap, sometimes revealing his private parts to the great amusement of the shoal of onlookers who always flocked to see him.

Achu was about to bend down and greet Nei Fon when Mr. Ndefru appeared at the door, jingling his car keys as most car owners usually do. No one had heard the car clanging down into the yard as it entered the driveway. But then, a customised Mercedes-Benz, made to measure Mr. Ndefru's person, wasn't supposed to make any noise at all.

Mr. Ndefru's appearance at the door instantly snubbed out the blazing banter and chatter of the old men.

"Massa, welcome back," Nei Fon managed.

"Yes, papa," Mr. Ndefru responded in a cracked voice. "How are all of you doing? I hope all's well and that you're having lots of fun."

"Well, we are somewhat okay," Nei Fon replied and hurried to add, "You know when palm wine is around, we're fine." He took the calabash of palm wine he was drinking from and shook it vigorously as if to let Mr. Ndefru see that there wasn't much of the wine left except the dregs.

Mr. Ndefru turned back and walked across the lawn to his own living quarters. He had to shed off the suit he was wearing to put on something more casual and comfortable after having been out since morning attending a series of important meetings convened by the ruling Party to work out ways of countering the newly formed opposition parties clamouring for a national conference. According to the opposition, a national conference was needed to discuss the government's stewardship of the country from the time of independence.

In his capacity as the chairman of the provincial branch of the ruling Party, Mr. Ndefru had been summoned by His Excellency, Dr. Prof. Amot, to do everything possible to subdue the opposition rallies that were taking place in his part of the country. A national conference was the hot-button issue, and the ruling party was resisting all attempts to convene one for fear that the skeletons it had in its closet would be revealed to the world.

Mr. Ndefru had returned home that afternoon completely exhausted. He dashed into the medicine chest in his bathroom and took some tablets to ease the nausea, dizziness, and stinking headache that were overwhelming him.

Achu ran into Mr. Ndefru's room, almost knocking down Ngwah in the corridor. Mr. Ndefru, who was full of tiredness, lay down to rest his weary bones. When he saw Achu, he jumped up happily, scooped him up, and tenderly wrapped him with his arms. Both of them clung to each other delightedly as they had done three months earlier when Mr. Ndefru had accompanied the acting assistant deputy minister of internal security on a visit to Achu's school.

The government had sent the ministerial delegation to the school to allay the fears of the students following the disturbances that had broken out after some unruly soldiers invaded the school campus to disperse a peaceful student union meeting convened to call government's attention to students' incessant demands for an improvement in their educational and living conditions. It was alleged that the soldiers had, in their infinite brutality, raped female students, arrested student leaders, and looted dormitories.

Mr. Ndefru had hardly had the time to say anything to Achu when suddenly, out of nowhere, while he stroked Achu's head, Cho crashed into the room and held out his arms to Achu. Achu immediately freed himself of Mr. Ndefru's tender grasp and ran into Cho's arms. They hugged each other warmly and impatiently and, entangled, fell on Mr. Ndefru, who was sitting on the edge of the bed. The atmosphere in the room was one of meditative exuberance. No one was talking, but the fruity smiles that adorned their faces were unmistakable signs of the bliss and felicity into which they had sublimated language.

Mr. Ndefru's room was full of delirious vibrations. Mr. Ndefru smiled at the two brothers clasped together by the sacred bond of fraternity.

For a boy that was barely seventeen years old, Cho Ndefru was tall—very tall and lanky. And he didn't have the overbearing portliness with which many affluent people and their children are usually associated. Mr. Ndefru himself was stumpy and had a fairly large midriff bulge that he carried around gamely. After all, a wealthy man who didn't have a podgy stomach had a very low consideration rating.

Cho was impatient to be alone with his brother Achu, far from the commanding presence of their father. Since they hadn't seen each other in about six months and had a backlog of gossip to catch up with, Cho took Achu by the hand, and both of them took leave of Mr. Ndefru. They ran out of the room and rushed down the corridor.

"Where are your things?" Cho asked, running out of breath from excitement.

"Where else?" Achu responded. "Of course, in your room."

"Great. Just great," replied Cho elated.

Cho and Achu entered Cho's room, and Cho sank into an armchair near the window. He was enthused with happiness at seeing his brother. Achu sat on the edge of the bed, and both of them looked at each other joyously.

After swallowing a lump that was clogging his throat, Achu held out his hand, and Cho took it. He held on to it for a while, and then with a slight pull, Cho flung himself to him. Both of them broke out laughing as they almost fell off balance.

"So, brother, how are you?" Achu ventured, still clasping Cho.

"Okay, I guess. You can see that I'm still in a trance. I still can't believe that you are the one in front of me." Achu returned, still dazed from the whiffs of emotion that mingled with happiness.

"Thank God," said Achu as he unbuttoned his shirt, revealing the hair on his chest and the gold pendant dangling from his neck. "It's wonderful to see you again after such a long time. So how's school?"

"Brother, please leave me alone. You know that I'm not particularly keen about school business," Cho responded instantly. "You know I'm going to school to please Daddy."

"Please don't say that again," Achu countered. "Education is the foundation for our future."

"I know," Cho retorted somewhat irritated. "That's what everybody says, but look at what's happening out there. How many graduates have jobs? And how many of those working are doing what they were trained for? I don't want to be a square peg in a round hole."

"That's being very negative," Achu commented. "Surely things wouldn't remain this way indefinitely."

"In any case, Daddy knows how I feel about this. I've told him I'm not interested in a purely academic education, but you know Daddy. He wants his son to have a PhD. That's all that matters to him, a PhD, so his friends can say his son has succeeded even if I end up driving a taxi as some of our country boys are doing in America. And it doesn't matter if the PhD is in some far-fetched, remote subject like determining the gallons of spit football players spit out on football fields or trying to decipher the sex of angels."

"But it's for you to convince him that a professional or vocational education is better at this time."

"You really think if I tell Daddy that I want to be a mechanic, builder, carpenter, welder, etcetera, he won't kill me?"

"Ni Cho, please credit Daddy with some common sense. Certainly Daddy won't kill you if you show him the merits of a vocational or professional education."

"I have the feeling that you've lost touch with reality. Look at all the big guys in government, the money people like Daddy make. Do you know any of them whose child is carrying plank to saw or playing with scrap metal? While my friends are going to be doctors, lawyers, engineers, professors, etcetera, you want me to saw plank? Please. And you expect Daddy to accept it, especially as he has the money to pay for what he wants me to become?"

"But that's not what you want to become."

"Correct."

"So why not be yourself? Do what you like and show Daddy that it is better to do what you like to do"

"Convince who? Daddy?" Cho asked with great misgiving. "I thought you are close enough to Daddy to know him better. You think you can change Daddy's views when his mind is set on something? Daddy wants everyone to call his son doctor."

"I think that's a legitimate wish on the part of every parent. To wish and expect the best from their children," Achu suggested.

"Please, Achu, let's halt it here because I have the feeling your own mind too is made up."

"It isn't. I'm just trying to be fair to Daddy."

"Fine. Be fair to him. Your turn will soon come. If I'm not mistaken, he has already told me I shall be going to school in America at the end of this school year, and the next in line will of course be you."

"Well," Achu looked up at Cho with vivid light in his eyes. "Daddy hasn't told me anything about it yet."

"But you've just come. Plus you still have one year to go. In any case, I'm not sure he's made up his mind fully yet. He just mentioned it one day when we were discussing my own program."

"That will be great," Achu exploded with joy. "You mean both of us may soon be in America?"

"If all goes well," Cho hedged. "Daddy has already contacted his friend the minister of national education to reserve two scholarships for both of us. But please keep your mouth shut before the information leaks out and embarrasses the minister. You know the number of students who are always clamouring for these scholarships each year."

"I do."

"Good," replied Cho. "Let's continue with this subject later. Before the old men of the village curse me for not greeting them, I suggest that we go and say hello to them."

"Brother, you can see far," Achu replied. "You know they felt I was despising them because I didn't recognise them?"

"That's the way they are. They want recognition, and when they don't get it, they make such a fuss over it; it's incredible."

"But that's precisely what happened to me this afternoon when I arrived."

"C'mon man, don't let that bother you. There's nothing you can do that wouldn't stir the frustration in these old men. They say you should greet them, but if you greet them with an empty hand, you are in trouble. Don't let what they say bother you. I know them since I see them every day. Please accompany me to greet them."

When Cho and Achu arrived in the living room, everybody had left. The spurt of activity that had been animating the Ndefru home had ceased. Fri and Ngwah were busy tidying up the place, wiping off the tobacco that littered the floor and mopping the palm wine that had spilled on the carpet. Lion, for its part, was busy chewing bones and licking the floor.

As Cho and Achu stood in front of the living room making up their minds about what next to do, Lion saw the silhouette of someone near the gate and began to bark inconsolably. Ngwah ran to the gate to see who it was. To his great surprise, it was Nei Fon, the frail old man whom every child in the village dreaded.

Nei Fon was known to everyone as a tough medicine man who could take away anybody's life at will through witchcraft, and nothing would happen to him. People flocked to him daily in their quest for solutions to their daily afflictions. Conventional wisdom in the village had it that government ministers consulted him to ensure their longevity in government. Football teams engaged in international or major local tournaments went to him to cook medicine so that the opposing teams would not find their feet.

Ngwah scrutinised Nei Fon before opening the gate. It was obvious to anyone who saw him that alcohol had done him in mercilessly. It had battered his face with unrepentant savagery. His breath stank, and he staggered along, swaggering as he entered the yard.

"Nei, what's the matter? Can I be of help?" Ngwah asked as he stretched his hand to help the old man.

"Leave my hand alone, you fool," Nei Fon croaked, swaying his walking stick with blind fury. "Who has asked, you fool, to come near me?"

Ngwah dodged, and the stick missed him.

"Where is my pipe?" Nei Fon groused.

"Your pipe, Nei? I'm sorry I don't understand your question. What happened to your pipe?" Ngwah asked innocently.

"I say where is my pipe, and you are questioning me? Did I speak with water in my mouth?" Nei Fon demanded angrily.

"I'm sorry, Nei, but I haven't seen your pipe. Where did you leave it?"

"You big fool, good for nothing houseboy," Nei Fon balled at Ngwah in an extravagant outburst. "Go and look for my pipe before my curse descends on you." He swung the walking stick again and missed Ngwah. "You are lucky that I don't want to hit you otherwise I would remove the few teeth adorning your dirty mouth."

"I'm sorry, Nei, but we've not seen your pipe," answered Ngwah trying wearily to be civil.

"I say where is my pipe?" the old man clamoured, snarling. "Go and look for it quick."

"Nei," Ngwah snuffled a reply, "I have just cleaned the house and didn't see any pipe lying around. If your pipe were here I'd have seen it and, of course, kept it for you. We haven't seen your pipe, Nei. Maybe you forgot it somewhere else."

"Maybe I forgot your mother, you say, maybe I forgot my pipe somewhere else. I don't want to talk too much," Nei Fon bellowed. "I say where is my pipe?"

He pressed on with unyielding firmness. "You think I'm drunk not to know where I left my pipe?" By now the steam of anger was pouring out of his eyes.

Ngwah was on the verge of tears. He didn't know what was happening to Nei Fon or what to say. Goosebumps grew instantly all over his body. He called Fri, and she ran to his rescue.

"Nei," Fri said as she approached the old man and took him by the hand and led him slowly to the living room where he had been sitting earlier. "What's the matter? I see you're not happy."

"Of course, I'm not happy since there's something the matter," he responded sharply and then laughed ruefully. "Just my pipe. I left it here and that your stupid houseboy says it is because I'm drunk that I don't know where I kept it. I don't know what that fool of a houseboy you people have is saying. I left my pipe here, and he's telling me rubbish I've never heard before."

"Papa, calm down, calm down," Fri tried to assuage him. "If your pipe is here, I'm sure we'll find it."

"I know it is here," Nei Fon said confidently.

Fri turned to Ngwah and winked.

"Ngwah, you should know how to speak to older people next time."

"But I was not rude to Nei—"

Ngwah hadn't finished what he was about to say when Nei Fon cut in, "You see what I was saying? This houseboy of yours is a big liar. He says he was not rude to me."

"Don't mind him, Nei," Fri said tactfully. "You shouldn't be mad at Ngwah because if he knew better he wouldn't be a houseboy."

"That's the kind of girl we like for a daughter," Nei Fon said with a vicious look that penetrated Ngwah's flesh, cutting him to the quick. "I knew that with you my pipe would be found in this house. Ask this idiot of a houseboy to go and bring my pipe from where he is hiding it. Are you sure he didn't steal it to sell?"

"Nei, don't worry. I know we'll find your pipe. Even if we don't find it, we shall buy you another one. I should have given you a pipe for a present a long time ago."

"My daughter, I can only say that God will hear your prayers because this is how children should behave to their parents instead of arguing with them. If it were that crook of a houseboy saying this . . . I wouldn't trust the lavish tongue of a liar."

In a moment of inattention on the part of Nei Fon, Fri turned in Ngwah's direction and smiled to him. The anger that had risen in Ngwah faded.

"Ngwah," Fri said loud enough for Nei Fon to hear. "Please go and bring some beer so Nei Fon can lubricate his throat. You've made him talk too much, and I'm sure that with this hot sun baking the earth, Nei Fon must be patching with thirst."

"You can say that again, my daughter," Nei Fon replied with excitement, flashing a wry smile. "But remember that the first drop of rain cannot moisten the soil."

"Ngwah, please make sure you bring the full calabash of palm wine that is in the storeroom," Fri said. Pa Fon rubbed his hands together and nodded politely.

"That's the language of wisdom, my child. Thank you very much. Thank you. I always knew I could count on you. You deserve everything people have been saying about you. Anyone who sees you knows that your father has a wonderful child. God will give you many children."

Fri rushed out of the living room to bring Pa Fon some cold beer from the refrigerator. She crashed into the kitchen when Cho and his mother, Ma Akwen, were engaged in one of their high-pitched spirited arguments. Both of them were visibly swelling with anger and screaming at each other.

"But you can't say things like that, Mummy, you can't." Cho squirmed.

"This is my house, and it is not for you to tell me what to say or not to say. I have a right to do here as I please," Mrs. Ndefru raged. "When you build your own house, you can do as you please, but until then I'm afraid you will have to toe the line in this home. And by the way, I don't want you to speak to me the way you've been doing. I don't know what you and your father want to turn me into in this house."

"That's unfair and very selfish of you to say that, Mummy, because you know us better than that," Cho answered fiercely. "Achu is your son, and you shouldn't be treating him like this. Why should you ask him to sleep in the boy's quarters when I have a big room and a mighty bed that can take both of us? Why, Mummy? Is that fair?"

"Fair or not fair, that's your problem and not mine. You say it is your room. It may be your room and bed, but as far as I know you never paid for them," Mrs. Ndefru blurted out gritting her teeth.

"You're right that I'm not the one who bought them. In that case, let Daddy be the one to say so and not you since he's the one that provides us with everything in this house." Achu blazed.

"Enough is enough," Mrs. Ndefru scowled down on Cho, bristling at his comment. "I'm not going to accept any more of your nonsense in this house."

"But Ni Achu hasn't done anything wrong for you to treat him the way you are doing," Cho answered back sharply.

Mrs. Ndefru picked up her slippers and jumped up, flaring hysterically. Cho ran out of the room. Her limbs were trembling while her lips quivered.

"God will punish you," she ranted with rage. "How dare you speak to me like this? And by which authority? Obviously by your father's since I won't be surprised if he's the one who sent you to provoke me. I have my two feet firmly planted on the ground in this house, and am waiting for both of you."

Fri who witnessed the scene strode out and called out to Cho tearfully with a clipped voice. Her body was trembling from surges of anger. Their mother stood outside the door growling, a frenzy of wroth ripping through her.

"But, brother," Fri whispered when she came close to her brother, "you know Mummy well enough not to engage in a heated argument with her. You know how she takes things."

"You're right. Maybe I shouldn't have," Cho replied with a frail voice. "But Mummy exaggerates all the time. What has Ni Achu done wrong?"

"Of course, nothing," Fri responded. "But you know Mummy. Do you have to do anything wrong for her to rave and rant?"

Cho stood still and listened to the desolation and depression rustling in his veins. Despair and distress were choking him. He looked up at Fri and saw the tears that had formed in her eyes ready to spill over. Tears immediately sprang from the artesian well of misery in the depths of his consciousness and flooded his eyes instantly.

Cho lay crushed under the heavy weight of grief.

Chapter Fourteen

Very early in the morning, at the crack of dawn, a voice stirred Achu from his deep slumber. Achu feigned sleep. After all, why would anybody in his right mind want to wake him up so early in the morning especially as he was on holiday? And why, he asked himself, had dawn come so fast, characteristically unbidden, when he hadn't slept a wink all night? Those rude and boisterous mosquitoes had not left him alone. They had frolicked around in sybaritic delight as they chased each other round the room puffing and huffing around Achu and pausing several times to whisper obscenities in his ear. In fact, one of them had, in a show of defiant intrusion in the face of Achu's resistance, forced a passage into his underpants and probed his manhood, pinching it several times and then scurrying away and returning again and again.

Before Achu could wake up to the voice he had just heard, Ngwah pulled the blanket from his body and stammered, "My friend, wake up. Wake up, you lazy fool. Madam instructed us last night to wake up early so as to get Cho and Fri ready for school, and you are still sleeping. Come on, you think you are a bride, or that I'm your houseboy? Wake up immediately. You are lucky I'm not in a bad mood this morning. Next time, I'll wake you up with a bucket of cold water."

Achu woke up, rubbing his eyes as Ngwah ogled him with a frightening stare.

"Oga, hurry up, eh. We have a lot of work to do, and don't think we have time to waste. If Madam wakes up and we aren't through with what we're supposed to do, I can assure you, there will be big, big trouble in this house."

Achu wasn't amused. As far as he was concerned, it was unseasonable to wake him up at that hour. All the same, he woke up sprightly without batting an eye. Madam's name carried with it the ring of authority. Plus, he wasn't going to blow his top in the presence of a strapping fellow like Ngwah, who had carved for himself a reputation in the neighbourhood for being an emboldened bully with brazen courage.

Ngwah was keenly aware of the raw reputation he had forged for himself, and so he carried himself about as if he was the cock of the walk. It was therefore not surprising that he delighted in recounting cock-and-bull stories of the many a young man he had floored for daring to challenge his superiority. Achu knew this and refused to be dragged into any situation that might whet Ngwah's appetite for brutality.

Ngwah ran into the kitchen hurriedly to prepare breakfast while Achu dashed into the garage to clean the two cars that would be needed that morning—Mr. Ndefru's slick and smart customised Mercedes-Benz and the Peugeot 505 Station Wagon that was used to transport the children to school. Madam's dashing BMW could be cleaned later since Madam wouldn't need it that morning. Mrs. Ndefru had phoned her boss at home the previous week to complain that she was bored with her work and as a result wouldn't be reporting to work for three days. The boss, Mr. Ekambi Laurent, had acceded to her request. In any case, he had no choice but to accede because Mrs. Ndefru could just have kept away without permission and nothing would happen to her.

As many a boss in Damenba knew, it was not easy being the boss of a wife, girlfriend, or close relative of a very big man like Mr. Ndefru because they usually took advantage of their relationship with the big man to lord it over their bosses. It was, therefore, always with gratification that Mr. Ekambi granted Mrs. Ndefru and others like her permission to stay away from work for a couple of days. He liked to justify this himself by saying that their salaries were, after all, not coming from his pocket.

After breakfast, Cho and Fri hopped into the back of the Peugeot car and lay back, giggling to each other as the driver drove them to school. Mrs. Ndefru, for her part, drove her husband to work as usual.

Ngwah and Achu cleaned the table and dumped the dirty dishes into the sink and then sat down on the back porch to play a game of cards. Cards were Ngwah's favourite game, and whenever he had a few spare moments from his generally action-filled daily programme, he would challenge his neighbours to it.

Ngwah and Achu were concentrating so hard on the game that they hadn't heard a car roll into the yard and into the garage. When they heard footsteps and when someone opened the door, Ngwah immediately threw away the cards under the bench on which they were sitting. He and Achu looked up with undulating eyelids and tried to cover up what they had been doing with a grin.

Mrs. Ndefru's eyes combed them rapidly, and then she puffed, "What are both of you gossiping about? You mean you don't have work to do? My God, how can two boys sit here and be chatting like two housewives trading gossips?"

Focussing on Ngwah, Mrs. Ndefru yelled, "Ngwah, have you swept the house and washed the bedsheets I left on the bed?" Then she turned to Achu, "And you, Achu, what have you done since morning? You think this is a hotel where you just come and stay and leave the work to others? I hope you aren't here to prevent Ngwah from doing his work?"

Before Ngwah and Achu could defend themselves, she scowled, "Achu, before you came here Ngwah had never been stubborn, and I hope you wouldn't make him change. And you, Ngwah, you're supposed to know what to do instead of just sitting around gossiping. Have you cleared the table?"

"Yes, madam," Ngwah answered in a low and frightened voice."But we haven't yet had breakfast, madam."

"You haven't yet had your mother you say you haven't yet had breakfast." Mrs. Ndefru snarled. "What am I supposed to do? Cry because you haven't eaten? Cook for you since Ndefru thinks I'm a cook? Idiots. Move from here. Must you eat before you work? Do you know how much food costs in this house? You say you haven't had breakfast. You expect me to cook for you? I hope for your sake that by the time I return you fools wouldn't still be sitting here. Take this bench away into the garage before I break it on your head."

Mrs. Ndefru turned round swiftly and slammed the door behind her and was swept away into her room by a tidal wave of rage. When she got to her room, she opened her gorgeous wardrobe. It had designer outfits of all kinds. She skipped over the drawer holding a throve of hairbrushes. It had hairbrushes with natural bristles, plastic prongs, and metal tips. Since she didn't have time to sit in front of the mirror to massage her scalp and untangle her hair, she opened the drawer with scarves, gloves, hats, muffs, stockings, and tights and selected a hat to wear.

She picked out a full-length dress that revealed her voluptuous neckline. She slipped into it and looked at her radiant and beauteous self in the large mirror that graced the room. Her small pearlike breasts, for a woman with two kids, jutted out unobtrusively from under the dress. Each time she looked at herself in that mirror, she quivered with the fear of contracting breast cancer and of doctors someday slicing her breast. The thought of a malignant lump and thus of a biopsy was a constant obsession to her.

Mrs. Ndefru took another look at herself, and her eyes captured every detail of the makeup she had applied to her face. Her favourite creams had lightened her fairly dark complexion and left chequered spots around the neck area. Most black women in her entourage were doing precisely the same thing, struggling desperately to neutralise the melanin in themselves so they could be fairer in complexion. And since it seemed that the Meroonca men preferred light-skinned women, women were going out of their way to procure the most popular skin cleansing creams. No one cared about the effects of the creams on the skin and on health generally.

Mrs. Ndefru entered the car and took one last look at her face in the rearview mirror, started the engine, and sped out of the yard.

About fifteen minutes after Mrs. Ndefru left, the phone rang. Ngwah and Achu ran to it, but Achu reached it first.

"Hello," Achu said.

"Is that Ngwah?" a female voice asked.

"No, madam. Can I help you?"

"Yes. Is Madam Ndefru at home?"

"No, madam. She just left the house. May I know who is calling please."

There was a hasty pause. Then the lady spoke up again. "I'm sorry, please. Just a second." Achu could hear the inaudible voice of a man in the background. After a few seconds, the lady returned. "Sorry I kept you waiting," the lady apologised. "When did you say Madam

left the house?" she enquired.

"About fifteen minutes ago, madam."

"Did she say when she would be returning?"

"No, madam," answered Achu.

The lady dropped the receiver, and Ngwah who had been standing by Achu's side was intrigued.

"Who called?" Ngwah asked.

"One woman. She asked for Mummy," replied Achu.

"Does she have a deep voice that rolls its r's?" Ngwah pursued.

"Yes. How do you know?"

"Well, did she sound young or old?" Ngwah questioned Achu further deflecting the answer to the first question.

"Come on, Ngwah, you can't ask me that," Achu quipped. "How am I supposed to know?"

"But her voice should tell you," Ngwah countered.

"I honestly don't know," Achu answered.

"I think I know her," Ngwah said calmly, and then divined, "She must be the same woman who calls here regularly at this time to talk to Madam. Each time she calls, Madam dresses and leaves the house."

"How do you know she's the same one?" Achu queried.

"Why? You think I'm some fool, eh? I know my Madam."

Chapter Fifteen

Mr. Ndefru returned home that evening with a doleful look hanging down his face, suggesting some internal torment. Anxiety seemed to have been stalking him when he stormed into his home. He carried visible signs that his bloodshot eyes had disgorged tears of mental affliction.

As he alighted from his chauffeur-driven official limousine, Fri ran to him jubilantly with outstretched arms. Mr. Ndefru brushed her aside without uttering a word.

Fri couldn't understand what was happening. It was out of character for her father to dismiss her as he had done unless there was something really amiss. Usually when her father returned home, it was with elation that he saw his family. How come this time he hadn't said a word to anybody?

Fri, like the rest of the family, knew that insufferable silence was her father's way of demonstrating that he was hurt. In such moments of deep distress, Mr. Ndefru would bark if he were forced to speak. And his bark was as good as his bite.

Everyone in the family knew that Mr. Ndefru's daily chores were such as to wreak him tremendous pressure. As a man perpetually on the move, his day was always charged. When he wasn't in his palatial office—located strategically along the Commercial Avenue where he served as the chief executive officer of the Damenba Allied Industries Corporation—he would either be chairing a branch meeting of his party, visiting his estates and plantations, or simply skulking the corridors of power in Zaounde, the seat of government and capital of the country. Mr. Ndefru loved to say it himself that even though he couldn't swim, he loved the challenge of sailing on the choppy waters of politics.

Furthermore, Mr. Ndefru dabbled in anything that looked promising, anything that could fetch him money. Accordingly, he wove his relations with threads of money. He had shares in almost all the major corporations in the country and rumours had it that he was fronting for His Excellency, the president of the Republic.

When Fri noticed her father's reticent attitude towards her, she ran to tell her mother. Mrs. Ndefru was busy repainting her nails when she stumbled in.

"Mummy, Daddy is back and looks very angry. He's definitely in a rotten mood," Fri announced.

Mrs. Ndefru raised her eyebrows and looked at Fri. "Why? Maybe your father is just tired," Mrs. Ndefru remarked.

"No, Mummy, no," Fri asserted knowingly. "I know Daddy, and he doesn't usually behave this way. Something must be amiss because he just went straight into the bedroom when he returned from work."

"Maybe your father has had a bad day," Mrs. Ndefru suggested. "These things happen, you know, particularly as your father works under extreme pressure."

"You're probably right, Mummy," Fri conceded. "But Daddy doesn't have to take it out on us. He really looked out of sorts."

"Let's go together and find out what's wrong," Mrs. Ndefru said. She put aside her makeup gear and ambled into the room followed by Fri.

Mr. Ndefru was lying down on his stomach and hadn't bothered to remove his tie and shoes. His wife sat on the bed beside him and shook him lightly.

"Nini, anything wrong? Fri says you don't look well."

Mr. Ndefru didn't move.

"Nini, what's wrong now, what's wrong? Any problem?" Mrs. Ndefru insisted.

Mr. Ndefru still didn't move. It was clear that he wasn't sleeping since his eyes were open. His wife looked at him all over and sighed. The air conditioners rumbled and grumbled.

"Please, nini," Mrs. Ndefru appealed in a furry tone. "Please tell me, anything wrong?"

Mr. Ndefru stirred, turned round slowly, and gave his wife a piercing look and then sighed. He was about to say something but turned his face away. An inner voice seemed to have decreed that he shouldn't say anything.

"Well, then fine," Mrs. Ndefru concluded with a tickle in her throat. "I hope you'll forever remain clamped up in this house." Her stomach rumbled like the skies do in anticipation of a fierce storm. When she stood up to walk out of the room with a tortured face of concern, Mr. Ndefru erupted like a volcano.

"Is it now that you're going to show concern for me? How come you are not with your devoted friend, Mrs. Anyere, with whom you spend the day roaming the streets in search of men when I'm at work? Please move out of this room immediately before I bare you in front of your own children."

Mrs. Ndefru gave a wicked smile and grimaced nervously.

"You're lucky that Fri is in the room," she retorted sharply seething at her husband. "I'd have responded to you in kind, and we'd see who of the two of us has more damaging revelations about the other." She walked out of the room painfully and slammed the door with violent force.

The suffocating heat of revenge hung in the air like a gladiator's sword ready to slice the throat of anyone who came too close to it. Fri glanced at her father and took his right hand into hers and massaged it gently as if to drain out the cloistered ire that had filled his veins. Mr. Ndefru guided her hand slowly to his aching back, which she usually massaged, and Fri threaded the flesh as if it were dough.

Later that evening Mr. Ndefru who had still not left his room rang the bedside bell, and Ngwah ran to him. Mr. Ndefru sent for Achu. Achu was watering the garden when Ngwah approached him.

"Achu, the master says I should come and call you," Ngwah said, intrigued.

"Me?" Achu asked. "But I thought Fri said Daddy isn't talking to anyone."

"That's what she also told me, but the master says I should come and call you."

"Ngwah, I hope you aren't playing another prank on me as you sometimes do."

"Of course not. Why would I? I for one don't know why the master wants to see you."

Achu dropped the water hose recklessly, wiped his hands, and ran towards the room. His heart was beating hard because he couldn't understand why Mr. Ndefru would want to talk to him when he hadn't spoken to anyone, not even Fri whom everyone said was his favourite child.

Achu stirred his mind to see what he might have done wrong to warrant a dressing-down or spanking since that was all he was expecting in retribution for his father's anger. Goose bumps crawled on him, and he cringed as if a caterpillar was walking on him.

Achu prepared his mind to receive whatever punishment Mr. Ndefru might decide to dole out to him. There was, after all, nothing he could do except to psyche himself up to the inevitable. After fishing fruitlessly in his mind for the reason, he decided that he wouldn't torment himself any longer because no matter how far he looked into himself, he couldn't see anything he had done either that day or any other day that would bring out savage instincts from Mr. Ndefru's usually tame demeanour.

Achu walked up to Fri, who was sitting on a bench reading by the kitchen. He waved to her weakly and hadn't the energy to say where he was going because fear had knocked out the strength in him.

Fri read the obsessive fear on Achu's face immediately. "Why, Ni Achu," Fri remarked. "You look worried."

"Yes, Daddy says he wants to see me, and I'm afraid since you told me that he is in a rotten mood and hasn't spoken to anyone. I don't know what he wants to tell me."

"Oh c'mon, Ni Achu," Fri replied dismayed. "I don't think it has anything to do with you. Besides, you know that you are Daddy's favourite."

"Fri, please. I know you just want to make me feel good."

"Because you doubt that you are Daddy's favourite?" Fri asked solemnly.

"What makes you think so?" Achu asked with earnest anxiety.

"Why? You think all of us in this house don't have eyes? Your name always comes first on Daddy's lips." So saying, Fri beckoned to her brother to come closer to her because she wanted to share a secret with him. Achu tended Fri his left ear.

"Daddy and Mummy almost fought in the room this afternoon. I was there," Fri said in a whisper.

"I beg your pardon," Achu said staring at Fri.

"I said Daddy and Mummy almost fought in the bedroom this afternoon. I was there," Fri repeated reluctantly for fear their mother might overhear them gossiping.

Achu continued to stare at Fri expecting more revelations.

"Daddy accused Mummy of always going out with Mrs. Anyere to look for men," Fri added innocently with great inhibition showing on her face.

The statement rang a bell in Achu's head, and he thought instantly of the telephone call he had received earlier that morning from a strange female voice. He recalled the shrill, dramatic ring of the telephone and how it had coursed through the living room, shattering the placid atmosphere at that hour of the morning. Then he remembered the interrogation to which Ngwah had subjected him and wondered if his father knew about the call and wanted to question him about it. Achu tried to dismiss the thought, but it lingered on irritatingly. What was he to tell Daddy if he asked him about the call and whether he had ever seen his mother with strange men. It was a puzzling question, and Achu couldn't figure out how he would wiggle free out of the situation.

Achu entered Mr. Ndefru's room without knocking. Mr. Ndefru was at his small table jotting down something in his calendar. The picture of his swarthy father framed with double mounds peered down at him. At the far end of the room were a tapestry and some family memorabilia—prize certificates, photographs, and displays of porcelain and figurines.

"Sit down on the bed, Achu," Mr. Ndefru said without taking up his head. "I'll be with you in a minute."

Achu sat down and licked his lips. The thought of what might happen to him jarred through him noisily. He tried to shrug it off, but it clung to him firmly. He continued to wonder why Daddy had called him and what he might tell him when he hadn't spoken to anybody since he returned from work. And why him of all people? Achu couldn't understand what was happening.

After scribbling whatever it was that he was writing, which looked to Achu from where he was sitting to be some form of indecipherable hieroglyphics, Mr. Ndefru turned round, looked at Achu, and smiled. Achu didn't know if he should smile back or not. He asked himself inwardly why he should smile under the circumstances given the rotten mood Fri had said Daddy was in.

Mr. Ndefru smiled again, and this time his smile elicited a slight parting of Achu's lips. Achu bowed his head in abject fear.

"Achu, what's wrong?" Mr. Ndefru asked.

"Nothing, Daddy," Achu responded. Fear showed all over his face. Mr. Ndefru smirked.

"Well then. You don't have to look like someone who's lost somebody." Achu cheered up a bit and raised his head slowly. It was heavy because of the onerous thoughts that were weighing down on it. He avoided Mr. Ndefru's eyes.

"Well, Achu," Mr. Ndefru continued with a grin. "I called for you because I have something to tell you, but I'm not sure you'll like it." He paused to see Achu's reaction. Achu's heart raced so fast it almost jumped out of his mouth. Achu looked at Mr. Ndefru furtively and restlessly not knowing what to respond. He wished Mr. Ndefru would release the bombshell on him immediately.

Seeing that Achu wasn't about to say anything, Mr. Ndefru scratched his beard and nodded understandingly with a smile.

"Okay, Achu," Mr. Ndefru said, "I have things to do and wouldn't be long. I suppose you also have things to do, right?"

"Yes, Daddy," Achu answered meekly. "I was watering the garden when Ngwah came and told me that you want to see me."

"Fine. Do you remember the promise I made to you in case you did very well in your final exams?"

"Yes, Daddy. You said you'd have a surprise for me."

"That's correct. I now have the surprise." Mr. Ndefru paused again to see Achu's reaction. Achu was still dazed by soaring anxiety. He turned his head towards Mr. Ndefru and mopped his drenching face. Mention of a surprise always titillates the imagination of children.

As the thought of what the surprise might be tried to retreat, Achu dragged it to memory and recalled that Mr. Ndefru had indeed promised him a surprise if he did well in his exams, but he hadn't given it any second thought at the time because it is in the manner of parents to use the bait of promises to lure the best that is in their children. At any rate, Achu wondered what a surprise the surprise could be. But then just thinking about the surprise brought into his mind some sweet thoughts. But then the sweet thoughts fizzled out just the way they had come like the evanescent fragrance of many a romantic relationship on the sly. Sweet thoughts are always too sweet to be true.

Achu looked at Mr. Ndefru from the corner of his eye and didn't say anything.

"Since I see that you aren't going to guess what the surprise may be, I might as well tell you," Mr. Ndefru said, glancing at Achu. "I have decided that you will continue with your education in Acada College next year. In fact, I am already in the registration process."

Achu wasn't sure he had heard Mr. Ndefru well. He tried to put meaning into the flow of words Mr. Ndefru had uttered, but the message didn't sink into him. Then he tried to connect the few dots of clues he could remember into a real picture of what he thought he had heard. Still, he wasn't sure he had understood Mr. Ndefru. He raised his head and looked at Mr. Ndefru and words abandoned him.

Mr. Ndefru knew Achu hadn't understood him. "Achu, I don't think you understood what I said, do you?" he asked.

"No, Daddy."

"I just said I'm in the process of registering you in Acada College for next year."

Achu opened his eyes wide and looked at Mr. Ndefru. When their eyes met, he burst out crying and jumped into his father's arms. Tears of joy distilled from his eyes and dripped on Mr. Ndefru's shirt. Mr. Ndefru held him close to his heart and patted his back.

Achu felt as if he was dreaming. Good news always has an element of the soporific. At one time, he had thought he was doomed and that the death of his father would crumple up his life, but Mr. Ndefru had served him with soothing words that buoyed up his sagging spirits. And those words alone had invigorated him, giving him hope in a future that had appeared so dark and bleak. Achu couldn't believe his luck and just continued to cry and cry. Before Mr. Ndefru realised it, Achu broke loose and tried to bolt away to impart the good news to the rest of the family. Mr. Ndefru held on to his shirt, and Achu staggered backwards and almost fell on the bed.

"I'll make another promise," Mr. Ndefru said tersely. Achu raised his starry eyes towards him while the tears continued to stream down his face. "If you do well in your General Certificate of Education examinations, I shall send you to America. Your brother will be leaving in August this year, and you will follow him next year."

Achu raced out of the room and crashed into an empty bookcase that Ngwah was taking into Mr. Ndefru's office. Even though the force of the crash was very violent, there was no dent on any part of Achu's body. The bountiful harvest of good news he had just reaped from Mr. Ndefru's mouth cushioned him against any physical or moral harm. It was a question of mind over matter. And the scalding tears that tore a burning path down his cheeks were nothing but tears of jubilation.

The first person Achu saw was his mother. She was reading a gossip magazine. With eyes blurred with tears, Achu announced excitedly with an emotion-choked voice.

"Mummy, Daddy says next school year I'll be going to Acada College and that if I do well he will send me to America like Ni Cho."

Mrs. Ndefru continued to read her magazine, pretending to be steeped in it to the eyebrows even though she could see Achu out of the corner of her eye. She made it appear as if she was unmindful of what Achu had just said.

"Mummy, I said Daddy has just told me I shall be going to Acada College and that if my performance is good, I shall go to America," Achu said giggling.

When his mother didn't react, he added, "Mummy, did you hear what I said?"

"Why? Am I supposed to dance because you will be going to Acada College and then America?" Mrs. Ndefru rasped. "Move from here and don't disturb me."

Achu lingered around for a while, not knowing why his mother had flipped at the good news. Could it be that she was still sore about the spat she and Daddy had had? Achu wondered. But why should she take it out on him when he wasn't involved? Or had Ngwah, with his big mouth, told her that it was he, Achu, who had answered the phone call from the lady who rolls her r's? Achu couldn't understand.

"I say move from here," Mrs. Ndefru growled with a piercing voice that attracted Fri. "Didn't you hear me say you shouldn't disturb me?" Content with herself and with what she had just said, she grinned derisively.

The warm tears of joy that had been flowing down Achu's cheeks turned into cold tears of bitterness and rolled down his cheeks irresistibly like the mad torrential rains that rush down the Chuforba hills and slopes, washing down in their anger all the top fertile soil.

Fri couldn't understand what was happening. She looked at her mother, but her head was buried in the newspaper.

"Mummy, anything wrong?" Fri asked curtly.

"It doesn't concern you," Mrs. Ndefru answered sarcastically.

"But I heard you screaming at Ni Achu. Surely something must be wrong."

"I say it's none of your business. You and your father better leave me alone in this house eh," she crowed.

Fri took Achu's hand, and they moved across towards the garden. The tears from Achu's eyes continued to flow uninterrupted.

"Ni Achu, what are you doing like this?" Fri asked. "You don't have to cry just because Mummy has spoken to you like this. By now you should get used to her."

More tears flowed down Achu's cheeks. Fri wiped them with her handkerchief and turned her own face away to hide the moistness that was developing from within.

"But, Ni Achu, what really happened?" Fri asked.

"I'm sure Daddy has told you that next year I shall be going to Acada College and that if I do well I shall be sent to America."

"Please come again," Fri said with great surprise. "Daddy says next year you'll attend Acada College?"

"Yes, that's what he just told me."

"Great. Wonderful. Just great," Fri exclaimed with ecstasy, jumping with happiness. "Have you told Mummy?"

"That's precisely what I did, and she drove me away just when you arrived."

"But that's great news. Going to Acada College is the best thing that can happen to any student, and Mummy should be very happy and proud."

"I thought so too, but I'm surprised that she is reacting the way she is doing," Achu replied.

Fri did not wait for Achu to finish the sentence. She ran to her mother agitated. Mrs. Ndefru had just lit a cigarette even though she had promised to give up smoking for fear of contracting chronic bronchitis and emphysema.

"Mummy, I don't understand you," Fri began. "Ni Achu says Daddy is going to enrol him in Acada College and that if he passes his GCE, Daddy will send him to America. Instead of congratulating him, you drove him away in anger, venting your spleen on him."

"Fri, mind your language," Mrs. Ndefru screamed. "All of you including you yourself, Achu, and your father can get lost as far as I'm concerned. What does Ndefru want to show me? That he can just walk into this house and accuse me for nothing?"

"But, Mummy, I'm talking about Ni Achu and not about Daddy," Fri said with a sinking heart.

"Don't give me any of your cheek," Mrs. Ndefru charged, foisting anger on her voice."Your father and Achu are the same. What does Ndefru want to prove? That he loves Achu more than all of us?"

"Come on, Mummy. I don't see the link," Fri mumbled.

"Of course, I don't expect you to. In any case, it is not your business. Since Achu moved into this house, I've noticed a change in your father's attitude. He can't do anything or go anywhere without Achu. Everything is Achu. Achu here and Achu there. What is he trying to prove?"

"I'm sorry you're feeling this way, Mummy, because knowing my father, I don't think he has any lesser feeling for any of us. Daddy loves all of us, Mummy, and I'm sure you know it," Fri concluded.

"Move away from here before I smash your skull, you idiot," Mrs. Ndefru bellowed."Someday you'll realise what I'm saying when it is too late. After they've taken over this compound."

Fri couldn't understand what was happening or why her mother was behaving the way she was doing. She ran out of the room hurriedly and went back to her brother Achu. The cigarette smoke had begun to mingle too warmly with the chilling words of her mother.

Fri and Achu clung to each other happily. It warmed the cockles of Achu's heart to know that Fri was showing solidarity with him because going to Acada College was after all the dream of every student who could afford to dream. And going to America was even a more distant dream.

Achu couldn't believe his luck. He had thought that the world in which he lived would sink under him with the death of his father. Now, from nowhere, not only was he certain of continuing in college, but he would be going to the best college that money and intellect could buy. Achu was overwhelmed with joy. For his fellow classmates without hope, going to Acada College was like the gullible pursuit of an elusive dream. But the dream had in Achu's case become a reality, and he was going to be walking buoyantly, full of pride and bounce, and living on cloud nine.

Chapter Sixteen

Cho returned from Wanta that evening wrecked by fatigue. He had gone there three days earlier to visit his father's coffee plantation and to see especially Mr. Ngu, the headman, who had been ill. The rumour mill in Wanta had it that Mr. Ngu had been poisoned by one of the labourers out of jealousy because Mr. Ndefru liked him to a fault.

Travelling in a Land Rover along the dusty road leading to the farm in Wanta usually took a heavy toll on the health of road users. Cho's body ached all over, and when he returned home, he immediately retired to rest. He didn't even have the stamina to supervise the unloading of the jeep as he always did to make sure that the bush meat he usually brought back on such trips was carefully distributed among as many family members as possible.

Cho had hardly covered his eyes when Fri and Achu barged into the room with fanfare.

"Ni Cho, I have good news to proclaim," Fri announced.

"Why don't you wait until I wake up?" Cho pleaded, yawning.

"No, brother. Good news like this one is best imparted when it is still young, fresh, and hot."

"Okay, go ahead."

"Ni Achu is going to Acada College next school year," Fri reported deliriously.

"Ni Achu is what?" Cho asked in amazement, stretching.

Daddy says I'll be going to Acada College next year," Achu confirmed.

Cho, who was too tired and emotional to say anything, leapt from the bed and clung to Achu, hugging him and stroking him on the back.

"What?" Cho managed to say with a faint voice. "This is great news and I am not surprised because you are Daddy's model of a son. He is always asking me to work hard and, to encourage me, he would say if I don't, you, as my junior brother, would overtake me.

I am therefore not surprised. This is just great and I think it calls for a celebration. Both of you better be ready for us to go and celebrate tonight. Please let me catch a little rest first."

"But, brother, you're tired. We have all the time in the world to celebrate this," Achu suggested.

"I say get ready," Cho deadpanned. "Today is your day, and we shall celebrate it tonight."

Achu was very excited because he would be making his debut into nightlife that day. He looked forward to it with great expectation especially as his classmates and friends loved to brag and recount stories about their exploits in the steamy nightclubs of Damenba. Many of them had taken up drinking and smoking because they felt it built in them a sense of worth. Some had even been more daring and had given in to the urge of drugs in imitation of the staggering number of musicians and show business personalities who, according to popular opinion, love to smoke and live on grass.

It was a little after nine in the evening when Cho and Achu left home. Cho was behind the wheel of his father's second car, a vintage old model Mercedes-Benz. Achu sat by his side. He looked much younger than his fourteen years in the sweatshirt and jeans trousers that Cho had given him to wear. Fri who had intended to go with them shirked going at the last minute when she remembered that she had agreed to bake a cake for her closest girlfriend who would be celebrating her birthday that very evening. At any rate, Fri promised to join them later depending on the time the birthday party would end.

The car romped down the dark untarred street leading from the Ndefru home to the junction where a few years before three trigger-happy soldiers from the Special Presidential Security Guards (SPSG) had gunned down several villagers who had unknowingly failed to alight from their bicycles when the head of state was passing. It was common knowledge in Damenba that whenever His Excellency, the president, was visiting any part of the country, which he did very rarely, every moving object had to stop and yield right of way.

After the junction, Cho increased his speed until he came to a point in the road where the wild and destructive rain that had fallen earlier that day had transformed the area into a muddy patch. A girl of unprepossessing appearance stood by the side of the road hitching a ride. Cho rolled down the car window and beckoned teasingly to her, slowing down so he wouldn't splatter mud on the girl. She ran towards the car, her huge necklaces, like chains, clinking loudly.

When she came near the car, Cho and Achu roared off laughing.

Around the Damenba Cooperative Store, passengers were decanting from a bus that had parked very carelessly at a bend in the road. Cho almost ran into the passengers and had to slam on his breaks abruptly. He and Achu cursed the driver generously.

Cho and Achu then drove past vacant lots that the townspeople had converted into a public toilet. It was an unsightly area where the stench of urine and faeces manacles the senses. Across from the vacant lots, young men were adrift in the street and were being tossed by hunger and misery from stall to stall.

There were the burnt-out buildings and dented cars with shard windows that served as a chilling reminder of the ebullition of demonstration that had taken place the week earlier. Thousands of students and the entire population had poured out into the streets of Damenba to protest against the brutal slaying by the forces of law and order of a student leader who had defied government orders and called on his colleagues to organise a sit-in on the university campus to press their demands for fairness in the way scholarships were awarded. In response, the men and women in arms had tried to dissipate the teeming crowd with tear gas and water cannons. Hell had broken loose. Government troops had fired into the crowds and the demonstrators retaliated.

As usual, even though no one believed them, the state-run mass media trumpeted the news that a roving band of armed youth had attacked peaceful policemen on the beat.

The car sped down the street gunning for Black and White, a gangbuster nightclub and watering hole for the cream of Damenba society. The Black and White nightclub had been made famous by the Hello Joes (British soldiers) sent on special assignment to Damenba in the early 1960s by Her Royal Majesty, the Queen of England. It was to this nightclub that the soldiers usually retired to jig-jig all night as they themselves liked to say.

Not far from the general post office, Cho and Achu were surprised when out of nowhere a petulant wind wearing the armour of defiance started to scuttle down the street frisking ladies against houses and flapping open their skirts. The ladies fought back valiantly. It reminded Cho and Achu of the raging wind that had blown months earlier with implacable brutality, lifting roofs from houses, overturning cars, and whipping up storms of dust all over the city.

The wind had hardly subsided when a group of prostitutes with ragged hair emerged from a stall by the side of the street into which they had fled to hide from the wind's blind fury. Prostitutes usually congregated in that area of town to flag down potential customers.

Two of the prostitutes, apparently teenagers, wore skintight suggestive miniskirts that exposed their fleshy, pulpy thighs. They were screaming at each other and cutting each other up with blades of invective. Each one accused the other of having eloped with her man the previous night. A few passersby stopped or slowed down to listen to them. The girls continued to heap insults on each other, and when Cho slowed down, they both ran towards the car beckoning to Cho and Achu seductively. As the prostitutes got closer to the car, they lifted up their miniskirts trying to show off their wares. Cho pressed on the gas and left them standing there flabbergasted. They forgot momentarily about the insults they had been doling out to each other and wagged their finger at Cho and Achu contemptuously, hurling obscene insults at them.

Cho and Achu roared off laughing and making fun of the prostitutes. They hadn't the slightest respect for prostitutes because they are women for whom any relationship is pursued with the zeal of a soldier of fortune and for whom any partner must be a victim.

Just as Cho and Achu were entering Massa Street, they ran into a roadblock manned by the Damenba Gendarmerie Detachment. A fairly young officer with a steel helmet approached the car waving a pistol nonchalantly as if it were a baton. Seven other gendarmes sat by a huge fireside drinking beer, smoking, and playing cards. Cho turned on the car's courtesy lights.

"My friend, let's see your car papers," the young officer said firmly with authority.

Cho showed him all his papers, and he scrutinised them with a torchlight.

"They're in order, sir," he said standing at attention. "Are you Mr. Ndefru's son?"

"Why?" Cho asked.

"From the name, sir. And I think I recognise the car."

"Yes, I am."

"Then I'm sorry, sir. Very sorry," the officer said apologetically. "I'm really sorry, sir. I shouldn't have stopped you, sir. I hope you'll forgive me, sir. Your father is a very big man, and I'm not supposed to disturb you, sir. I'm very sorry, sir." The officer then turned to his colleagues. "Gentlemen, this is Mr. Ndefru's son."

All the officers abandoned what they were doing instantly and stood at attention.

"So where is oga going now?" asked the young officer.

"To Black and White," Cho answered casually.

"Uuh, that's a senior service club, sir. I've just been hearing about it but have never set my foot inside it." The young officer looked at Cho and Achu expecting an answer. When he saw that no answer was forthcoming, he continued with a smile. "Okay, sir. But don't forget us now."

Cho dipped his hand into his pocket and combed it for some money. He took out a 2,500 CFA francs note and handed it to the officer.

"Thank you, sir. I'm sure God will be your angel." The officer who was at attention touched his cap in deference to Cho and Achu and rolled away the stone that served as a gate. Cho and Achu drove off.

The closer Cho and Achu approached the Black and White nightclub, the livelier and livelier the city centre became. Music was blaring from loudspeakers along the Commercial Avenue, and many young boys and girls were flocking to the various clubs and cinema houses that lined the avenue.

The Commercial Avenue was the busiest street in town at any time of the day. It was along it that girls wanting to have fun hung out to grapple their emotions to sentimentally rudderless guys. The omnipresent hustlers and hawkers too were always there selling at dirt-cheap prices everything that was in the shops next door. And if someone decided overnight to become an expert in any field, all they had to do was to walk down Commercial Avenue, and a crafty hawker would award them the academic degree of their choice. Doctorate degrees, understandably, fetched the highest prices. Which was normal given the insatiable craving of many Merooncans for the title "doctor."

Cho who was just seventeen years old and still in high school had once left home to go and buy something along Commercial Avenue and had returned home after barely two hours with a degree in ornithology. Transcripts and seal provided.

Cho and Achu cruised farther down Commercial Avenue towards Mwetta Quarters, and slowed down when they approached the Apostles Church. Next to it was an abandoned crummy and rundown building that was well-known to everybody, including the ubiquitous police officers who were everywhere else except where it mattered most. The building was a kind of Damenba drug stock exchange for it was there that the government tethered citizens washed ashore like pebbles by the high tide of Damenba's economic morass. From their crest of poverty, these helpless citizens peered down for hope into the churning byzantine depths of Damenba's hopelessness.

Cho was explaining to Achu what the building was used for when a naked young man emerged from it. He had a lush field of hair growing wildly on his head in which lice grazed freely. And much to the chagrin of the women, who could not have him, the man's dangling manhood was of commendably desired length and of appropriate tensile strength and tumescence.

The man staggered into the street, speaking alone to himself, and undecided as to where he was heading for.

Cho and Achu arrived at Black and White when the full moon that hitherto had been casting its shadow on the Station Hill began ducking behind the clouds. They were parking when another car swept past them and stopped. Two girls of unblemished wholesomeness alighted. Their long hair waved to the light wind that was passing as they waited by the side of the road for their date to park. Achu almost lost a rib from the poke that Cho gave him in his desire to draw his attention to the two artistic creations of nature.

The atmosphere in the nightclub was electrifying. Since Wednesday night was ladies' night, the club was full of customers. Cho and Achu made their way to the bar from whence they could watch a bevy of girls twirling their waist on the dancing floor, their voluptuous eyes beckoning alluringly to avid tongue-wagging white tourists gulping down pints of local beer. A group of predatory males perched on tall barstools watched and sneered as glamorous girls glided past flaunting their heaving buttocks provocatively. Before Cho and Achu could sit down, Cho recognised many people. As the son of Mr. Ndefru, most of the VIPs in Damenba knew him because they were his father's friends.

Mrs. Mofor's husband, the director of customs, was there. He was well-known in town for always finding solace in the backrooms of nightclubs. He and Cho waved to each other briskly. He was sitting in a corner with a girl the age of his granddaughter, and both of them were making goo-goo eyes at each other. Cho's eyes combed the room, and he noticed a girl he remembered seeing a long time ago. She was sitting alone opposite Mrs. Mofor's husband. Cho walked across to her.

"Miss, excuse me. If I'm not mistaken you must be eh . . . eh," Cho said staring at the girl as her name slowly faded out of remembrance.

"And excuse me, sir. If I'm also not mistaken you must be eh . . . eh," the girl responded with good grace.

Both of them laughed, and Cho bent down to hug her.

"Hi, Lum. Long time no see."

"That's true, Cho, but don't give me that your mess. You know where I live, don't you?"

"Lum, please. You're mixing up your boyfriends," Cho responded instantly.

"I've not been privileged to be invited to your house."

"Okay, okay. Don't rub it in now. I thought you knew my home."

"I don't remember you inviting me to it," Cho shot back sarcastically. "Today is probably my day. Procrastination, they say, is the thief of time."

Lum didn't say anything. She wore an enticingly cloying perfume that Cho loved. He held on to her and wouldn't let her go. He was going to whisper some sweet adulating words into her ear, the kind of passionate talk that ignites a romantic fire, but the music was so loud that his voice was faintly audible. Cho turned round and waved to Achu.

"Who's that?" Lum enquired.

"My brother."

"Cho, c'mon. I never knew you had a brother. You mean your pa has . . . you know what I mean?"

"Come on, Lum, you know better than that." So saying, Cho waved to Achu to join them. Achu walked over to their table holding two bottles of soft drinks.

Cho introduced Lum and Achu. "Lum, this is my small brother. His name is Achu. Achu this is Lum, a former girlfriend who decided to abandon me to take up freelancing."

"Cho, please," Lum protested, a little shyness clothing her face. "Achu, don't mind Cho. We've never gone out together. In fact, we've met casually a few times at parties but never gone out; I think, unless I'm mistaken."

"That's right. I was just joking," Cho answered. "The last party we met at was the one given by Dr. Nifor's son to celebrate the appointment of his father as fourth assistant deputy minister of education. The poor man was fired barely four months thereafter."

"Certainly not because of the party," Lum exclaimed.

"I wouldn't think so," Cho replied. "But who knows? It might have been because of the ruling party."

"Maybe because of some offence such as embezzlement, misuse of state funds, or something like that?" Lum asked.

"You must be kidding," Cho interjected."You know of anyone in this country, let alone a minister, that was fired for some such reason?"

"Come to think about it, I don't recall," Lum responded, nodding, her eyes dilating. She searched her mind for something else to add when three girls who had been on the dance floor returned to take their seats. A young man whom everybody in Damenba knew to be a lady-killer escorted them. It was said that girls flocked to him because he was bringing back chivalry into romance at a time when it was fast losing its shine. In any case, he was also known to be an expert in ducking in and out of various jobs and in mucking in with all the frivolous girls in town. Cho spotted him wearing a small earring and bangles.

As the girls drew near their table, Achu stepped aside to give them way. They sat down near Lum.

"Cho and Achu, let me introduce you to my friends," Lum pointed to her friends as she introduced them. "Grace, Shiri, and Teresa."

Cho and Achu greeted the girls warmly and exchanged pleasantries. Just then, two other girls walked in and sat at the table near them. They were outlandish in the way they dressed, and many people in the club turned to look at them. One of them was well-known in town for bed hopping. She slept with any man she met as if sleeping with a man would soon be going out of style. She was one of those divorced women who, for reasons of social expediency, clung to the "Mrs." title.

The other girl was a bubbly rambling girl whose face was her fortune. As rumours had it, she was the girl who, at fourteen, gave birth to a bouncing baby girl and dumped her in a latrine. Literally throwing out the baby with the bathwater. Now she had reached the ripe age when it was fun to lie about her age, and she was going out with Mr. Fonyuy, a filthy rich businessman.

Fonyuy was not a particularly well-esteemed person because he was uncouth and exceptionally haughty although steeped in the lore of monumental ignorance. But that didn't matter to the mistresses he kept all over the country. He was an extravagantly generous man, and that's all that mattered since each of his mistresses could expect to be the beneficiary of a car or a house; and sometimes, if luck was on one's side of the bed, one could wake up with both.

Folks in Damenba loved to recount the funny thing that happened to one Ms. Mercy Jigja alias Hot Pepper. She and Mr. Fonyuy had a torrid affair that was the talk of the town because it was so hot that Mr. Fonyuy had to abandon his wife and family to check into a lavishly furnished apartment he was leasing for Mercy. The two lovebirds could be seen together everywhere in town holding hands and eating each other's resilient lips. Pleasure, when illicit, pleases pleasurably.

But then, as it always happens, rumours started flying all over the place that Hot Pepper was seeing a young student in Bongla College whom she was sponsoring with the money Mr. Fonyuy was giving her. The news must have reached Mr. Fonyuy because one afternoon while Hot Pepper was at work, he ordered one of his trucks to divest the apartment of all its belongings and take them to his home. When Mercy got home and found the apartment empty, she collapsed; and on gaining consciousness, she couldn't stand the shame and humiliation and had to leave the town.

The chitchatting on Achu's table was going on pleasantly when Mr. Enoh, a senior executive in the Damenba Hotels management board, approached Grace and asked her for a dance. She stood up graciously, and they glided to the dancing floor.

"Come on, what are the rest of us doing?" Achu asked, standing up and giving his hand to Lum, "Let's also go and dance."

Lum, Shiri, and Teresa stood up followed by Cho and Achu. The five of them danced together in a circle. Achu was having so much fun that he refused to leave the dance floor. He danced frantically as if he had been starved of music. The last time he danced to such bruising waist-breaking music was a year earlier during the silver jubilee celebration of his college.

When the girls were tired they left the dance floor and went to their seats, but Achu continued to dance alone. Three unescorted ladies were also sweating it out on the dance floor. By the time Achu returned to his seat after the nonstop series of popular tunes, he was exhausted and drenched in sweat. He looked round and didn't see Cho and Lum. Shiri and Teresa were sipping their drinks leisurely.

"Don't tell me my brother has left," Achu said with surprise.

"But you don't have to look that surprised," Shiri responded with her nose in the air. "Are you afraid to be left alone? We're not going to eat you. We don't eat people."

A diamond smile lit Teresa's face. She turned sideways and pointed with her eyes to the corner where Cho and Lum were sitting. Achu turned round and saw Cho and Lum entangled in a discussion of what looked like a numinous subject from the way Cho was gesticulating. Achu gave Teresa a full-length smile, and Teresa smiled back timidly and then blinked.

Teresa had an articulate kind of captivating and rustic elegance. When Shiri took leave to go to the ladies' room, Achu asked Teresa for a dance. She stretched out her hand warmly as if she'd been waiting for the invitation and added the bouquet of a winsome smile. She knew many of her friends who went out on the beat every weekend hoping to dance the night away but returned home frustrated and in faltering spirits because none of the guys would dance with them.

Achu took Teresa's lissom hand and pulled on it gently, trying to heed Cho's injunction that in everything he did to a woman he had to be a gentleman or at least appear to be one. First impressions matter a lot. The crudeness could always come later after the triumph like it usually happens in most relationships, including marriage.

On standing up, Teresa accidentally stepped on her own dress and lurched over the table overturning a bottle of soft drink. Achu caught her in his arms and her full-blown chest cushioned the impact of the collision. Both of them looked at each other with some longing for a few seconds. There was a discharge of soothing emotions, and they held on to each other for a while, grubbing in each other's mind for something sentimentally precious that might be lurking in it. A dewy smile hung from Teresa's lips with the freshness of a flower in first bloom.

"I'm sorry," Teresa managed to say in a drowsy voice. It was as if she had run out of breath.

"C'mon, you don't have to be sorry," Achu answered in a whisper. "It could have happened to anybody." Looking at Teresa's chest gave him ideas as to the erotic delight that those with privileged access to the backroom of Teresa's sentimental life could enjoy.

"Granted," Teresa acknowledged, arching her shoulders. "But it happened to me, not to someone else."

"Please forget it, and put this out of your mind," Achu decreed. "Let's go and have fun on the dance floor."

Teresa slid close to Achu and gave him a radiant smile. They waffled to the dance floor. By the time Achu and Teresa returned from the dance floor, Shiri had left unceremoniously, taking French leave and leaving her friends' purses unattended to on the table. She must have left with the group of white men who had been eyeing her all along and whistling each time she passed near them to go and dance. She had been aware of the men's glances when their eyes met her enthusiastically inviting bosom.

Achu looked in Cho's direction and saw his brother fidgeting with Lum's hands and whispering something into her ears. Lum was laughing heartily, and Achu surmised that Cho must have been sweet-talking her since sweet words are the appetiser on the table of seduction.

Chapter Seventeen

It was about 4:25 a.m. when Cho and Achu returned home after dropping the girls. They slipped in quietly, not wishing to wake up the household, which was sound asleep. They raced into the kitchen and took out some bread from the refrigerator and ate with some sardine. They were so hungry they could eat a horse. Then they retired to their room to catch a little sleep before daylight could chase the night away. They were so worn-out and badgered by fatigue that they couldn't discuss the wild time they had enjoyed in Black and White and especially their encounter with the girls. That could be done later on in the day particularly as they had planned to see them later that evening. They needed to compare notes and harmonise their strategy.

Cho and Achu must have been sleeping for just about twenty minutes or so when the door to their room swung wide open, and the lights were flicked on. The fluorescent bulbs twinkled nervously before emitting light that shone with intense brightness.

"Get up, you little devils, get up," Mrs. Ndefru bellowed. "Your nighttime revelling is over." She pulled the blanket from over the two brothers.

Cho and Achu turned and tossed and continued to sleep.

"I say get up, you two young rascals. Get up. Today is not yesterday, and I don't want to have to repeat what I've just said again. Get up, you fools," Mrs. Ndefru hollered and began to shake the boys vigorously in order to peck out the sleep from them.

The boys stirred and sat up. Sleep had subdued them. They didn't know where they were or what was happening. They were seized by panic, and their eyelids quivered as their eyes came in contact with the bright light. They shielded their face.

"You two tell me where you've been and make it quick before I kill you today," Mrs. Ndefru said indignantly. "Make it quick because I've had enough of your nonsense since Achu moved into this house."

"Mummy—" Cho was about to say something.

"Mummy my foot. So I'm your mummy eh?" Mrs. Ndefru cut him short. "If you think I'm your mummy you should have told me where you were going."

"But we told Daddy where we were going, Mummy," Cho responded.

"But you told your mother you say you told Daddy," Mrs. Ndefru screamed with towering rage. "Both of you are taking me for a toy in this house, eh? Ndefru comes in and refuses to speak to me maybe because one of his girlfriends has not cooked for him. But he speaks to you. And because all of you think I'm nothing in this house, both of you decide with the consent of Ndefru to go and hang out late without telling me."

"But, Mummy, you were not in when we were leaving so we told Daddy," Achu ventured an explanation.

"Shut up, you devil, shut up. When people are speaking in this house you should be quiet," Mrs. Ndefru yelled. "I was in this house all day and only left for a few minutes this evening to go and see my hairdresser."

For Cho, that was the unkindest cut of all more than flesh and blood could bear. His blood was boiling and emitting fumes in the form of sweat that glistened on his brows.

"Mummy, what do you mean by when people are speaking in this house Ni Achu shouldn't speak?" Cho asked his mother in a fit of paroxysm.

"What do you think it means? Of course, it means what it means," Mrs. Ndefru shouted back. "Don't you ever question me again." She moved closer to Cho and wagged her finger contemptuously, pinning her eyes on him as if taunting him. Cho jerked his eyes out of her control.

"Mummy, you don't think you are exaggerating?" Cho screamed. "What has Ni Achu done wrong to you in this house? If you don't want him to live here better throw him out there on the street than treat him the way you are doing. In fact, I'm the one who suggested that we should go out and celebrate his admission into Acada College. What's wrong with that, Mummy?"

Achu enveloped his head in his hands and shuddered with fear. Tears poured out of his eyes prodigiously; and anger, anguish, dejection, and rejection sidled up to him.

"But if you and Ndefru love him so much why don't you rent a house for him and also find a woman for him to marry since that's all he seems to be interested in. Isn't that what he's been teaching you to do?" Mrs. Ndefru asked scornfully as she turned her back to leave.

"That's a cheap shot, Mummy, that's a cheap shot, and you know it," Cho said as his voice faltered and trailed away. "I thought you'd someday change, Mummy."

Cho broke down and started crying. Achu put his hands around him and comforted him.

"I don't know why you are crying, Ni Cho. By now you should know, Mummy. Please dry your tears and sleep."

Achu was stung and stunned by the daggerlike words of his mother. He lay down beside Cho and sleep, his usual bride for the night, eluded him. He couldn't sleep as a zillion thoughts buzzed round him. Thoughts of dejection and death kept him awake, and alive.